TO TAKE A SOUL

SARA SULTANE

To Take a Soul

Copyright © 2022 by Sara Sultane
All rights reserved.

No reproduction without permission.

Library of Congress and Publisher's Cataloging-in-Publication data

Identifiers: LCCN: 2022906410 | ISBN: 979-8-9859902-3-2 (hardcover) | 979-8-9859902-4-9 (paperback) | 979-8-9859902-5-6 (ebook)

Subjects: LCSH Iranian Americans—Fiction. | Witches—Fiction. | Magic—Fiction. | Love stories. | Paranormal fiction. | Fantasy fiction. | BISAC FICTION / Romance / New Adult | FICTION / Fantasy / Romance | FICTION / Romance / Paranormal / Witches | FICTION / Fairy Tales, Folk Tales, Legends & Mythology | FICTION / Occult & Supernatural | FICTION / Magical Realism | FICTION / Middle Eastern & Arab American |

Classification: LCC PS3619.U4555 T6 2022 | DDC 813.6—dc23

Book cover and interior design by Natalia Junqueira

For more information, visit:
www.sarasultane.com

Content Warnings

Misogyny, mental health issues, substance abuse, sexual content, assault, kidnapping, violence, blood, murder

To Take a Soul

For the girls who are consumed by love . . .

ONE

Maya

The evening air was biting, its icy sting a reminder of the months ahead. Tonight, we were going to a charity event, but I was still in the mood for the last slice of pumpkin pie in our fridge, a piping hot tea, and a novel that would immerse me into its pages. I longed for the unknown and the rush of adventures beyond my reach.

My father and little brother, Milad, were already waiting in the car as I stepped onto the pile of crunchy brown leaves that lined our driveway. The cold seeped through my clothes. I wore a long-sleeved black dress with a high neckline and heeled boots.

"You should've brought a coat," my father said.

Milad, never one to hold back, quickly countered, "It won't hide her nasty personality."

I kicked the back of his seat with my knees, making a satisfying thump.

"I'm fine. I think this is made of wool." I touched the sleeve of my dress.

Winter was approaching, meaning another year had passed with me on autopilot. How was I almost twenty-one with nothing to my name except a high school diploma and an old car? When I was thirteen and looked at the twenty-one-year-olds, I thought they were all full-fledged adults. I thought I would be an adult by now, that I would have a career and a house and all my life figured out. I was still just a kid in a grown body. I had no idea what was going on, and that scared the shit out of me. When was adulthood supposed to kick in, and was it ever going to happen to me? This coming year, I had to make some serious decisions. I didn't want to work at Mimi's forever. My life was one big waiting room at a doctor's office, and I wanted to change that.

Much like the days of the week, the car ride slipped away as we drove toward the venue. The Twin Oak Estate emerged before us, one of Mist Creek's hidden gems. A massive barn-like structure stood proudly, adorned with expansive windows. Curtains draped gracefully from the lofty ceiling while delicate string lights crisscrossed the space, casting a warm glow. Three crystal chandeliers hung between the vines that trailed along the beams, adding an enchanting touch to the place.

Surrounded by the lively chatter and laughter filling the room, I couldn't shake the nagging feeling of being an outsider. Despite the cheerful atmosphere, a subtle unease settled within me.

We were assigned to the table we had bought with my oldest friend, Alie, her sister, Lena, and their parents. Alie's parents were first-generation Indian Americans.

"Salam aleikum," I said to her parents in their dialect, where the salam sounded more like *slaam*.

Milad echoed after me in his own way. My father took a seat next to Alie's father, and my brother settled beside him. I was wedged between Milad and Lena, unable to sit next to Alie as I had hoped.

"I love your makeup," I said to Lena. She always experimented with her makeup. Alie shared her sister's distinct features: sleek black hair, round brown eyes, and a uniquely shaped Cupid's bow. We were sitting at the roundtables in the front, next to the performers. The volunteers had done a great job of pulling this together. It was all very high-end; there were flower arrangements on all tables. The champagne glasses were spotless, like they had just been polished, and the tablecloth was the expensive kind, soft to the touch. Our table had beautiful pink lilies whose scent reminded me of when my mom lived with us. That was before she decided to leave and reconnect with her Persian heritage. In me, however, there was a lingering absence of that, and perhaps that wasn't good enough for her. Or perhaps I wasn't good enough for her. I had let myself become too Americanized. I often wondered if she knew what she was getting into when she decided to marry my father. At least he hadn't left us.

This year, the event aimed to support children in need, drawing aspiring artists from our community, including Mist Creek's renowned A-list talent, Toby Swenson. The program promised a series of performances and an auction finale.

"Ladies and gentlemen." The announcer's voice boomed through the venue, attempting to hush the crowd. "We gather once again to raise funds for the less fortunate. This year, we are privileged to witness the extraordinary talents of Mist Creek's finest performers."

Milad tapped my arm. "Pass me those." He pointed at the snacks he couldn't reach.

"Keep your voice down. It's embarrassing," I whispered. Milad reached over anyway and took a handful of crackers.

"Let's give a warm welcome to Sam Wessel," the host said. With everyone else, I started clapping.

Lena leaned in. "He's actually really cute, but he couldn't sing if his life depended on it," she said.

He was cute in a rugged way. Tall, tousled brown hair and a daring smile. Lena was right. The poor guy wasn't great. Toby rolled his eyes, exchanging whispered comments with his wife beside him. The lackluster applause followed Sam's performance until the host rose to introduce the next artist.

Milad leaned over again, but this time, I elbowed him.

"Can you stop!" I hissed.

He groaned, dumped a handful of salted peanuts in my drink, and grinned. I didn't want to give him the satisfaction, so I said nothing and looked back up at the stage.

Sitting in the crowd, a sudden surge of inspiration coursed through me. For the first time in a while, I felt like I was so close to finding my path. I needed to be at home, making a vision board for my future.

Weariness settled in, overshadowing my enthusiasm, as we had already endured two underwhelming singers and a ballet act by a group of kids. My father, ever determined to instill goodness in us, always dragged us to these events. I knew he had worked really hard to get here, and his success didn't come overnight. Clearly, I was aware of how important it was to help people, but I didn't need to witness half of Mist Creek perform to understand the lesson.

"... Please give it up for Adam Pave," the announcer went on.

An average-looking guy went up to the stage with a mic. He had a cute, dimpled smile, but his teeth were crooked. His curly hair was nice, though. It effortlessly drooped a little on his forehead.

"Gosh, another singer," I said under my breath.

"No, it's not. Don't you know him?" I shook my head, confused.

Was I supposed to know him?

He performed a skit reflecting his experiences as a Black man, cleverly representing both sides of the coin. First, he was the voice of mainstream media and their portrayal of people of color. Then the narrative shifted as he assumed his own identity, offering a heartfelt response to the accusations against them. He expressed the constant struggle of feeling unwelcome in his own country and the persistent need to prove his patriotism.

As he performed, a wave of emotion washed over me, causing literal goose bumps on my skin. Though my light skin allowed me to blend in easily, I saw how people's gazes and interactions differed when directed at my brother. His complexion was darker than mine, and although his dark hair was similar to mine, it was much curlier. I couldn't imagine how it must have felt living here without the privilege I had. I was the whitest in our group. Most of my friends were children of immigrants, but they seemed so relaxed and at peace. I just never have felt like I belonged anywhere, really. Not here, where I was born and raised, and not in Iran, where my mother was from. I should be more grateful for all the opportunities I had here. Whenever my mother took us to Iran, I was reminded of how fortunate I was. We visited our family almost every year when we were younger. We even had dual citizenship.

"Isn't he wild?" I leaned back and whispered to Alie over Lena.

"We've seen this performance before. And I'm pretty sure he came to our school once."

"Impossible! I would have remembered," I said.

She shrugged and continued recording him. "He's all over the internet. Maybe that's where I've seen it."

"That's my future husband," I said jokingly and looked back at him.

The world around me transformed into a blur as his performance unfolded, leaving me utterly speechless. In my eyes, he went from a six to a solid ten. He was suddenly so attractive. I had never noticed the power of charisma that men had, letting them transform and captivate with their words. He had a mesmerizing presence on stage. My gaze followed him as he gracefully exited, melting into the sea of faces in the crowd.

When we got home that evening, I had spent hours on the internet trying to figure out who this guy was. I read every article about him and saw all the videos I could find until my eyes were sore from looking at the screen. He was a local talent with an impressive resume. He wrote books, gave TED Talks, and performed his skits. He had accomplished so much for his age, which only heightened my sense of failure. I was still here, doing nothing. I was in awe many of the following days and tried to see if I could catch one of his shows, but I never did.

It was almost Christmas, and the streets were filled with shoppers. The Salvation Army Santa stood in his worn-down red suit at a busy corner, collecting donations. His bell rang intermittently, cutting through the hurried footsteps and cheerful voices. I stood behind the window of Mimi's on Proctor Street, my gaze unfocused until a figure caught my attention. He appeared, dragging his bike alongside him. Despite the lack of direct sunlight, he wore sunglasses, adding an air of mystery. As he strolled by the store, his eyes passed over me. It was a fleeting moment for him, a passing glance that held no significance. While, for me, it carried the weight of all my daydreams. The sight of him sparked the promise of hyperfixation. A whirlwind of thoughts and possibilities began to swirl in my mind, each one intertwining with the next. Images and scenarios danced before my eyes. It was a pattern I had come to recognize, where my mind would latch onto stars of TV shows or characters from books, weaving intricate narratives that occupied my waking hours and infiltrated my dreams. There were times when I wished I could turn it off.

What if he, too, felt the same pull toward me as I felt toward him? The thought of it dragged me away.

A bustling bar unfolded in vivid detail. With a confident stride, he would approach me, his eyes filled with intrigue. "What are you having?" he would ask, his voice barely audible over the noise. So, he would lean in, his lips brushing against my ears, "You're too beautiful to be drinking alone." But instead of pulling away, he would linger, fully aware of the effect he had on me.

"Maya!" My boss, Alyssa, called.

I jerked. "Yes!"

"It's almost seven. Bring in the rack." She rarely caught me doing nothing, so she never scolded me when I zoned out. This Saturday, I had asked for the day off, but then Hellen got sick, and I had to cover for her. I rolled in the rack with the Christmas tumblers and locked the doors.

"I'll count the register myself. You can go," she said.

"Alright, thanks." I removed the green apron, grabbed my things, and went out the back. Dissie was waiting for me at Olympia Café two blocks down. Delnaz was her real name. One time, she was so drunk she was swaying from left to right. We started calling her Dizzy Delnaz, then it morphed into Dissie and stuck ever since. Dissie was also *Irani* and my most recent friend. I had known her for less than a year, but we quickly became close friends. She was a couple of years older than me. She was also trying to find her way out of this town but got stuck working for her sister at her diner.

I headed down the street, past the already closed stores, and down to Olympia. Most of Mist Creek's singles would come to this area on weekends to get lucky, and it was always the same sad crowd. Still, I loved Olympia Café because it had the most natural light. Even in the evenings, red, pink, and orange light streamed through the big windows.

I spotted Dissie sitting at a table by herself, talking—no, arguing on the phone. Dissie was one of the most beautiful girls I knew. Her eyes were vibrant green, her hair dyed blonde, her pouty lips tinted like she was kissed by cherries.

I decided to give Dissie a minute and instead made my way to the counter to place my order. Lizzy was working; we used to go to the same high school but weren't in the same friend group.

"Hi, Lizzy, can I please have a cup of quince tea and the apple pie?" My eyes lit up at the sight of the last piece behind the glass. Their apple pie was the best in town.

"You did not just order tea!" Dissie appeared beside me, wrapping her arm around me in a sideways hug. Her voice filled with disbelief.

"I've only had one cup today." Drinking tea three times a day was something I picked up in Iran years ago. When my mom moved out, I had to teach myself how to brew it because my father was a traditional coffee drinker. So, I started going to Mimi's for tea and questions so often that Alyssa eventually gave me a job. Now, I had an entire tea routine in the morning.

"We'll also have two Long Islands," Dissie said, putting down her card. "My treat."

Lizzy didn't care. She'd serve us alcohol even if I was the one ordering. I carefully balanced the tall glass of tea wrapped in a napkin in one hand, the apple pie in the other, and hurried back to the table before it got highjacked by someone else.

"I love that color on you," Dissie said, putting down the Long Islands.

"*Ghabel nadare.*" As a rule of thumb, in Middle Eastern culture, when someone complimented the clothes you were wearing, you offered them the item. They went overboard with politeness and etiquette in that sense.

Dissie smiled and took a sip from her drink. She liked it when I leaned into my Persian side.

"Oh, by the way, I don't know how your bra ended up at my house." I pulled the bag out of my tote. "I guess it must've wound up in my laundry because I found it in our downstairs bathroom. So random."

She looked in the bag. "Thanks, I was looking for this," she said and put it away. "I have so much shit to tell you. I'm talking to this guy I met at the diner, and before I go on, do not tell Lena and Alie."

"Why, do they know him?"

"Well . . . I'm actually talking to two guys." She smiled, and I knew the next thing coming out of her mouth would be great. "One of which may or may not be Shabaz."

"Stop!" I was on the edge of my seat, leaning over my pie. Shabaz was Alie and Lena's cousin from their father's side—the more religious side of the family. Dissie wasn't exactly breaking girl code, but Alie and Lena hated Shabaz because he always outed them.

"Maya, don't turn around just yet." Her eyes tracked someone behind me. "Adam just walked in." Frozen in place, I held my breath. Twice in one day, it felt like fate was nudging me. I had told Dissie about Adam but might have failed to mention how obsessed I had become overnight.

"Now you can look," she said.

It was him! *Why is he here? Who is he waiting for? A date, maybe? Oh, damn, he's not single. What kind of girl is he into?*

A million questions raced through my head.

"You should go talk to him," Dissie said a little too loudly for my liking.

"I'm good," I whispered and glanced back, only to find him looking at me, too. I turned back, flustered, and accidentally took a sip from the wrong glass, expecting hot tea but drinking a mouthful of the Long Island Iced Tea.

"You lost a perfect opportunity there. He's gone now," she said. "Since when are you afraid of talking to guys?"

"I'm not afraid! I just don't have anything to say to him." If I was afraid, I wasn't going to admit to it. Perhaps I was starstruck like a loser or envious because he had his life together, and I didn't.

"You read all these romance novels. I'm sure you could steal a line or two. Also, didn't he write a book? You could've asked him about that and then it wouldn't be so obvious how hard you're crushing on him," she said, leaning back and taking another sip from her drink. "Although your flushed cheeks would give you away, but you could blame the Long Island for that." She shrugged.

"I haven't read any of his books." *Yet.* I ate a heaping spoonful of the pie and washed it down with the now not-so-hot tea. "Anyways! Enough about that. What the hell are you doing with Shabaz?" It was easy to distract Dissie. Ask about any guy on her roster, and she could go on forever.

"Fuck Shabaz, you should see the other guy I'm talking to. He's also a D—" She shook her head and waved a hand in my face. "What is that deer horoscope called? The same as you."

"Capricorn?" I asked, uncertain where she got deer from.

"Yes! He's also a Capricorn, and he is British, tall, sexy, and mysterious." Her finger lazily stirred the ice in her drink, creating a gentle clinking sound. "But he's acting hard to get," she added with a hint of frustration.

"Well, let me see him. And we're not done talking about Shabaz!"

"I don't have his socials. And fuck Shabaz," she said, looking up from her drink with a grin. "Literally."

"Stop, Dissie!" I said, wide-eyed. "You did not!"

"Don't you dare judge me! You almost slept with Jonathan last month. And also, I was really horny, and he was right there, so . . ." She trailed off with a shrug as if it were a perfectly reasonable explanation.

Jonathan and I broke up a year ago. We started dating during our senior year, and although I loved him, I didn't expect us to last. I believe he loved me, too, until one day, he switched. Overnight, he became distant and didn't care about me or anything I said.

Nonetheless, I stayed with him until I found out he cheated on me with Britney. They were still together to this day. A month ago, I met him at a party without her, and I almost slept with him out of spite because she knew we were together and didn't care. Luckily, I didn't go through with it. He was really messy in the end—could get a little possessive sometimes, and I was not about to get tangled up in that again.

٢

TWO

Maya

Last year, I bought myself an excuse for a car. The faded paint peeled off some places, revealing the scars I had left behind. Sometimes, when I turned the key, it growled in protest. It was all I could afford at the time, mainly because I refused any financial help from my father.

The night had left frost on my car. I used the scraper to clear the icy layer from the windshield, each stroke numbing my fingers around the handle. After fumbling with my keys, I finally managed to open the door, but even inside the car, my breath formed misty clouds.

Right before the Christmas holidays, there was another instance when Adam strolled by the store, briefly looking inside.

Wouldn't it be cosmic if I saw him right now? Maybe then he would realize there was magic between us—something putting us in constant proximity. I often envisioned my life as a web of magical connections, but I wanted more. I longed for the ability to perceive beyond the veil and unravel the hidden mysteries of the world. As a teenager, my khale Hana was friends with the Romanis in Iran. They taught her palmistry, tarot, and whatnot. I would have gladly settled for even a fraction of her skills—if you believed in that sorta stuff. My grandma, for instance, was very superstitious. She taught me all kinds of things, going beyond mere instruction. Her rituals became ingrained in my daily habits because they let me believe something else was out there for me. Something other than this repetitive life.

Sometimes, my attention would waver, and that day was no exception. I turned the corner from 19th Street to Clay, and a jolt shot through my body as my foot slammed on the brakes. My car came to a stop mere inches from him. *I just called it!*

There, in the middle of the street, materialized out of thin air, was Adam. As if I had manifested him into existence. Maybe that seer stuff wasn't that far-fetched after all.

Adam turned to face me, his expression strangely unfazed. He pulled his left hand out of his pocket and waved me off as if it was nothing.

Why was I always left with chills when I saw him? Were moments like these meant to paint a bigger picture? Because I refused to believe that these accidental encounters happened for no reason. Or maybe I was a dreamer, a hopeless romantic, moping over a boy who was clearly not interested. Yet, in that instant, as our eyes briefly met, a flicker of curiosity danced in his gaze.

I arrived at Dissie's place; she lived with a girl whose parents had bought her the apartment they lived in. It was a unit in one of the nicer neighborhoods close to where Stacie lived. I was going to crash at Dissie's because the girls and I were going to the New Year's Eve party Stacie was throwing. I didn't know much about Stacie besides that her parents were crazy rich and had left for their annual ski holiday.

Pregame was always at Dissie's because the rest of us lived at home. Pregame was also our chance to catch up on a month's worth of gossip.

As soon as I got there, I plugged in my straighter to fix my hair. Dissie was rummaging through her wardrobe, searching for the perfect outfit, while Lena applied the base of her makeup in front of the mirror. Alie was lounging on the bed, scrolling on her phone, already dressed and ready from home.

"Does this look effortless enough?" Dissie asked, holding up her hair in a high pony and examining herself in the mirror. "I don't want him to think I did all this for him."

"Who, 'The Sub' or 'Manbun'?" Alie asked. The Sub was one of the guys on rotation on Dissie's roster, Manbun, whom I had never heard of.

"Can someone pour me a shot?" Lena said while trying to pump out the last drops of her primer.

"Me too!" I said. "Alie, get up."

"I have single-use cups somewhere in the kitchen," Dissie said. "And, no. It's Alex from that bar we went to a few weeks ago."

Alie poured us each a generous shot of tequila and downed her own straight away. "Anyone want seconds?" she asked while pouring herself another one. I put my hair in a messy half updo and lined my eyes before taking the shot. I couldn't risk messing the eyeliner even with a single shot.

"Ohhh. Alex," Lena said after a while. "He's one of your better picks."

"You can have him. I'm only entertaining it because this other guy is not giving me the time of day, and he needs to know his place."

"Are you talking about 'The Tall Brit'?" I asked. They all had nicknames and were rarely referred to by their real names. I didn't remember the names of most of them because they never stuck.

We arrived around ten, a bit later than planned. I had never been to Stacie's house before but wasn't surprised by its size. They weren't the kind of people who would do their own gardening or cleaning. It looked like they had people taking care of everything. A layer of frost painted their yard, adding charm to the scene.

When we entered through their massive white doors, I instantly felt the heat hit and the windburn on my cheeks and ears. The house was packed with people, most already drunk. Laughter and cheers mingled with shouts of excitement. Every corner of the house seemed to be alive with activity.

Shortly after, we merged with the crowd. The air was thick with the mingling scents of alcohol, sweat, and perfume. It was a sensory overload: the warmth of bodies pressed close, music pulsing, and conversations overlapping. I fidgeted with my sleeves as I tried to navigate through the sea of people.

Jason, who lived on my street, approached us. "The three musketeers," he said, flashing a wide grin. "Who is the fourth?" He nodded toward Dissie, who was speaking to "The Sub"—Alex. He must have seen us walk in together.

"That's Dissie," Alie said.

"Mmmm." He was studying her, undressing her with his eyes.

"Stop being so creepy," I said, elbowing him in the ribs, although not hard enough to avert his eyes.

"Here, have a drink, neighbor." He poured half his drink into my cup and raised his in a toast before leaving. I always thought he had a crush on me, but he never acted on it. Just like he wasn't going to approach Dissie. I hadn't planned on drinking too much but then one became two, and two became three. Alie was drinking straight from a bottle, and Lena on her third or fourth.

As the countdown to midnight approached, the crowd buzzed with excitement. "Ten, nine, eight . . ." The voices grew louder, arms raised in the air, fingers counting down. "Three, two, one . . . Happy New Year!" The room exploded with a roar, and the party erupted into a frenzy of celebration.

For a good while after that, I was on a roll. I slipped into a blissful, carefree state, dancing and befriending strangers. After some time in that euphoric haze, panic gripped me as I desperately scanned the place for the girls. The room seemed to warp and shift as if the walls were melting. *What if they went home and left me here? What if everyone I know has already gone home? Where is Jason? I can trust Jason. Are the walls melting? Fuck! Fuck! Fuck! I'm so drunk.*

I saw colorful blobs in the air while running around like a headless chicken. My heart only stopped pounding against my chest when I saw Lena and let out a relieved sigh. She was in the bathroom. *Of course!*

"There was no soap in the bathroom," she said. "Who doesn't have soap?"

I followed her into the kitchen like a child who had just lost her mother and found her again. While she was washing her hands in the kitchen sink, my eyes were fixated on the flies trapped with us in the house. *Why are flies so stupid? Flying in triangles and squares—into the window, again and again.*

The cool part was I could slow them down, make the wings go in slow motion, zoom in, and pause. *What the hell is going on with me?* Then I felt the beating of my heart again going crazy behind my ribs.

Lena was about to head back in when I stopped her.

"I don't feel so good, Lena." I wasn't lightheaded, but now her face was morphing. *Are those scales on her skin?* I closed my eyes to shake it off.

"Drink some water. It'll help," she said. Then, when I opened my eyes again, she looked normal. "Here."

I took the water from her and drained the whole glass.

"Do you think Jason would roofie me? Does this smell funny to you?" There was still a bit of drink left in my cup. *Wait! No! I finished the drink he gave me. Oh my god. I'm going to die!*

"Jason would never do that. Roofies are supposed to make you unconscious. Do you feel groggy?" Her words were comforting but not enough to fully ease my mind.

"No, but this is not normal!"

"Are you dizzy? Do you want to find a place to lie down?" she asked.

"No, not at all. But where is Dissie? I need the spare keys. I'm gonna head back."

"I have the keys here," Lena said, pulling them out of her purse. "She said she might go with Alex. Do you want me to go with you?" She lit the screen on her phone. A picture of their cat in a Halloween costume popped up, and the time read twelve thirty-eight.

"I just need to find Alie f—"

"No, it's fine. Really. I'm just drunk," I said. "Stay. I'll find Dissie and tell her I took the keys." I didn't want to ruin their night, too.

Lena and I went into the big living room, where she found someone to talk to. I climbed a chair to get a better view. As I towered over people's heads, scanning the room with my heightened senses, my eyes started pulling literal data on the ones I recognized. The words materialize letter by letter in a Matrix-like font as if they were being typed out in real-time with a distinctive clicking of a typewriter.

Name: Anna

Age: 23

Reference: Lizzy's cousin

Note: Not wearing her signature lipstick

Name: Kevin

Age: 22

Reference: Error

Note: Wearing Anna's lipstick residue around his mouth

This is not normal! Fuck! Fuck! Fuck! A guy carelessly bumped into me, stepping on my shoe. "My place later," he shouted over my head. It was like I wasn't even there. I walked past people and went to the bathroom to pee. I hadn't been in there more than a minute before someone pounded on the door. "Come on. I can't wait any longer," a guy was saying. I hurried washing my hands, remembering there was no soap, yanked the door open, and darted past him to the kitchen to wash my hands. The walls of the house seemed to be closing in on me, and I had to get out of there.

Fresh air hit my face, and I could finally breathe. Between the sound of the wind that pushed through the leaves and the music from inside, I heard someone giggle and a car door close.

I looked back at the house, and something bizarre was happening again: colorful sound waves rippled in the sky, coming out through every crack of the house.

Holy shit! Am I having a bad trip on stamps? Isn't that something you're supposed to put on your tongue? Could someone have put it in my drink? Fuck! Fuck! Fuck!

Something is definitely wrong. I need to get rid of this feeling, these thoughts. I can focus on my mission: finding Dissie, but why? Why did I need to find her so badly? Did I want something from her?

The questions popped up like a game show.

What if I'm stuck like this? What if I have to live my life permanently high! Dad will be so disappointed. Fuck! Good thing I'm not going home.

I was so uncomfortable and couldn't wait to get under a blanket. All the sounds around me were muffled, like a distant hum. I stepped out onto the oddly quiet street lined with parked cars. Amid the stillness, a flicker of movement in the backseat of a car caught my attention. I could recognize Dissie's dyed blonde hair anywhere. She was straddling a guy; either The Sub had gotten lucky, or The Tall Brit finally had succumbed to her beauty.

I turned around and walked down the street. When I took out my phone to text Dissie that I had taken the keys, I saw that it was almost two in the morning. I had no idea how long I had been standing outside.

Clutching my coat tighter around me, I convinced my-self that walking would help; I was sure of it. My head was pounding, and I felt nauseous, but that was all normal after that much alcohol. Maybe I hadn't been drugged after all.

How long did it take us to get there? Eight minutes? I'm a fast walker. I can do it in three minutes.

"Not driving home, I hope," a voice called out behind me. Star-tled, I turned around, and there he was, making his way toward me. I stood, frozen in my shoes, too stunned to speak.

I watched him with my new cyborg vision and couldn't stop the data from appearing before my eyes like a hologram.

Name: Adam Pave

Age: 23

Reference: Public figure, speaker, author, my latest obsession.

Note: A shameless grin on his face.

This was the first time we were in such close proximity to each other. His eyes were like dark pools of desire, drawing me into their mystery. When he grinned, his dimples appeared, teasing and playful. Like most people, his teeth weren't exactly perfect. *Jagged is the right word, Maya, but I'll let it slide this time.*

My favorite thing was a nice set of teeth. I had a good set myself, but it could've been better; the arch could've been wider.

"I almost ran you over today," I blurted out, the words seemingly coming out of nowhere.

"An apology would do," he said, still smiling. "I'm Adam." He reached for a handshake. *As if I don't know that already. I would know your dog's name if you had one.*

"Sorry," I said with a smile I couldn't hide, so I bit my lip and reached for his hand. "Maya." My cheeks flushed with warmth.

"Happy New Year, Maya," he said, scruffling his curly hair.

"Happy New Year." I smiled. "On your way home?" I asked, my curiosity getting the best of me as if it were any of my business.

"Yes, I live just down the street." He nodded ahead and rubbed a hand down his neck. The effortless gesture was tempting.

Out of nowhere, a car pulled up, startling both of us. It was Jonathan's car, and I couldn't help but feel confused. After all, he didn't know Stacie. *Luke!* The pieces started to come together in my mind. *Luke, Jonathan's good friend, was at the party.*

Time slowed as Jonathan's intimidating stride closed in on me, his shoulders swaying with each step. My heart pounded in my throat, its rhythm echoing on my tongue. Desperately, I swallowed to control the overwhelming feeling, but it only intensified.

I had to keep my fingers apart because, when they touched, the pulse drove me crazy.

Without warning, Jonathan punched Adam in the face for no apparent reason. Adam was left stunned, trying to process the sudden attack, when Jonathan grabbed my arm, yanking me toward his car.

"Get in the car."

I didn't get a chance to protest before I was shoved into his car, and he drove away. As I settled into the backseat, I found myself unable to move, hands trembling. *Speak up! He isn't a stranger. It's just Jonathan.*

"Honestly, what the hell is wrong with you?" I finally found the courage to yell at him. "Is it because I didn't want to sleep with you?"

"I dumped her, Maya. I wasn't myself with her. I haven't stopped thinking about it ever since that party. I tried to be normal with her, but I couldn't. Luke told me you were here, and I contemplated not coming at all, but I need you. I can't be with anyone else, and when I saw you with that dude—" He exhaled, then looked at me through the rearview mirror. His hand reached out, gently resting on my knee. I couldn't tell if his knuckles were swollen or if that was how they always looked. "I'm sorry I grabbed you." His voice carried a hint of remorse.

There was no point in yelling or arguing with him because it would never lead anywhere. I could tell he was driving me to his place. Meaning Britney wasn't there.

He wouldn't do anything. He never forced himself on me. There is nothing to be scared of.

I ran my hands along the velvet fabric covering the seat. The seats were covered half in fabric and half in faux leather. I loved the French pronunciation of faux—*fuh, fuh, fuh*. It sounded more like a swear word. Jonathan looked at me through the mirror every other second, probably wondering why I was so quiet.

Is that a person on the road? "Watch out!" I screamed.

In an instant, he slammed on the brakes, sending me hurtling from the backseat to the front, crashing against the dashboard. I got a severe blow to the head and felt a dull throbbing in my nose. A guy stood completely still on the road. We could have killed him if I hadn't noticed him. I started hearing ringing in my left ear from the shock, but it quickly stopped.

What a cliché—a couple driving on an empty road, then a girl in a soaked white nightgown blocks their way—but we're not a couple, and this is not a movie.

It was dark, and we couldn't see his face. The headlights only lit up his body. He still didn't move, even though we stopped and didn't hit him. I didn't know what to think. Two almost-accidents in one day—I had to be cursed.

"What the hell . . ." Jonathan said.

We both scrambled out of the car, Jonathan before me. I wrapped my arms tightly around myself, but the wind pierced through my clothes. Tiny needles prickled the insides of my ear. Jonathan stood a few steps ahead of me, his gaze fixed on the guy still standing motionless in the darkness.

"What's your problem, dude? Move!" Jonathan said.

The guy came closer, and I realized it was Adam. Just moments ago, he had been standing outside Stacie's house. I couldn't believe my eyes. None of it made sense.

Adam's voice cut through the air. "That was dramatic, don't you think?" His tone calm and collected. I felt sick to my stomach. *Is any of it even real?*

When Jonathan registered that it was Adam, he almost stumbled back in disbelief.

"Get out of my way!" Jonathan said, trying to sound convincing, but his voice gave him away.

"Maya, I can take you home," Adam said as if he knew me like that. Completely ignoring Jonathan's existence. Jonathan found his confidence, got into position, and suddenly remembered what he was made of. He charged toward Adam, driven by pride and anger, but Adam moved too fast, anticipating the move. Jonathan was effortlessly overpowered by Adam's calculated moves. He released his grip on Jonathan's arm, tossing him onto the sidewalk like a rag doll.

As Jonathan struggled to rise from the ground, it was clear that he had reached his limit. I could tell because he wasn't looking at either of us. *Oh, this is definitely going to bite me in the ass.*

Adam came toward me, his steps carrying a sense of purpose. "Are you okay?" he asked.

I didn't speak. I couldn't get the words out.

"My car is not far from here," he said. I couldn't explain why I followed him or why I trusted him.

"How did you do that?" I finally asked.

He stopped in front of me. His hand reached my face, and he tucked a lock of hair behind my ear. I felt a soft tingle spreading under his touch.

I shook off the feeling. *How Bollywood of you! It's not going to work. I might be under the influence, but I'm not stupid.*

But when his fingers brushed against my skin, I couldn't help but shiver. Something was twisting within me. A shuddering feeling I couldn't get rid of. Perhaps it was nothing. Perhaps it was just the fact that I could smell the cigarettes on his skin, and it bothered me. If it was any other guy, I would have slapped his wrist away from my face.

"What you saw is exactly what happened," he said.

What is that supposed to mean? I wanted to say, but I was distracted by his forearm. Biteable and smooth skin tightly wrapped around the muscles, marking the blood-pumped veins. Every second, I would find new things about him to be attracted to. Again, ringing in my ears, now both of them. We walked for about two or three minutes without talking. My hands were frozen into fists in my pockets. My feet took independent, rhythmic steps until he stopped and pulled a key out. A car in the driveway of a big house blinked. He wasn't lying. He did actually live down the street.

"I can drive you home if you like."

"Can you take me to my friend's house? She is waiting for me." I lied. Best to be sure before going with him. I shouldn't have gotten into his car, but I was so exhausted and didn't want to think about it.

"Where does she live?" he asked.

"Not far from where the party was. I'll guide you once we get closer." I should have known better and made the responsible decision, but I didn't want to. So, I opened the door to his car and stepped in.

There was something about him that I wanted. He had something that belonged with me, and I simply needed to be close to that energy. He might not have known it, but we were magnetic.

"Will you tell me how you did that?" I asked again when we started to drive. I couldn't finish the sentence out loud because what if I was the one seeing things? What if there wasn't anything to be explained. What if I was going crazy?

"I don't know what to tell you. You seem like a nice girl—has he been violent with you before?" Either he avoided my question, or he misunderstood entirely. Why was he asking about Jonathan being violent? He didn't do anything to me.

"No. He hasn't," I said. "Turn left here, and then all the way down to that No Parking sign. Then you turn right." He followed my instructions without uttering another word. His brows knitted together with frustration. Was he regretting getting involved? I couldn't see the left side of his face where Jonathan had punched him. Was he going to bruise? I had so many questions and no time at all.

"This is her." I pointed at the building. "Thanks for driving me." He gave me a smile full of pity and drove away. I hated him for that pity.

I had forgotten the mess we had left behind and started gathering the scattered clothes from the floor and putting them on the desk. Next, I pulled out the hide-a-bed, creating extra sleeping space for Alie and Lena. It wouldn't be the first time we all crammed up against each other.

I had collapsed on the pull-out bed and woke up five hours later with Alie's knee digging into my back. I don't remember them coming in or making any noises. Lena and Dissie were both knocked out on the bed. Lena was still in full glam, but Dissie had washed her makeup off before going to bed.

My father would be sound asleep, so I knew it was safe to go home without having to explain myself. He knew I was sleeping over at Dissie's, but I didn't want him to know how fucked up it had gotten.

Our house was on 66th Avenue West, only a fifteen-minute ride from Dissie's. It was the very last house on the street. Over the last few years, my father had been renovating the place. He made it look like a new house with a new door, arch windows, and matte brown roof tiles. He also painted the house a fresh white. The brightness of the color went really well with the surrounding forest.

I sneaked inside as quietly as I could so I wouldn't wake anyone. I could hear my brother snoring all the way by the front door. I hurried upstairs because I couldn't wait to wash all this sweat and alcohol off my body. My morning was going to be a lot more interesting than I had anticipated. As I entered my bedroom and closed the door behind me, I came face to face with Jonathan. Swiftly, he clamped a hand over my mouth, silencing me. His other hand firmly gripped my hair, yanking me closer to him.

"Not a single word—do you understand!?" he said.

I nodded, trying to control my breathing, tears stinging my eyes, but I refused to let them spill.

"Did you sleep with him?" he said into my ear while tightening his grip on my hair. His voice dripped with accusation. I shook my head, and he loosened the hand over my mouth and nudged me. "Answer me! Did You?" he whispered, voice harsh.

"I swear—" I fought to steady myself. "I swear I didn't."

"If you so much as think of him, I'll come for you. Do you understand!"

I managed a feeble *yes* as tears streamed down my cheeks. He let go of me, pushed the chimes hanging from my curtain rod to the side, and climbed down. I had forgotten he used to sneak in here when we were together. It all happened all too fast; before, I could think of how tough I could or should have been.

The chimes swinging from side to side were from my grandma. She made them herself and told me to hang them in my window for protection. They clearly didn't do much protecting anymore.

I rushed to the window, locking it with trembling hands, and took a deep breath. Then, I licked my forefinger and traced it along the window frame. Then I licked it again and made an X on the glass. A ritual my grandma had instilled in me. It also helped me calm my nerves.

I wanted to sob, scream, really cry out. For the first time, I was scared of him, scared of what he would do, scared of everything.

I couldn't wrap my head around it. Jonathan wasn't like that before. When did he even get to this point? I knew he could be possessive sometimes, but this was unusual behavior, even for him.

When the initial shock had passed, I went online, trying to figure out what kind of psychedelics I could've ingested. It could have been a number of things: foxy, ketamine, LSD, MDMA, PCP, mushrooms, or even ecstasy. LSD was the most common one with hallucinatory effects. And you could get it in liquid form, making it very convenient to add to a drink. Perhaps Jason put it in his own drink and forgot it when sharing it with me. I would have to ask him.

At least seven or eight hours had passed since the peak of my high. I wasn't hallucinating anymore, but I wasn't completely normal either. An article online said the drug could last up to twelve hours.

I went in, took a long shower, and then tried to sleep the rest of the buzz off. I couldn't wait to move out of this shit town and start a new life. Maybe even change my name—become someone else, someone without a crazy ex.

٣

THREE

Maya

I had one of those lucid dreams again—floating in the clouds, shadowy beings looming over both Jonathan and me, forcing us still. Time slowed to a crawl as their presence drained us empty, leaving our skin a lifeless shade of gray. Then the scene changed, and I was lying on my bed, trapped in a nightmare. Adam leaned in, his lips pressing against mine, but his kiss was suffocating, like he was trying to pull out the air from my lungs. When I woke up, I was drenched in sweat, sheets clinging to my skin. The dreams had only occurred a handful of times, but it was enough for me to believe something was wrong.

Less than a month had passed since the incident with Jonathan. I saw him with his girlfriend, Britney—on my birthday, actually. He gave me a friendly smile like it had never happened. As if I had imagined all of it, and maybe I had.

I didn't tell anyone about Jonathan, not even Dissie, whom I shared everything with. I wasn't sure why; perhaps I thought my fear would disappear if I pretended it never happened. Perhaps it never actually did. Because, when I confronted Jason, he told me he had put LSD drops in his drink. The moron had completely forgotten it when he poured half of it into my cup. He apologized profusely and told me he never intended to drug me. I only believed him because of the genuine shock on his face.

Yesterday, my grandma called me three times, which wasn't unusual for her. Once a week, she wanted updates on us, and unlike all my aunts, she was not a news broadcaster, so I could almost tell her anything. Although I never mentioned any of my partying, she always told me to be careful when going out. I hadn't told her about Adam either, but sometimes, she stirred me to the topic of love and boys as if she already knew.

I decided to call her back on my way to work so it wouldn't be too late in the evening in Tehran.

She always let it ring three times before picking it up.

"*Allo,*" she said. She didn't speak English and was the reason Milad and I had learned Farsi early on.

"Hi, Mamani." All her grandkids called her that ever since we were kids.

"*Salam jegaram.*" Which technically meant *Hi, my liver*, but in Farsi, it was a term of endearment.

"I was worried sick yesterday when you didn't answer my calls. Milad said you were at work. Are you working every day? How will you have the time to think, to prepare yourself for the future. Have you even read the books I sent with your mother?" She had mentioned this before, and although she knew I didn't see my mother, she sent some books with her from Iran, knowing full well I couldn't read Farsi. My mother knew that and never bothered to send the books my way.

"Not yet," I said, hoping she would let it drop.

"*Jegaram*, I told you the books are important. Now tell me about the boy you like." She jumped topics like that, always on the next question before getting an answer to the first.

"I don't have a boyfriend if that's what you're asking."

"Oh, but you will, and it will hurt and it will be wonderful and it will be grand, but don't forget that men never appear as they truly are. Just stay on your path, read the books I have sent you, and you will find your soul in honey-colored eyes that will transform you. You would be a fool to trust them all," she said. *Cheshmaye asali* was always used to emphasize the beauty in a person, sometimes even for people who didn't have honey-colored eyes. Most Middle Easterners wanted their daughters to get married to a man who could provide for them. My grandma, however, was a romantic.

"*Chashm*," I said, agreeing with her, or she would keep going forever.

At work, customers trickled in and out, their conversations melded with the hissing wind from outside. I was arranging the shelves and aligning the rows of colorful tea canisters when I saw Adam on the other side of the street. He stood outside Meyer's, leaning against the building, eating a sandwich, and casually looking over between each bite. I sneaked glances at him while pretending to fill the jars.

"Maya," Alyssa called from the other end, "can you go downstairs and check if we have any matcha bamboo whiskers left?"

"Sure." *And pink tea infusers. We're always out of those.*

I went through the string curtain and down to our basement; it always smelled so funky down there. I couldn't decide whether we had mold or if it was the smell of wormwood tea. I guess if we had mold, the health inspectors would know.

"Also, see if you can find any of the pink reusable tea infusers," she called from upstairs.

"Yeah," I shouted back. *As I said. She needs to put in a new order. We're running low on everything. Did I tell her that already? I think I did. Is that the phone ringing? Not my problem. I'm hungry!*

First, I went through the basket of silicone tea infusers. There were no pink ones left. They were always the first to go for some reason. I found a bunch of the bamboo whiskers and went back upstairs. As I passed through the string curtain again, my heart dropped to my stomach. Adam was here, talking to Alyssa.

"I like green tea but maybe something more aromatic." He looked at me and quickly looked back at her.

"Of course. Let me show you a few options," Alyssa said.

The phone rang and stirred me from my paralysis. I hurried over to pick it up.

"Mimi's Tea House, how can I help you?"

"Hi, how are you? I'm calling from F-Track International regarding a shipment release. Is there a manager I can speak to?" the guy said.

"Yes, one moment, please." I walked toward them. "It's about a shipment release." I handed her the phone. She pressed the phone against her stomach to mute it and looked at Adam.

"I'm so sorry. I have to take this. Maya will help you find whatever you need." She put her hand behind my back and gently pushed me closer to him. My eyes followed Alyssa back to her office. When she was out of sight, I looked back at Adam.

"How can I help you?" I said.

"I'm looking for a tea that is not as addictive as this one," he said with a box of tea, pointing it at me. *Is he talking about the tea or me?*

"I just keep coming back for more. I don't know why."

Has he been coming here while I wasn't at work? Am I delusional to believe that? What took him so long?

"Maybe you should avoid tea altogether," I said instead of all the stupid things I was thinking.

"That's not an option," he said. I couldn't tell if he was flirting with me, and I didn't want to play his games.

"What do you want?" If Alyssa ever heard me speak like that to a customer, she would freak out. *Always be polite, always smile. Make sure they leave the store satisfied. Blah, blah, blah.*

"I want your number so I don't have to come here whenever I want to see you," he said. *So, he had noticed me working here. Interesting. I wonder how often he had come by only to find Hellen at work.* I pushed the thought back. It shouldn't have mattered.

"Are you stalking me?"

"How else would I get your number?" he said with a wink and a dimpled smirk. *No! Stop it. Get a grip! But he's so charming. Dammit, I'm so fucking easy.*

I couldn't resist it. What harm would come from getting to know him? Perhaps he could inspire me to make something of myself. It would be foolish not to surround myself with accomplished and capable people. He certainly was that.

I reached out, waiting for him to place his phone in my hand. He did without hesitation. I typed in my number and gave him his phone back. *Who cares? I certainly don't. He's just an average guy.*

After work, I was supposed to meet with Dissie, but she canceled on me because they needed help at the diner. So, instead, I drove to the other end of town to buy mushy chocolate chip cookies from Hen & Co.

Finding a parking spot proved impossible and forced me to circle the block multiple times. Eventually, I gave up and left the car in front of a gated entrance, hoping I wouldn't get towed. Five minutes tops, and I would be back. Hen & Co. was two blocks down the street. They were the last store to close because they always had so many customers. People mostly came for their legendary cheesecake, but I loved their cookies. Usually, they had a few left around closing hours.

I was about to sprint down the street with my wallet and keys in hand when Dissie's voice froze me in place. "I don't give a damn what you want. You came to me looking for help. This is the price. Take it or leave it," she exclaimed, determined to stand her ground. Her voice came from the alley a few steps ahead of me, but why had she lied to me about work?

"Absolutely not. Tell me where he is." *British! Is that The Tall Brit?* His voice was much lower than hers, but he spoke with so much ferocity it made me shiver. What was she doing? Who was this guy she was dealing with?

I kept close to the wall and inched forward with cautious steps. A gasp or a moan escaped her. They were farther down the alley than I had thought. He had backed her up against the wall, grabbed her from the roots of her hair, and pulled her head backward. *Wait, what if this is them role-playing?*

Either this was what Dissie looked like before an orgasm, or she was in some kind of elusive trance. Her eyes were showing whites, her mouth gaping. The sight before me defied all logic and reason. From her chest, tendrils of smoke began to rise, curling and twisting like ribbons. His hand hovered above her chest and mouth, delicately pulling at the wisps of smoke. My mind struggled to process what I saw.

What the . . . I took another step and accidentally kicked an empty can. *Fuck!* When I looked back up, nothing was the same. He was tenderly cupping her cheeks, kissing her. *Impossible. I . . .*

"Dissie?" I said.

I wasn't high, wasn't dehydrated, and wasn't drunk. They both turned to me. She looked flustered while he straightened his shirt, grinning like a wolf.

"I thought you were supposed to be at work," I said.

"I wasn't needed after all," Dissie said as she walked toward me. He was right behind her, his gait confident, leaving no room for doubt and my assumptions in the shadows behind him. "Then I met—" She looked at him, hesitating. *Hmm, you look like an Andrew—no, your accent sounds like an Andrew, but you—you are something else.* The Tall Brit reached his hand out.

"Aldridge," he said. *Aldridge . . . Close enough.*

She wasn't lying; he was handsome. Tall and commanding, with eyes that held a mesmerizing depth. His dark hair and brows made him the male version of a siren—someone who would take you swimming only to drag you beneath the surface the minute you let your guard down.

"Maya." I took his hand.

"Pleasure to meet you," he said and turned to Dissie. "I have to run. I'll see you tomorrow, yes?" Dissie nodded.

"What the hell was that?" I asked when he was out of earshot.

"I'm sorry. I should've called," she said. "FYI, you just cock-blocked me."

I looked behind me to double-check before speaking. "Stop playing with me, Dissie. What did he do to you?" I wasn't going to dance around it.

"What are you talking about?" She looked genuinely concerned. "Are you okay?"

What—this can't be happening. I saw it . . . didn't I? I exhaled a long-held breath and dragged both hands over my face. *I'm not crazy. I'm not crazy. I'm not crazy.*

"Never mind. I'm just tired. Do you need a ride home?" I asked her.

"If you're headed that way, then, yes."

During the ride back, we didn't speak. She was on her phone, unaware of the awkward silence. I put on the radio to distract myself, but the image of him drawing smoke from her kept going in a loop in my mind. There were only two ways to explain it. Either I was deranged and losing touch with reality, or I was psychic, and my dreams were a warning against Aldridge.

What kind of name is that, anyways?! Did I manifest this ability? Am I an actual seer now?! I'm not crazy!

I dropped Dissie off and was about to make a U-turn when a car honked at me.

Fuck! What is wrong with you! If he had hit me, it would've been my fault entirely. I didn't even look in the mirror. My hands were shaking, and I couldn't make them stop. The other car backed up and parked behind me. *Shit! Did we collide, and I didn't feel it?*

I didn't dare turn but saw through the mirror that his door had opened. *Fuck! I can't deal with this right now.* I closed my eyes for a second, breathing in slowly. There was a light tap on my window. My eyes widened like saucers when I saw it was Adam. I rolled down the window, still unable to collect my thoughts.

"Hi," he said.

"I'm so sorry. I didn't look, and it's the second time with you, and you're probably thinking I shouldn't be driving at all, but I swear it's not always like this—"

"Hey"—he placed a hand on my shoulder—"it's fine. Nothing happened. Are you okay?" His touch burned through the layers of my clothes.

"I'm fine," I breathed. "I wasn't paying attention, and you always appear out of nowhere like fucking Houdini. I mean, even in your car, really?" I knew I wasn't making sense, but it spilled out of me.

"Can I come in?"

I motioned toward the passenger seat, inviting him inside.

"What's going on with you?" he asked with the same look in his eyes as Dissie. People were starting to pity me.

"I have to ask you something. You need to explain how you managed to appear in front of Jonathan's car that night."

He looked confused as to why I would ask that. "I ran a shortcut. I can show you right now if you want." *A shortcut. I'm not crazy.*

"I'm sorry. My drink was spiked at that party, and I haven't felt like myself ever since. Something changed, like a flip of the switch. I have lucid dreams. I know what people will say before they speak the words. And then Dissie and the smoke out of her chest but then it didn't happen, and they were just making out. But I swear, for a second, I thought I saw him pulling it out of her. Next, you and your car appear out of the blue. It doesn't make sense. I can't explain it. I don't think it's fun anymore. I'm just scared. I'm scared of myself, scared for Dissie—or of Dissie, I'm not sure. Scared of Jonathan, and Aldridge, and—"

"Wait, back up." When he stopped me, I realized how insane I must have sounded to him. What a way to make an impression on people.

"Repeat that again," Adam said in a completely different tone.

"Forget what I said. It was just unfiltered vomit."

He frowned impatiently. "Tell me everything from the beginning," he demanded. And, for some reason, I couldn't deny him.

"This is all hypothetical!" I said, waiting for him to understand that it was going to sound insane. He was dead still, so I went on. "Let's just say I saw this guy putting a hand over my friend's chest and then smoke floated out of her. What would you think was going on?" I asked.

"You saw smoke come out of her chest and mouth?" he asked.

I stifled the gasp with my hand. I couldn't believe it! "I never said mouth. How would you know that?"

"Maybe she was smoking. You said his name was Aldridge?" Adam asked, paying no attention to my utter disbelief, and it started freaking me out.

"Are you kidding me? I just told you I witnessed literal magic, and you are completely unbothered by it."

"I'm just confused." His voice softened. "I don't know what you think you saw," he said. *Oh my god, what is happening to me?*

"Didn't you just say your drink was spiked? Maybe you are suffering the side effects." He was right. Something was wrong with me.

"I need to go home," I said, trying to appear calm.

He was confused for a second but complied and didn't look back. I wanted him to stay, talk to me, and tell me I wasn't crazy. I didn't want to be alone, but no one would believe me. I didn't even believe me.

٤

FOUR

Maya

Dissie and I were both off work and had decided to meet up at Olympia for brunch. While there, I tried to get my mind off Adam, but it was so damn hard because I was spiraling into my imagination where things were different—where I controlled the narrative. I didn't know him, but I had read some of his work, his haunting poetry that painted sunsets and secrets of the heart. With each word, he cast a spell over me. I created stories in my head, conversations I would have with him, some romantic, some angry, and some steamy.

I couldn't help but wonder why we crossed paths, why his gaze locked to mine, why it felt like we belonged together. How could a tiny spark ignite a roaring fire within me? That was my problem: I took a grain of sand and formed a desert. The excitement of a new romance made me want to jump in headfirst. The fact that my heart could be broken into tiny pieces was a thrill, a stupid high I was chasing. I wanted it, even if it was short lived.

Adam and I had left off in a weird place—or, rather, an awkward place. A part of me couldn't shake the nagging feeling that getting involved with him might not be a good idea. Despite the doubts, my obsession with him held my mind captive and clouded my judgment. The day after, he called me, but I couldn't bring myself to pick up. I was too messed up, my mind in turmoil, tangled in the aftermath of what I had seen. I was losing touch with reality.

Eventually, he texted me, apologizing for his blatant disregard for what I had said, still not confirming that he believed me.

"How are things going with Adam?" she asked me, sipping her cappuccino. She could always tell what was on my mind. Even when I didn't want her to. I hadn't told her what happened after I dropped her off that day. That would be admitting to being unstable, and I didn't want to circle around that possibility anymore.

"You read minds now?" I said and smiled. "I was just thinking of texting him, but I'm not sure what to say. He texted me yesterday, asking if I wanted to hang out. I said no, and he responded. 'Alright, I'll try again tomorrow.'"

"You can say, 'It's tomorrow, now . . .'" she suggested. I had been writing and deleting the same text for the past twenty minutes; Dissie made it look so easy.

"When you and Adam get more comfortable around each other, we can do a double date. I have a feeling Adam and Aldridge would hit it off," she said.

Not in a million years, I wanted to say. "Are you guys *dating* dating?" I asked instead, hoping he was in the revolving door on his way out. Even if he had done nothing to her, my gut feeling was never wrong. Aldridge was bad news.

"Maybe," she said with a mischievous smile. My phone buzzed, and she leaned over eagerly to see. "Is it from him?"

I hadn't thought it through. He was asking where I was. What did I think would happen when I wrote that? Dissie took the phone from my hand.

"Don't send anything!" I warned when I saw her typing.

"Relax. I wrote back, *Olympia*, not *I wonder what your hands feel like on my skin, your tongue parting my lips*." She dragged a lazy finger across my arm. I snatched my phone from her in horror. Sometimes, it was scary how accurate she was. "I could've done that, but I didn't," she said.

"Wow, you're so poetic," I said. "What if he—" Dissie grabbed my arm, her nails digging into my skin. I could tell by the way her eyes darted to the door and back at me that he was there. *Fuck! If I turn, he will see me. What am I thinking? He'll see me whether I turn or not. How is this even possible?*

"Maya," Adam called, and I had to look. He was dressed in all black. The two top buttons of his shirt undone—in the dead of winter. Was I supposed to smile? Wave? Both? I smiled as he walked to our table.

"I was just around the corner when you sent that text. What a coincidence, huh!"

"Absolutely," Dissie replied, offering her hand. "Dissie."

"Nice to meet you, Dissie. I'm sorry for interrupting you—" He barely got the words out when Dissie waved a hand in the air.

"Actually, I'm meeting a friend in a minute if you want to take over," Dissie said, looking expectantly at Adam. She was making it too obvious, and I could feel the heat rising to my cheeks. She thought she was helping, but she was not! She was putting him on the spot. Clearly, he wasn't going to say no now.

"Well, yes, of course," he said sincerely, eliminating my doubts. "I would love to go for a walk, but it's freezing, and I didn't bring a jacket. If you like, we could go for a ride."

Dissie coughed. "She would love that," she answered for me. Adam still awaited my reply, acknowledging I had been set up.

"That'd be nice."

Once outside, I followed his lead. His hand found the small of my back, gently pulling me aside, when a woman tried to walk past us. My skin raged under his touch, even through the layers of my clothes.

His hand brushed mine when he opened the passenger door for me.

"I'm gonna go get a cup of coffee from across the street. What would you like? Coffee, tea, lemonade?" he asked.

"I'm good, thank you."

"I'll get you something," he said before closing the door after me. He was so hot, I couldn't breathe. His car smelled just like him: a breeze of freshness, sandalwood, and sensual, musky notes. You would think he had broken a perfume bottle in here.

In the pocket of his car door was a book. A Nabokov, to be exact: *King, Queen, Knave*. I hadn't heard of that one, so I read a few lines of the first page and then went to the middle and then the last. He had written numbers all over this book with a pen. *Blasphemy!* Toward the end of the book, there was a marked paragraph with *melodramatic 43* written on top. There were no other clues as to what these numbers meant. So, I put the book back where I had found it and scooped up another book in the same pocket. This was a tiny notebook with the softest paper I had ever touched. When I turned the pages, I stroked the side of my hand across the paper. All those numbers were notes written in eye-catching and somewhat unreadable handwriting. I found number 43 and read a passage about a wife wanting to kill her husband. Suddenly, the car door opened, and Adam got in. I was so embarrassed because I forgot I was snooping around in his car.

"I'm so sorry," I burst out. "I was looking in the book with all the numbers and found the notebook and got carried away," I said, setting the notebook back.

"Don't worry about it," he said, smiling. His dimples, the heat of his gaze, was all too much.

"These are your notes?" I asked to distract myself.

"Yeah, I'm surprised you could read my handwriting," he said, handing me a coffee cup and a water bottle. "I know it's early, but I got you hot buttered rum. They make it with Jamaican rum, spices, and heavy cream. It's so good I just wanted you to taste it."

I wasn't a fan of rum or whiskey, but his enthusiasm was infectious, so I wanted to give it a fair chance, suppressing any grimace that might creep onto my face.

"Thank you," I said and removed the lid to whiff how boozy it was. It smelled like an Indian chai latte with liquor.

He took us out of downtown and headed south. Driving past my old high school, the familiar sight stirred my memories.

Then the park where my parents first met came into view, taking me back to carefree days. As the car turned and the scenery changed, I broke free from the clutches of nostalgia.

"Do you annotate all books like this?" *Like a psycho.*

"No, that was just an exercise my agent had suggested to help me practice plot development." Casually reminding me how much of a big shot he is. *Am I projecting? Maybe . . .* He reached for his cup and took a sip.

"So, you change the storyline of the book?"

"Change, correct," he said, wiping the edge of his mouth with his thumb. *Maybe he could do that to me. Fuck! Get your head out of the gutter.*

"Wow, correcting Nabokov, are we!" I said and raised an eyebrow.

"Not like that." He smiled sheepishly. "Have you ever read any of his books? He is crazy!"

"I've only read *Lolita*, and my vomit wanted to vomit. But it's wild how he makes you empathize with the wrong person," I said.

"Exactly! Humbert is charming and likable."

"Calling him 'charming' might be pushing it a bit." I stole a quick glance at him before taking my first sip of the hot buttered rum.

"Oh my god! This is the most amazing thing I've ever had." It felt like a warm hug: sweet, creamy, and nutty, with a dash of cinnamon. He looked pleased with himself by my reaction.

As we arrived at St. Cassandra Cliffs, I realized that, although it was just a short distance from my home, it had been ages since I was last here. Because of the season, we had the whole viewpoint to ourselves.

"Do you like to read?" he asked with a hint of curiosity.

It was my turn to catch him off guard and strip the public persona off of him.

"When I get the chance, I like to read, yes. I have phases. I was stuck on romance and fantasy for a long time. Then I switched to spiritual self-help books and then poetry," I said, cocked my head a little to the side, and forced his eyes to meet mine. "I read your book, too."

A shy expression crossed his face.

"I really liked it. 'Moving Mountains' is my favorite poem."

"Thank you," he said, clearly wanting to end this conversation.

"You must have heard this before."

"Yes, but people who interview me usually just skim through my stuff. It can get overwhelming sometimes because then I think of all the parts I'm not super satisfied with and regret ever publishing anything."

I was surprised to hear he, too, had doubts about himself.

We both fell quiet, and I wondered what I was doing there. Doubt crept in, and anxiety coiled inside me. *I'm such a fool. Is he even worth the trouble? I shouldn't be the chaser here. I'm setting myself up for failure. Why did I think he was interested in me to begin with? Dissie was the one who pushed him to it.*

"Can I ask you something personal?" he asked, interrupting the spiraling thoughts. What could he possibly want to know about me? *Bra size? Body count?*

"Sure."

"The guy from New Year's Eve . . . Are you two—"

"No!" I cut him off. "We were . . . a year ago. I honestly don't know what happened that night. He wasn't like this before. One day, he just woke up different. Do you know what I mean? He changed so drastically, you would think something traumatic had happened to him," I said.

"Did he really change overnight?" he asked, suddenly very interested in Jonathan. This was not what I had imagined when he wanted to ask me something personal.

"I guess."

"Interesting," he mused, tilting his head slightly. "Have you heard from him since that night?"

"Uh-huh."

Curiosity filled his eyes, and he pressed further. "What did he want?"

"Why do you want to know?" I asked, not bothering to hide my skepticism.

"I just want to help."

"I'm not a charity case, Adam!" I almost spat the words in his face.

"And I'm not trying to be a fucking philanthropist," he retorted. We jumped from the calm before the storm right into the hurricane.

Why is he triggering me? And why do I still want him? Fuck! I rubbed the middle of my eyebrows with my forefinger and thumb, trying to think.

"One day—" he said, breaking the silence between us. His gaze fixated on the cliffside. "I was grabbing a sandwich across from where you work. I saw you standing by the door, talking to some guy," he paused as if performing on stage, creating suspense.

"The—I started making excuses just to pass by Proctor, hoping to catch another glimpse of you." He turned, his eyes meeting mine. "You've captured my attention in a way no one else has. So, no! I don't think you're a charity case. It's genuine interest and attraction." A smile tugged at the corners of his lips. "And this was before you tried to run me over with your car." His smile widened to a grin.

The weight of his confession settled.

"You're not making this easy," I said breathlessly, torn between desire and uncertainty.

"Would you rather have me be a jerk?"

His question hung in the air, and we left it at that. Curiosity killed the cat, they say *Miaw*, because I couldn't stop myself.

۵

FIVE

The sun rose, casting a warm golden glow across Elias's eyes. He sat behind the wheel of the 1968 Ford Mustang his father—my brother, Edgar—bought him. The road stretched endlessly while the scenery unfolded before us. After months of cold and barrenness, the forest slowly came alive, with fresh leaves unfurling on the branches.

"I know you're jealous of my new baby," he said as his hands glided over the steering wheel. His father was only looking out for his safety because Elias was such a daredevil.

"I am not swapping cars with you."

"Worth the shot." He shrugged. I always let him borrow my Camaro when I wasn't using it—which was most of the time, but he wanted unrestricted access.

Edgar had three sons. The twins, Elias and Daniel, and the youngest, Theodor, had just turned fifteen. Elias and Theodor had elemental abilities, Elias's coming in pretty late but still present. Daniel, on the other hand, got the short end of the stick. Although he was born without any elemental powers, he was still no less of a Dūshev, just as strong and already able to aḍhār. Aḍhāring was something we learned after mastering our elemental skills. It was the ability to travel through thin air by "bending" time and space to create a shortcut between two locations.

Being the first set of twins in our family, Elias and Daniel left us uncertain about what to expect from them. Their powers were unevenly divided between them—unlike the soul they shared.

"What's the plan for today?" Elias asked.

"Saltwater and pace manipulation, but you're still a little behind on split-focus," I said. He wasn't, but I wanted to rile him up before starting so I could catch him off guard.

"Piss off!" he snapped. "I'll split-focus your face."

When Elias turned eighteen, his powers kicked in, and so he had to be assigned a master. Not all my brothers decided on this path, but for me, it was the only thing giving me solace. In our world, we only had each other; everyone else faded away with time.

It wasn't hard to mentor Elias. He wasn't like my other nephews; he learned effortlessly and was always eager to push harder. I was just as good when I was his age, but I sure as hell wasn't as fast.

We arrived at Griffin National Forest, a sprawling expanse of tall trees and the air thick with humidity welcoming us. The mud and the bark were soft and dank. Beads of sparkly water were perfectly placed on the green leaves. Thin rays of sunlight peeked through the tall trees.

It was precisely the kind of environment that suited Elias's powers. We reached a small clearing, and Elias closed his eyes, focusing on his powers. A subtle shift in our surroundings became apparent, as if the moisture in the air responded to his call. Droplets began to gather and dance in midair, defying gravity.

"Show-off." I scoffed. "That is not what I meant by split-focus."

"I know." Elias's voice held a hint of mischief. With a subtle flick of his wrist, he released a sphere of water he had been gathering above my head.

"*Ebn el kalb*," I swore under my breath.

"Relax," he said, grinning. Instantly, a wave of warmth spread over my shoulders as the water evaporated, leaving me dry in an instant. The bastard wanted to prove me wrong before we had even started the lesson. He had a decent grasp on evaporation. Whenever it rained, he never bothered with an umbrella, effortlessly drying himself faster than the rain could soak him. However, he hated saltwater. Because of the density, it was a greater challenge for evaporation. Knowing this, I always brought gallons of water from the Dead Sea.

The faint scent of the sea reached me as I poured the water from the Dead Sea into smaller cups. Elias groaned, and his tall figure slouched slightly. "We just got here. Give me a break," he said.

"I'm preparing it for later. Right now, I want you to focus on your pace," I said.

"How?" Elias asked.

I picked up a branch with lots of twigs and leaves and handed it to him. "I want you to slow down so we can see these droplets shrink to nothing."

"Easy," he said.

"Let me finish—while drying the bark of this tree," I added, pointing at a random tree.

I circled around him to break his concentration. He furrowed his brows and shook his head, trying to dismiss the distractions. Despite my attempts to throw him off track, he remained determined. I watched the branch go dry in an instant, same with the bark on the tree. I slapped it out of his grip, demanding him to try again. "Again!" *Again, again, again.*

We practiced like that for hours. I didn't think he would master it by the end of the day, but he did.

For the grand finale, I positioned myself strategically behind him, gripping his shoulders to divert his attention forward.

"Now, I need you to channel all your concentration into the humidity surrounding us," I said, releasing my grip on his shoulders. "Hold it there." I adʰāred over to grab a cup of seawater and back again to splash it against his back.

"What the hell, Adam!" he exclaimed.

"I told you to focus," I said and splashed him with another cup before he had the chance to react.

In his frustration, he grabbed a nearby bough and hurled it at me, followed by a punch to my collarbone. I couldn't help but chuckle at his reaction, but my grin faded as I noticed the anger burning in his eyes. He leaped at me, his body crashing into mine, and with a surge of energy, he pushed me to the ground, his breath ragged and the vein in his forehead pulsing.

"Stop it!" he yelled. The weight of his body pressed down on mine, with one elbow digging into my chest. I could feel the raw strength in him, and the excitement of it coursed through my veins.

"No! You're just going to learn how to handle it," I said.

His body trembled, and his gaze hinted at desperation, but he was still unyielding. I didn't realize it 'til my hands got dry and cracked between the fingers that he was attempting to evaporate my body fluids.

"You don't want to go there!" I pushed him away and switched positions with him. His breaths came in heavy gasps. He had been struggling with saltwater for too long. I wanted him to master it, but I didn't want to break him. Maybe I was too harsh, but he had to learn the hard way. My father wanted us to master our skills to perfection. There was no room for errors, especially if we found ourselves in the face of danger.

"You have no idea what it does to me," he said breathlessly.

I reached for the last cup, my hand resting firmly on his chest. "Focus." I tilted the cup, urging him to act before the water made contact. His heartbeat quickened in response, his body vibrating with anticipation, the air seeming to buzz with energy.

The water inched closer to the cup's edge, surrendering to gravity's pull. The water transformed into delicate, feather-like salt, gently falling like snowflakes. I could almost taste the salt on my tongue; it was a beautiful demonstration of the power he wielded.

I rose to my feet and extended a hand to help Elias up from the ground.

"I knew you could do it. I'm proud of you," I said, pride evident in my voice.

Elias brushed off the dirt from his hair, a hint of a smile playing on his lips as he licked them, trying to suppress his joy.

"You are ruthless!" His eyes sparkled with satisfaction.

As we climbed into the car, exhaustion settled in our bones after hours of intense training. Elias took the driver's seat, and the engine roared to life, its hum filling the cabin. The sun was dipping below the horizon, and a blanket of darkness was slowly covering the landscape. The forest, a silhouette of towering trees behind us. Elias adjusted the rearview mirror, catching a glimpse of his tired eyes. A smile tugged at the corners of my lips, a silent acknowledgment of his progress.

"That was intense," he said.

I nodded in agreement, leaning back against the seat. "You're making incredible progress, Elias."

"It's clear that I will surpass you very soon," he said, grinning.

Elias pushed further and worked harder than we did back then; he desperately wanted to impress the elders.

I turned to him. "Is that so?" I asked, amused by his cockiness. "Well, don't get too ahead of yourself. You still have a lot to learn."

Like Elias, I was an apprentice and underwent all the necessary training to become a Dūshev. We didn't care about these things when I was his age. I was an apprentice under my father. All the ones with more than one ability were taught directly by him. My true element was air, but I could also control electromagnetic waves. After truly mastering the elements, we were taught to adʰār and, finally, how to take a soul.

Over the years, my father had become somewhat paranoid and more meticulous in teaching the next generation, which was understandable, considering the few strays in our family. He was becoming a helicopter parent to his grandchildren and was not pleased when we moved to Mist Creek seven years ago. In fact, he didn't want any of us living in the States. Two of my brothers were killed by the police for simply being in the wrong place at the wrong time, and a third was killed in a hit-and-run. All three couldn't adʰār, or they would have been able to save themselves.

"You know, one day, I'll be giving you orders left and right," he teased, knowing I never intended to become an elder. "Adam, bring me food. Adam, massage my feet."

"You wish," I chuckled.

I knew he was only half kidding. Being a Dūshev meant a great deal to him. He had a clear goal in mind—to become an elder and sit next to my father.

The only way to become an elder was to father a son, which was never my priority. I had recently decided I wanted to become a person outside my family, and writing became my outlet, a passion that freed me from my father's ambitions for me.

With a final turn, we came to a halt in our driveway. Elias killed off the engine, and we both stepped out, the sound of the closing car doors disturbing the quiet evening. The two-story Victorian house stood before us, a place that technically belonged to Edgar but one that he let us live in.

"I meant to ask you, did you ever run into Aldridge?" Elias asked as we walked toward the entrance.

I had briefly told Elias that Maya had seen Aldridge take her friend's soul. But, of course, she remained unaware of what she had witnessed, and I had no intention of informing her. My brother, Aldridge, was one of those strays in our family, actually the worst one. Aldridge needed to be dealt with before he would expose all of us.

"No, I haven't," I sighed.

"What about the girl?" Elias pressed, curiosity leaking out of him.

"What about her?"

"Did he actually take her soul?"

"Oh, I—um. No, he didn't. I met her. She's fine." Why did I sound like a flustered teenager? I was making a fool out of myself. He wasn't asking about Maya.

"Oh?" he said, raising a brow, his expression mischievous. "You thought I was asking about Maya. Please elaborate. Don't let me stop you," he taunted.

"Don't even start, Elias." I wasn't about to get into that with him; I could barely explain it to myself.

"Interesting," he mused. "One might assume you're being a bit possessive over a mere girl." He turned and made his way upstairs, leaving me to my thoughts. He would have a field day if he had known how utterly infatuated I was with this *mere* girl.

Alone in the living room, I sank into the couch and wondered how it had happened. I was making excuses for myself, convincing myself that curiosity was my only motive. How had I lost control of the situation? I had been so careless and almost risked exposing us because of her empty shell of an ex-boyfriend.

I wasn't planning to get involved with her, and the irony of it wasn't lost on me. Maya had become more than just entertainment; she had become a source of unrest and spiraling desire. I couldn't resist the tug from this beautiful girl with doe eyes and long lashes. What had started as curiosity evolved into something much deeper. Day by day, I became increasingly aware of her presence even though she was not physically there. I could feel her desires entwined with my own, stirring a restless longing in me. I felt her fears echoing and coiling in the pit of my stomach. I remained a helpless observer, not knowing how to reach her while the weight of her presence wrapped around me like an invisible cloak.

"Are you still here brooding over *Maya*?" Elias said, dragging her name mockingly and interrupting the circus of my thoughts. Out of reflex, I sent a tiny shock wave through his chest, catching him off guard.

"Dick!" he exclaimed, jumping slightly before joining me on the couch. He turned on the gaming console and handed me one of the controllers. I took it so I could force myself out of the loop. I never thought I would feel that way, at least not so soon, and not with a random girl I barely knew. The mindless gaming helped. It was a diversion from the thoughts that threatened to drown me.

SIX

Maya

For the midwinter break, my father had booked a trip to Los Angeles for him and Milad to see the Warriors versus Wizards game. They had left this morning, when I was at work. I couldn't go because I had work on Monday.

Instead, I changed into my new set of matching leggings and hoodie and an old pair of sneakers. The new fit was supposed to encourage me to start working out. However, I wasn't delusional, so I didn't buy new sneakers as well.

The air was cool and carried a hint of dew. I made my way to my car, already dreading the next two hours in the gym. I stepped in and slammed the door closed when I realized something wasn't right. My seat was adjusted—pushed all the way back. *Did I do this?* I pulled the seat to where it was supposed to be when, suddenly, chills ran down my spine, and unease washed over me. *You're fine. Relax!* I looked in the rearview mirror to check if anyone was behind me, but, of course, there was no one.

Still, the faint scent of cologne seemed to linger in the air. I shook it off with a turn of the key, but the engine made a hopeless sound. I tried again and again, but it just wouldn't start. *Well, maybe this is a sign I shouldn't work out. It is Friday, after all.*

"I might have disconnected the battery," a deep voice whispered behind my ear, causing me to jolt in surprise. Before

I could scream for help, his hand covered my mouth, and I was pulled back against the seat. *I just checked! There was no one! Absolutely no one!*

"Don't worry, it's easily fixed," he said, his voice both calm and unsettling.

I always imagined I would fight back if I was assaulted, but the reality was far from it. Panic surged through me, and I desperately gasped for air, an agonizing ache coursing through my body. The world blurred around me before he released his grip, allowing me to take ragged breaths.

His hand closed around my neck, his grip tightening. "It might please you to know that you're of use to me—for now." *I know this voice!*

Before everything went dark, I caught a glimpse of Aldridge's sinister face, carving his features into my memory, leaving me to wonder what I had done to deserve this.

I woke up on a thin mattress in darkness with the musty scent of mold filling the air. Breathing felt unsafe, but it wasn't like I had a choice. My hands trembled, and my breathing was uneven.

My shoes and socks were missing, triggering a deep-rooted panic in me. It all stemmed from a vivid memory of when I was five, at the beach with my parents. I could still feel the sensation of small black beetle-like bugs crawling on my feet.

My top underneath my hoodie was still tucked into my leggings, which was a good sign, considering where I was.

As my eyes adjusted to the darkness, I could make out the details of the room. A steel door with bolts caught my attention. I got up and tried to open it, but despite my desperate attempt, it refused to budge. Dirt crunched beneath my feet as I returned to the mattress. My toes were cold and numb, on the verge of breaking off.

Although screaming was pointless, I couldn't help but cry for help. It occurred to me that I had to come to terms with my options. I could either fight for my life if given the opportunity or give up and let things be.

Time slipped away, and I lost all sense of day and night and didn't know if I had been there for hours or days. With each passing moment, the cold intensified, and I couldn't bear it any longer. Tears streamed down my cheeks, trailing down and into my ear canal. My stifled sobs filled the confined space, a haunting reminder of where I was.

After what felt like an eternity, the door swung open, and a tall blonde man entered, leaving the door slightly ajar. From where I sat, I could see the stairs outside the room. *Get up! Run!* My instincts screamed at me, but all I did was stay frozen because I had never seen this guy before. At least with Aldridge, there was a twisted sense of familiarity.

The stranger kneeled down in front of me. "You know, the Lord works in mysterious ways. He might tempt a hungry man with poison but never allow him to feed, then reward him with sweet nectar when he least expects it," he said.

He got up and didn't let himself hold back when delivering one kick after another, each blow landing with bone-jarring force. I was tossed against the wall, the impact reverberating through my chest. I clung to a flickering hope that someone would burst through that door to save me, to make him stop.

Desperate to shield myself, I raised my arms, protecting my face. Each breath became a battle, my ribs pressing painfully against my lungs, robbing me of air. The coppery tang of blood filled my mouth. Soon, my senses began to fade, and the world around me darkened. I fought consciousness, but he refused to let me slip away. I was sprawled on the ground when he kicked me awake, my body convulsing with pain. With a creak, the steel door opened, and Aldridge stepped inside. Surprise flashed across his eyes before his attention shifted to the man.

"You fucking imbecile," Aldridge lashed out, gripping the man by the collar and slamming his head against the wall before he could respond. The crack of his skull echoed in the room. "I said to scare her, not break her bones," he said to the man, who collapsed with a thud. He was motionless when blood streamed down his temple.

"Apologies, darling." He pulled a phone out of his pocket—*my phone!*

"Password?" he demanded. Still reeling from the shock, unable to think straight, my mind scrambled to remember the digits.

"Privacy is the least of your problems."

"Seventy-two, seventy-two," I muttered. There was little point in resisting, not when the lifeless body of a grown man lay just a few feet away, reminding me of the consequences of defiance. With the password successfully entered, Aldridge called someone, putting it on speaker, but no one picked up. Just as frustration etched his face, my phone suddenly started ringing.

"How lucky you are," he said, holding up the screen, showing Adam's name.

Drawing closer, he reached out and took my hand in his. His touch was surprisingly gentle, the contrast unsettling.

"Make it count." A wicked grin spread across his face in anticipation.

"Adam, tell me if you recognize this voice." Instantly, my arm was wrenched behind my back, the excruciating pain threatening to snap it out of its socket. I screamed, my back arching in a desperate attempt to lessen the pressure. I cried, knowing Adam couldn't help me through the phone.

"Please," I begged when he eased his grip on me.

"He hung up. Can you believe it?" Aldridge said and dragged me out of there with the grace of Frankenstein's monster. It didn't even hurt when my skin scratched the rough-faced stairs. The worst seemed to be over. Upstairs, the remnants of a forgotten life came into view—shabby furniture, faded wallpaper peeling off, and empty picture frames on the floor. Our footsteps creaked on the worn floorboards as dust particles danced lazily in the air, swirling around us as we walked.

We stepped out, leaving the broken-down home behind us, and emerged into a wooded area. It was clear a storm had broken. The wind was still very present, picking up my hair and leaving a stinging sensation on my skin. My body grew stiff, chilled to the bone. I was dragged along, my arm held firmly in his grip. As I struggled to keep pace with him, I looked back at the abandoned house that was claimed by nature. Ivy vines snaked across the weathered wooden panels as if reclaiming what once belonged to them.

Desperately, I scanned my surroundings, hoping to catch sight of a road or any sign of human activity. The unfamiliar scene stretched before me. My car was parked on the side of the house. *If only I knew where he kept the keys . . .*

"We have one final act and then you're free to leave. I suggest you stay out of the claws of Adam for your own sake." Aldridge released his grip, causing me to tumble to the ground. Sand and dirt from the house clung stubbornly to my bare feet, driving me mad. *This is not important. Focus!*

With Aldridge's silence enveloping me, I allowed myself to surrender to the moment. I closed my eyes, sensing an intangible shield of protection encircling me. In a sudden motion, Aldridge grabbed my hair at the base of my skull, holding my head upright, directing my gaze toward the emerging figure. *Adam! That can't be . . .*

"Let her go, Aldridge." Adam looked completely unbothered by the situation, as if it was only a slight inconvenience.

"It's a simple trade. My soul for her," Aldridge said.

I started coughing, gasping for air. The fit of the coughs only intensified, racking my body. The overwhelming sensation of suffocation took over, leaving me unable to draw even the slightest breath. Every ounce of air seemed to be sucked away by an invisible vacuum. It felt as if my airway had been completely sealed off and that I was trapped underwater. I writhed and juddered, desperately gasping for air. My phone dropped by my feet and then so did Aldridge. He was on his knees beside me, enduring the same.

Suddenly, the illusion shattered, dissolving into nothing. In an instant, all signs of pain vanished, leaving no trace of its existence. I knew I didn't imagine it because I was lying on my side with tears welling in my eyes when air flooded back into my lungs.

Aldridge burst into laughter, his amusement evident. "I bet you wonder how I did that," he said.

As if on cue, a deafening clap of thunder hit the gloomy woods. The ground quivered in response, sending tremors up my legs. A dome of air seemed to ripple around us and disappear again. *Boom!* And it rippled again, threatening to collapse. *Boom! Boom!* The dome shattered. There was a sudden release from the previous quietness. The air felt alive again, carrying with it the scent of damp earth and the rustling whispers of nature.

A glowing blast of energy surged toward Aldridge, streaking through the air and creating visible ripples as it traveled. A guttural scream erupted from Aldridge as his hands flew to his head, his fingers digging into his temples and beads of sweat dotting his brows.

And then, in the blink of an eye, he vanished before me. He closed his eyes, and his body disappeared into thin air within seconds. It began with his hair delicately dissolving like sugar in a hot cup of tea. The transformation spread from the outer parts of his body, moving toward the center of his chest, until nothing remained but stillness and his lingering essence—a trace of his haunting scent. *I'm not crazy! I'm not crazy! I'm not crazy!*

"Dammit!" Adam's voice sliced through the silence, tearing me from my train of thought. His soft footsteps thudded as he strode toward me and kneeled.

"Give me your hands," he said, his voice gentle yet firm. Uncertain, I extended one hand, thinking he wanted to help me stand.

His eyes met mine with concern. "Both," he insisted.

As his hands enveloped mine, a warmth spread through me, removing all the pain in my body. It was as if a soothing balm had been applied all over me, relieving me of every ache. The soreness in my arm, the pressure in my lungs, and the throbbing headache were all gone, leaving behind nothing else but relief. I watched him in awe. *I'm not crazy!*

"I'm sorry it went this far. I should have taken precautions," he said.

With his help, I got up, my focus shifting back to the old house.

He kneeled, grabbed my phone from the ground, and handed it to me. "I'll see if I can find your car keys," he said. In an instant, he vanished before my eyes. *I'm not crazy.* There was no way I was imagining that.

A brief moment passed, and just as suddenly, he reappeared, holding the keys in his hand.

"I'll drive you home," he offered, which I was grateful for. My brain was left in scrambles, and the last thing I wanted to do was drive myself in this state. I followed him to the car, letting him open the passenger door for me, but he stopped me with a gentle hand on my shoulder before I could get in.

"Maya." He reached for my face, cupping my cheeks in his hands. "Are you okay? You haven't said a word."

"I'm fine," I said. "*I don't know what you think you saw, Adam. Maybe your drink was spiked.*"

He sighed, and his forehead touched mine. Our barrier had been crossed, and I didn't mind it one bit. He was so close. *Stop it! Don't fall for it!* But it was too late. All I could do was lick the wounds of my scraped knees and pull Eros's arrow from my chest. I was so fucked.

"Look, I'm sorry. I will tell you everything, I promise."

Even though he was the reason Aldridge kidnapped me, Adam actually came, and he saved my life, but I still needed answers. I just wasn't sure I could handle much in that state.

I stepped back, not letting his touch affect me. "Everything!" I demanded.

"Everything! I promise."

I settled into the seat, pulled my feet up, and brushed the dirt off with my hands. Adam joined me in the car, slipping into the driver's seat. As he turned the key, the engine hummed to life, and we moved forward. The familiar road reassured me I was safe and going home. So, I leaned back, closed my eyes, and let the air conditioner's cool breeze ground me.

"How were you able to find me?" I asked, my voice barely above a whisper, the words escaping my lips as I kept my eyes closed. My curiosity mingled with exhaustion, but I had to know what had led him to my rescue.

"I can feel your presence," he said softly. "Not just now, but sometimes, in the middle of the day. Sometimes at night, as if I have a direct line to you, a deep awareness of where you are and the emotions you experience," he said.

I opened my eyes and turned to him.

"How is that even possible?" The doubt lingered in my mind, a trace of skepticism tugging at me.

"I don't know. I swear I have no idea," he said, briefly meeting my eyes. I saw no deception. Instead, I saw a confusion that mirrored my own. I decided to allow myself to believe in the extraordinary, to believe that there was something magic between us.

"I can drive myself from here," I said as we neared his home.

"No, it's fine. I don't mind," Adam replied.

We pulled up to my house, and a tinge of apprehension settled around me. I couldn't help but notice the absence of lights. Yet I didn't dare ask Adam to stay. I took a deep breath, steeling myself to face the loneliness of my empty house.

"Are you going to be okay tonight?" He reached for my arm.

"I'll be fine." *But I wish you would stay with me.* I pressed my lips together in a thin line to reassure him before going inside. I closed the door behind me, bolting both locks. I stood there for a moment, my senses heightened as if waiting for any sign of an intruder. With a cautious step, I made my way upstairs, carefully navigating through the empty rooms, making sure I was truly alone before going to my own room. Although fear lingered in the back of my mind, I pushed it aside and decided to take a much-needed shower.

V

SEVEN

Maya

I groggily woke up to the persistent ringing of my phone buried under the pillow. It was Adam calling, but I didn't pick up because I didn't want him to know I was sleeping. Instead, I dragged myself out of bed, feeling the weight of exhaustion in my limbs. I realized it was already nearing noon, and the throbbing ache in my head intensified. I had slept way too much. I shuffled to the bathroom, washed my face, brushed my teeth, and tested my voice before calling him back.

He picked up on the first ring. "Maya."

"Hi," I said, attempting to mask the desperate itch to speak with him. "You called?" I didn't want to sound desperate, even though I wanted an explanation, and it couldn't come fast enough.

"I also texted you. I wanted to know how you're feeling," he said.

"I mean, I'm fine, but we still need to talk." I wasn't going to settle for anything less than an elaborate explanation.

"I know."

"You can come over here if you want," I said and regretted it immediately. It sounded desperate. "Or we could go for a walk or a drive." *Does it sound casual enough?*

"Okay, see you in a bit," he said.

We hung up, and I started to panic; I didn't know if he would magically appear at my door or drive here like a normal person.

Frantically, I scurried around my room, picking up all the scattered clothes, shoving them into my closet, and changing into a pair of jeans and a T-shirt so it didn't look like I had just woken up.

Because I had slept with my hair wet, wrapped in a towel, it looked like a bird's nest; it was always curlier when I did that. So, I ran my hands under the water, finger brushed the hair down, and added mousse to tame it.

Then I went downstairs to inspect the house; it looked fine, just as I had left it. So, I went into the kitchen and filled the double tea kettle with water. It was a Persian tea kinda day. I needed all the healing I could get, and drinking Persian tea felt like a hug from my grandma. I cracked three cardamom pods with my teeth, crushed a few dried rosebuds in my hand, and threw them into the top kettle with the black tea leaves. When the water started boiling, I added a pinch of saffron to the tea mix. The tea needed to steep for fifteen minutes to get the perfect balanced flavor. That would give me enough time to run back upstairs and look myself in the mirror, but then the doorbell rang, and my stomach churned with anticipation.

Was I supposed to be ready to go outside? We didn't exactly decide anything. Is he coming inside? Where would we sit or stand—the living room? No. Kitchen?

As I walked into the hall, I saw Adam through the window panel of the door. He smiled, his dimples showing, and it eased the sourness of my stomach. He was so very handsome, even in a boring gray hoodie.

"Hi," I said awkwardly, opening the door wide enough for him to enter. He was holding a yellow Hen & Co. paper bag.

"I brought cookies," he said and handed me the bag. I closed the door and peeked inside.

Impossible!

"Chocolate chip cookies. They are the best." He noticed the shoe rack by the door and instinctively took off his shoes.

"I know. I get them all the time. Have you been stalking me?" I joked, leading him into the kitchen.

"Come on now," he responded defensively. "We have two good bakeries in the city."

"Fair enough." I shrugged. "Do you want some tea? I was just about to have a cup."

"Yes, thank you," he said straight up. Of course it didn't matter. I was used to it. There was no *Taarof* in the Western culture; they always kept it real. *Taarof* was the Persian word for a custom that came into play when people offered you something. Especially as a first-time guest in someone's house, it was considered impolite to accept anything before it was offered three times. This custom was common in all of the Middle East and Asia.

"Do you live here with your family?" he asked.

"Yes, with my father and little brother." I poured us both half a cup of the concentrated tea and topped it with the hot water from the bottom kettle. "Do you want to look around?" I liked snooping in people's homes and always offered the same in return. I found it quite fascinating to see how people lived and what trinkets they collected. There was always a story to how things ended up in someone's home.

"Sure," he said.

Either I was procrastinating for my own mental health, or I was very nervous. Either way, I was talking way too much.

He followed me, tea in hand. "Not very exciting here." I gestured to the living room. "I'm mostly in my room or in the kitchen."

Then I took him upstairs and crossed the hall to my brother's room.

"Beware! Milad's room is a war zone," I said before opening the door. Luckily, it didn't stink. Still, it was utter chaos. My brother's room was the classic teenage boy's room: a gaming station with two screens and a keyboard that lit up in rainbow colors when it was on. A chair that served as a basket for clean laundry. The floor was decorated with his dirty socks, work-out clothes, and his nasty boxing gloves. And the sheets on his bed were always halfway torn off.

"I'm not allowed in here, so count yourself lucky." I took a cord from his desk and shoved it under his mattress.

"Why did you do that?" Adam asked.

My brother and I had done things like that so often that it almost became second nature. I smiled, unable to come up with a good explanation.

"I see," he said, understanding what I was doing.

We crossed the hall to my room. "And this is my room," I said and gestured for him to have a look as I took a sip of my tea before it turned cold.

He grabbed the bell hanging from my door handle before entering. "A bell," he said.

"It's a *doorbell*. Get it? Ha-ha." I guess I was so used to it jangling that I never actually heard it anymore.

"This room is warded," he said under his breath when he took a step inside.

"What?"

"Oh, I see. So many crystals and books! You have so much stuff in your room." His eyes wandered around the space, brimming with curiosity, before he sat on the side of my bed. *What is it with men who don't know the difference between outside and inside clothes? I will let it slide. Now that the sheets are dirty . . . If I could just peel off those outside clothes . . . Push you down . . . No. Stop it! Focus. Talk about something else.*

"My mom left the crystals when she moved. My dad wanted to get rid of them, but I thought they were too pretty—"

"Don't worry, I don't judge." He stopped me.

"What do you mean?" I wasn't ashamed of my parents being divorced. It was better for both of them.

"If you are Pagan or into Wicca, I mean."

"I'm sorry, you lost me. What are you talking about?"

"I mean, you clearly believe these"—he picked up the marbly white gemstone—"are more than just pretty rocks, since you have carefully placed them around your room. Selenite by the door, carnelian and rose quartz near your vanity, and this on your bedside table." His thumb ran over its smooth surface.

"What are you, an expert on crystals now?" I scoffed. "Or are you trying to make me look witchy to downplay everything that happened yesterday?" I asked, getting a bit annoyed with him. There was nothing magical about me. There would be no filter over my mouth this time. He looked apprehensive; maybe he didn't feel like he could trust me. "Adam, whatever you tell me will never leave this room. I promise you." I said and took the snarkiness out of my tone.

He shifted slightly, carefully placing the cup of tea on my nightstand before leaning against the headboard. With a gentle expression, he replied, "It's not like anyone would believe you." His words struck a chord within me.

"Then, tell me."

"We call ourselves Dūshevnici," he said. His eyes locked with mine. "Over the years, it's been shortened to Dūshev. A Dūshev is made with intention. We are born, yes, but entirely different from humans. Even other practitioners cannot measure with us. We have power over the elements. We wield it, bend it, and make it an extension of ourselves. You've seen it with your own eyes, the damage we can cause, the harm we can do. We can teleport through thin air and appear anywhere—unless it's warded, of course."

"Wait, is that what you meant when you said my room is warded?" I asked, not even sure I understood what he said.

"Yes. It means I cannot, under any circumstances, adhār into your room. I can travel within the wards and out but never in," he said.

"*Ad*-what?"

"Adhār—appear, teleport, or whatever you want to call it. It's not something we are born with but something we learn after we have mastered our elemental power, just like a child has to learn how to walk."

"Damn . . . So, you can just go anywhere you want?" I wanted him to keep talking, but I couldn't help interrupting and asking him questions. I sat across from him on the bed, leaving enough distance between us.

"As long as it isn't warded, then, yes. While it might seem magical and convenient most of the time, it's truly draining. If I overuse it, my body will start to protest and work against me. We have the power to adhār for a very specific reason. We must be able to appear and disappear to do our job. Our sole purpose is to distribute souls amongst humans. You can say it's the vegan version of Hermes." He scoffed.

"What?" I wasn't sure I heard that right. *Hermes distributed souls . . . ?*

"We take souls from people who waste them and give them to children—technically, boys born without souls. I have yet to come across a female born without a soul. My father's theory is that if you are born into this world with a womb and have the power of creation within you, you are predestined with a soul because the soul is created in the womb. Although it's still possible for a woman to destroy her soul."

"How?" I asked, eager to know if I had destroyed mine but afraid to ask.

"Extreme drug or alcohol abuse can cause it. Physical or mental trauma, any extreme distress can damage a soul. With the soul comes humanity, compassion, and morals. So, if we, as Dūshevs, don't get to the soul before it's destroyed, it will go to waste. People without souls slowly lose themselves."

"Who decided you could play god?" I asked before I could stop myself and rephrase the question. I was asking out of curiosity and didn't mean to sound so judgmental. Although I probably was a little.

"Believe me, we know what it means to hold that much power. My father taught us that and built a legacy around it. We do not simply exist to be superior to the human race and play god. Our purpose is to balance the order of nature. My father was the very first of his kind, gifted by a goddess. However, he saw it as a curse in the early days until he understood the soul's journey. He was finally able to see how he could change the world for the better. Without him, the world would fall apart because there are only a finite number of souls, and not all souls match their vessels. My brothers and I are created to correct that flaw," Adam said, hiding his pride.

I wasn't sure my brain could fully grasp it. There was nothing ordinary about Adam, and maybe the attraction was my simple human soul drawn to this supernatural creature. Surely, that was why he was alluring beyond comprehension. *Is my attraction even real?*

"What happens to the people you take the souls from?" I asked, but deep down, I knew the answer. *They die.*

"They die." He repeated the words from my mind. "On rare occasions, some live on for a few years."

How is that fair? Why did they get to decide who was worthy of a soul? If it's my soul, do I not have the right to destroy it?

"What about Aldridge?" I asked.

Adam sighed at the mention of him. "My brother is—"

"He's your brother!" I exclaimed. "You don't even look alike."

"Yes, he is my brother. All my brothers have different mothers, so we don't always look alike. Our mother's soul is transferred to us during pregnancy, so when we take our first breath, our mothers take their last," he said.

"So, none of you ever met your mothers?"

"All of us except Aldridge. Just as someone can be born without a soul, some people are born with multiple. A flaw of the universe, you could say. That was probably why she survived giving birth to a Dūshev." He paused. "It's worth mentioning that not all women can carry our children. Often, they get miscarriages."

"What is the deal with him, though?" I didn't want to mention Aldridge's name. It seemed to bother him.

He sighed again. "Aldridge has been in constant conflict with our father and the elders. He isolated himself years ago and refused to see any of us. I didn't know the scope of his issues with my father until he ordered anyone who saw Aldridge to take his soul as a form of punishment." He paused, his voice filled with a profound sense of conviction. "I ended up being that someone not so long ago."

"And now he will do anything and kill anyone to get it back," I finished for him. I knew there was something about Aldridge that rubbed me the wrong way. I just hadn't imagined it was that bad.

"He won't come for you again," Adam reassured me. "He isn't that stupid. He knows I can get rid of him. Trust me."

"If—I mean . . . This is very overwhelming. I feel like you're making this shit up, leaving me with more questions than before."

"Shoot," he said. "I promised to tell you everything, and I will."

"How many brothers do you have? Are there others like you? Are you immortal? Do mermaids exist?"

"I am the thirteenth son of the first Dūshev, and I have twenty-six brothers and a bunch of nephews. No, there is no other like us. We are not immortal by any means, but we do age at a different rate. And as far as mermaids go, I have never met one," he said with a curl to his lips.

Twenty-six. Holy fuck! Different rate? How different? Slower or faster. No mermaids, what a bummer.

"Is Adam even your real name?"

"Yes. Adam Pave, short for Pavlenko. My grandfather was Russian. He married my Egyptian grandmother. In fact, my mother was also Egyptian, so I'm twenty-five percent Russian and seventy-five percent Egyptian."

"You—Oh. I didn't realize you were Arab," I said before thinking. I knew Arabs weren't exclusively White. Of course, I knew that! *How dense am I even?* I didn't want to sound stupid, so I skipped the thought and kept going before he could catch on.

"And you age at a different rate. What does that even mean? Dog years?"

He smiled and hesitated for a second. "I was born in 1645. The first eighteen years of our lives pass like normal human years. After that, it's different. Time is a weird construct. All these societal and cultural changes seem so grand when you look back, but everything is diluted when you are in the heat of the moment. We age at a slower rate. It's estimated to be fifty or fifty-five years per human year. By that logic, I am between twenty-four and twenty-five years old," he said.

1645! "Oh my." I gasped. "And I thought you were too old for me before. Imagine that," I muttered to myself. *Fuck! I wasn't supposed to say that out loud! I need a shovel to dig my own grave. This is so embarrassing, dammit. Think fast. Change topics!*

"Did Aldridge take my soul?" I asked, knowing I didn't feel any different.

He got up and walked to stand in front of me. If I were to have stood, we would've almost touched.

"Do you want me to check?" There were sparks in his eyes, and for a second, he made it sound like he was asking to kiss me.

"Can you?" I asked breathlessly.

He pulled me up by the hand and stood even closer, his body lined up with mine, heat emanating from him. His right hand went behind my back, and his left hand gently lay over my chest. "Relax," he said. *Fuck!* I closed my eyes so I wouldn't have to look at him. My eyes would give me away, reveal my desire for him. I could easily melt away, lose myself in him. His hand moved toward my neck, and his fingers grazed my jaw. Chills ran down my spine. *Fuck!*

"You're fine," he said casually, letting go of me. I felt utterly exposed as if standing naked and drenched in sweat. He walked to my window and started playing with my chimes, Unaware of the state he had left me in. I shook the feeling off and tried to be as nonchalant as him.

"When I first saw Aldridge, his hand only hovered over Dissie's chest when he tried to take her soul." *He didn't touch her like you touched me.* I wanted to say but then I thought better of it.

It took him a moment to consider. "Well, I wasn't attempting to take your soul, was I?"

"Oh."

"Or perhaps I just wanted an excuse to touch you, just like you wanted an excuse to be touched." He grinned.

I felt the heat rising to my head. "My god, you're full of yourself."

I couldn't help but feel a mix of fascination and horror. Adam reassured me that Aldridge wouldn't return, not even for Dissie. Still, Adam's morbid world unraveled before my eyes. A world of monsters that people didn't know about. I was allowed a front-row seat, but I didn't know if I was supposed to watch my back or let my guard down.

EIGHT

Adam

There had been no sign of Aldridge since the day he tried to hold Maya against me. I hadn't exactly told Elias why, but we diligently combed through every hotel, inn, and motel in the city in our attempt to find him. I wasn't worried about him returning; he wouldn't risk it. Still, it had changed Maya; I couldn't blame her. There was so much information to take in and process. Aldridge might have scared her away from us—from me, which was probably for the best—but I couldn't let her go just yet. I reached out to her several times, only getting vague answers for replies. She needed time. I understood that, but that day felt different. Something was wrong, and I knew it before my phone rang and before I saw her name across the screen.

"Are you okay?" were my first words because I needed reassurance.

"Can you meet me at the parking lot of St. Joseph's Hospital?" Maya asked. She sounded fine, but she definitely wasn't.

"What happened? Are you okay?" I asked as I grabbed my keys, contemplating whether to aďhār or drive. It was in the middle of the day. I couldn't just appear out of the blue.

"I'm fine. Call me when you get here," she said and hung up. I let out a breath, even though something was tugging at me. I knew she was safe, but it didn't stop me from spiraling the entire drive to the hospital.

Before I arrived, I received a text from her. *I'm parked in section F66*, it read.

She was standing there with her arms crossed, leaning against her car. *She's fine.* I parked the car and got out.

"Maya," I said as I walked toward her. She straightened and shook her head, which made me stop in my tracks.

"I have a question." I couldn't move, dreading the feeling brewing inside me. "Did you take his soul, Adam?" *Shit . . .*

I hadn't thought much of it when I took his soul, except that he lived in the same city. By the time I saw him again, a few months had passed, and the clock was ticking. That's when I first noticed her. She didn't pique my interest at the time; I was only intrigued by how she was clinging to him. I could tell by how she carried herself, how she bit her lip and flipped her hair from one side to the other, how she desperately sought his attention. Still, Jonathan wasn't going to give Maya the attention she wanted because he had nothing to give.

She didn't tell me how or why, but they broke up sometime last year, probably shortly after I took his soul. She was too good for him anyway, even before.

Now, his time had come, and she had pieced it together. I could have told her, I should have told her, but I didn't. I had told her everything else, though, more than I had shared with any other girl, and now I had to deal with the aftermath.

"I had no choice. I already explained this to you." I tried to emphasize, but this was my life, and the work I did was simple. I was in the business of souls, and I couldn't change what I was.

"Were you ever planning to tell me?" She spat the words out like she hated every cell of my being.

"Yes, of course, but no matter what, it wouldn't change his fate."

"Of course not! You made sure of that," she said. She blamed me, and there was nothing I could do about it.

We were not here to play heroes. In fact, many stories depicted us as villains. The fairytales and movies about vampires were based on us. Although we didn't drink blood or live forever, there were many similarities.

"What if it was me? What if your father told you to take my soul and give it to someone else?" she continued.

"That would be different." It would. I wasn't lying. I would find a way.

"How would it be different, Adam? You don't have a choice, do you? And you can't change someone's fate, can you?"

"No," I raised my voice, matching hers. "But I would try. I would find a way, even if it meant going against my family. Do you not see how obsessed I am with you!"

She looked away, and I was too scared to step forward. I wanted to touch her, to tell her I was sorry, to tell her I wished I could do something to make it go away.

"The doctors say he had heart failure and might not make it," she whispered.

"I'm sorry," I said, walking closer, but she stepped back.

"I need some time to think about all this," she said, opening her car door. I desperately searched for something, anything, to make her reconsider.

"Wait," I said, instinctively reaching out toward her.

"Please, Adam," she pleaded, her voice filled with sadness. The unspoken emotions in her eyes shattered everything in me.

As much as I wanted to hold her and beg her to stay, I knew it would only lead to more pain. Reluctantly, watching her leave, I let my arm fall and slip back to my side. The sound of her car engine faded into the distance.

٩

NINE

Maya

Jonathan died the night he was admitted to the hospital. I couldn't help but feel guilty, even though I had nothing to do with it. It didn't even cross my mind until I got the call from Jonathan's brother and went to see him at the hospital. It dawned on me that Jonathan's change of behavior was unnatural, that it happened overnight, and suddenly, everything aligned.

I didn't let myself believe it until I heard it from Adam himself. I thought he would have had the courtesy to tell me before I had asked him because I deserved to know. Of course, he didn't tell me straight up; it would make him look bad. Not that I could have prevented what happened to Jonathan. Adam must've taken his soul back when we were still together—I didn't ask him when it was. In fact, I hadn't spoken to him since. He had called, but I couldn't bring myself to answer. I wanted to talk to him, hear his voice, and let him fill me with excuses and justifications to erase the chafing guilt.

Most of all, I felt guilty for falling for him. Admitting it to myself was the hardest part, since I didn't know what way was up. I was torn between all my desires and my moral compass. All this time, I had been searching for a feeling of contentment and a true purpose, but I didn't know it would come with the heavy burden of conscience. How was I supposed to look away while his whole existence revolved around stealing souls and leaving people to die?

To meet Adam felt like finding the missing piece to my puzzle, the answers to my questions, and the possibility of being truly loved and cherished by someone. I wouldn't have been conflicted if there was nothing between us, but no matter what, I couldn't pretend away the desire to be with him.

That was one part of my dilemma. The other part was Dissie. I was supposed to meet with her but then Jonathan died, and the days slipped through the cracks again. I wondered if she had heard from Aldridge, if she was still seeing him, and if he would come back to take my soul.

I promised Adam I wouldn't tell anyone about them, but I couldn't watch while Dissie walked straight into a death trap. On the other hand, what if I told her and that she didn't believe me? What if she thought I was crazy? What if Aldridge had some power over what she could and could not remember? Maybe if I finished early at the fair, I could meet up with Dissie.

Without asking me, my father promised Miss Peterson I would help her at The Figlow Lodge Art Fair because her daughter had gotten the flu. Miss Peterson was the event organizer at the art fair, and even though I didn't want to, I couldn't say no because she was literally the nicest person ever.

Figlow Lodge was huge, but the stalls and art stations were still crammed together. The air was thick with the chatter and excitement of noisy kids. I hadn't expected so many to show up; people squeezed together, navigating through the crowd. The scent of stale coffee wafted through the air, blending with the faint hint of pine from the lodge's rustic décor.

The mayor even came. He gave the shortest speech ever given. Still, his words resonated through the room, capturing everyone's attention. Miss Peterson went up to speak when the mayor stepped down.

"Good afternoon, everyone, and welcome to another year at The Figlow Lodge Art Fair!" Her voice carried over the crowd, vibrant and enthusiastic.

"Yet again, we are here to inspire you with our activities. This year, you can let your imagination run wild at our craft stations, where you can create masterpieces using various materials like paints, beads, papercraft, and a clay modeling station, perfect for those who love sculpting and molding. With the guidance of our skilled instructors, you can create anything you like. So, whether it's the returning favorite: face painting, DIY crafts, or clay modeling, there's something for every artist here at The Figlow Lodge. I'm encouraging everyone to dive into the world of art, let your creativity soar, and enjoy your time at the fair!" Excited whispers spread among the children.

A hand pressed against the small of my back, triggering an involuntary reaction. My heart plummeted, and a wave of anxiety crashed over me. "Excuse me," the man's voice broke through. Startled, I turned to face a man trying to maneuver past me. I managed to step aside. The sound of my heartbeat pulsed in my ears, and my breathing was shallow and rapid. Attempting to regain my composure, I took a deep breath.

When I looked up again, Miss Peterson was heading toward me.

"I need you to help me at the paint station before the parents let their kids actually run wild," she said as she guided me through the crowd to a table with two huge boxes of acrylic paint tubes. "The smartest thing is we do it like last year." She handed me a stack of paper plates. "Let the kids pick their colors and squeeze a little on their plates—shoot! I forgot the brushes. Wait here!" she said and sprinted away.

I sorted through the tubes. Some were dried empty, but there were plenty of unopened ones. Suddenly, an overwhelming sense of being watched washed over me. Instinctively, I shifted my gaze to the right, where Adam was speaking with one of the clay instructors, who was pointing past the painting section. My heart raced with the thought of his proximity. Adam thanked the guy and appeared to be heading toward me. *Is he stalking me? How did he know I was here? I'm not ready to talk to him.*

Returning to the table, Miss Peterson placed a plastic container full of brushes in front of me with a thud. "Adam!" she called out, beckoning him over. A smile passed between them before his eyes met mine. I discreetly shook my head, signaling that I couldn't do this right now, especially not in front of everyone. Nevertheless, he continued to make his way toward us.

"I'm glad you could make it. Jared is setting up for you guys. Let me show you where he is," Miss Peterson said, leading him away. Why did I always make everything about me? He didn't come to the fair for me. Although he did look back at me while following Miss Peterson. My eyes faltered under the weight of his defeated gaze. How many times could I push him away before he never came back? Would he understand that I needed time, or would he give up?

My phone vibrated in my pocket. It was a message from Dissie. I had texted her earlier, asking if she wanted to grab something to drink after five.

Can't. I'm closing and then The Brit is picking me up ;) . . .

I reread the message twice, hoping the words would rearrange themselves into something else. *I have a bad feeling about him Delnaz.* I wrote back, hoping her real name would help with the urgency of my plea. Putting my phone away, I noticed a child approaching with her parents. Soon, more kids joined, and one kid became ten, and I was giving away paint faster than *nun Barbari* during the morning rush.

Hours went by until the last lingering families trickled home, and we began packing up, gathering brushes and plates, wiping down tables, and stacking chairs. I didn't see Adam again, and his absence left an emptiness in my stomach, but Adam couldn't be a priority right now. Dissie hadn't responded to my text, which wasn't unusual when she was at work, especially an hour before closing. Still, I just couldn't shake this negative feeling. I had to get there before Aldridge. I couldn't convince her over the phone, but she would listen to me face-to-face.

After wrapping up at the lodge, I rushed to my car. I had roughly thirty minutes before the diner closed and, at most, an hour before Dissie would lock up and leave. Thoughts were racing through my head. What if she left early and I didn't make it? Was her sister there, too? Were any of the guys at work or only the girls? Could they even stand a chance? What if he had already taken her soul in the past few weeks?

I neared The Nob and spotted her standing behind the counter. I could finally breathe. Luckily, Aldridge was nowhere in sight. So, I drove around the block and parked near the staff entrance. Until that point, I hadn't thought about calling Adam. What would I even say? *Sorry for ignoring you. Please come save my friend. Tsk . . .*

It was suddenly so quiet I could hear my own breathing. I kept glancing through the rearview mirror, half expecting to find Aldridge lurking behind me, but he wasn't there; I was being paranoid. *Should I call Adam? No. Stop being desperate.* Still, I took my phone out, looking at the last message from Adam. *I could text him "Coming to The Nob" and pretend it was for Dissie. No! Stop embarrassing yourself.* Then a shiver coursed down my spine, and a cloud of dread engulfed me. Without thinking, I hastily typed *Nob* before hitting send. *There is no one in the back seat,* I told myself. With a deep breath, I stepped out of the car, locked the doors, and tried to compose myself. He was here; I could feel it, even though I couldn't see him yet.

I buried my trembling hands in my pockets and turned toward the diner's back entrance. That's when I saw him emerge from the shadows, just a few feet away, his wolfish eyes piercing into mine.

He approached with measured steps, gradually closing the distance between us. I wanted to move, escape his grasp, but fear made me immobile. His hands caressed my face with a deceptive tenderness as if he meant no harm. His nose trailed along my shoulder, reaching the nape of my neck. Still, I couldn't move a muscle, unsure if I was even breathing.

"I can sense his filth coating you." He was smiling from ear to ear, still cupping my face, grazing my temple. "And you have given me no choice, darling."

He weaved his fingers into my hair, grabbed it, and pulled my head backward. I braced myself, expecting a release of fog or swirling smoke, but nothing happened when his hand was above my chest.

His face bore a few scattered scars, and his eyebrows were thick and undone. His scent enveloped me as I stood in his pres-ence—a heady blend of woody notes, warm and rich like cloves and cinnamon, perhaps even a hint of frankincense. The scent was oddly captivating, the only tangible thing to cling to amid the unfolding nightmare. My vision blurred, and a force com-pelled the life within me to surge outwards. It slipped past my lips, coursing through my chest. Like a glove being pulled off, he pulled the air from my lungs and the blood from my veins. Yet there was no pain—rather, a strange sense of relaxation, a surrender to the inevitable. The taste of blood burned in my throat and reminded me that this was not a good thing. *I should want this to stop.* My limbs remained unresponsive, refusing to obey the commands of my brain. I couldn't fight or call for help. I felt weightless, trapped in a dream-like state. My feet seemed as heavy as concrete blocks, yet without the pull of gravity.

Every signal of movement my mind tried to send through my body was dulled down to nothing. He drained me of everything I had, leaving my body sweaty and my muscles sore. I was the trapped fly, constantly slamming my head against a closed window, not seeing the glass barrier.

In the realm of dreams and unconsciousness, vitality flowed through my body, infusing me with life at once. I caught snippets of Adam's voice, his words a jumble of incomprehension yet comforting. I felt the warmth of his hands encircling my waist, his scent enveloping me like a soothing embrace. I closed my eyes because I was safe again.

When I woke again, I regained control over my limbs. I was in my bedroom, lying on the bed, the familiar texture of my blanket under me. Adam sat at the edge of the bed, facing me, his hand tenderly clasping mine. The touch of his skin against mine stirred a wild longing within me, a desire that disregarded all the dangers of his world. None of it mattered, for, in that moment, I wanted him, regardless of who or what he was.

"How are you feeling?" he whispered.

"I'm fine. How did we get here?" I replied, pushing myself up onto my elbows and sitting upright. "Who let you in? Is my father home?" . . . *Had they met?*

"I drove us in your car—found the keys in your bag. Your brother let us in. I told him you were drunk, and he watched me carry you all the way to your bed and showed me out the door. I teleported back into the hallway before he walked up the stairs. I needed to make sure you were alright." His hand tightened around mine for a fleeting moment. "I can leave if you want," he said, his voice just above a whisper.

"Will you stay?" I asked, hoping he wouldn't say no. My brother was here, and my father would come home soon. What if Aldridge came back again? I was putting my family in danger, but what choice did I have?

"Maya," Adam said, his hand finding mine, caressing me with utmost gentleness. *Did he ask me something I didn't hear?* Then he touched my cheek and turned my face to his. I felt my cheeks heat up.

"How did you end up in that alley?"

"Uhmm—I . . . Dissie told me she was meeting him after work, and she doesn't know what you—he is," I said.

"What were you thinking? Why didn't you tell me? Do you understand the danger you put yourself in?" His voice had an edge of frustration, making me feel like an idiot. Of course, I didn't think I would run into him. I thought I would catch her before she met up with him and prevent it—how, I had no idea.

"I was just having a main character moment."

"This isn't some game, Maya. You can't go on a suicide mission because you're mad at me. What if I didn't make it?" He sounded annoyed like I was a child he was forced to take care of.

"Do you think I went there because of you? Dissie is in danger because of your brother. Not everything is about you!" I retorted, pulling the blanket over my head and turning away from him. "I don't want to be a bother to you. You don't have to stay."

Adam got up immediately, and I felt a pit in my stomach. His shadow loomed over me as he stood, blocking the gentle glow of the lamp. To my surprise, he circled around the bed and kneeled in front of me. His face mere inches from mine. With a gentle touch, he cupped my face, his thumb softly caressing my cheek. His voice, barely above a breath. "I'm not leaving you." His eyes filled with unwavering devotion, erasing any lingering doubt.

At that moment, time seemed to stand still. I could feel his breath against my cheek, his gaze locked on my lips. The anticipation hung between us. Every fiber of my being yearned for the connection, for the press of his lips against mine.

What if it isn't magical? What if I feel nothing?

But then he leaned in, kissed me, and ignited sparks and fireworks like a fire alarm going off. His fingers delicately threaded through my hair. I could feel the hint of a smile on his lips as they melded with mine and the touch of the delicate and invisible bristles that marked my skin.

He nestled beside me, pulling me closer; his arms circled my waist in a possessive embrace. I rested my head on his shoulder, hoping the steady rhythm of his heartbeat would help me breathe.

١٠

TEN

MAYA

When I woke up, Adam wasn't there. I don't know when he left, but it must have been while I slept. The curtains were drawn, but the glow of my phone illuminated the room as I scrolled through the different group chats, my mind still drowsy with sleep. Suddenly, the door swung open. Milad barged in, switched on the light, and flexed his nonexistent muscles in the mirror.

"Get out!" I exclaimed.

"This is my domain now because I have dirt on you." With a triumphant smirk, Milad continued his grunting sounds, flexing his biceps.

"Close the door," I said before he turned to leave. Milad, being the brat that he was, left the door ajar. I stayed in bed for another hour, staring at the ceiling, before finally getting up from my warm bed and changing out of my pajamas. I didn't have a bathroom connected to my bedroom; we only had one upstairs and one downstairs. As always, Milad had splashed water all over the tiles. My socks got slightly wet, but I didn't bother changing. Instead, I rubbed my feet against the green carpet and all the way down the stairs. My dad wasn't home, which was unusual for a Sunday morning. He would, typically, be in the kitchen, flipping pancakes before he sat down to read the paper or watch the news. My dad watched every news channel there was, both in English and other international ones. My father's usual spot remained empty, the Sunday paper untouched, the television silent.

I was too tired to make traditional Persian tea, even though it was the first day of Nowruz. Instead, I started the kettle with some jasmine green tea with three cardamom pods and then went back upstairs and crossed the hall to Milad's room.

"Have you talked to Dad?"

Milad, lost in his world of video games, lazily lifted one side of his headphones. "What?" he muttered, his attention divided.

"Have you talked to Dad?" I repeated.

His response was tinged with sarcasm. "You mean, did I tell Dad a boy carried your drunk ass home yesterday? No." Stretching out his hand. "That'll be twenty bucks," he said.

"But honestly, how embarrassing for your life! It wasn't even nine, and you blacked out." He paused his game and turned around. "And who was that guy, your boyfriend?"

I clenched my jaw, avoiding the topic of Adam. "Can you just tell me where Dad went?" I didn't know what he was to me after just one kiss. Momentum led him to kiss me, nothing else.

"Oh! I didn't tell you," Milad said with enthusiasm. "Dad asked me to update his phone, and a text popped up from someone called Daisy. It said, 'You can't tell anyone about yesterday.' It was the only text from her."

"I don't want to hear it," I said, leaving his room. The last thing I needed was to know who my father was messing around with.

"I swear, if you even think about touching the last cookie, I'll punch you in the face. I'm saving it for later," Milad's voice echoed after me. I hurried downstairs, managing to take the tea off the heat just in time, when my phone vibrated in my pocket. I retrieved it and saw my grandma's nickname, *Mamani,* on the screen.

"*Sale no mobarak,*" I greeted her, attempting to mask my guilt for not calling her last night to wish her a happy Nowruz.

"I will not be here forever to teach you the ways of life, young lady. Do you know what time it is? I have waited all day," she said.

"I'm sorry, I just woke up. *Bekhoda,* I was about to call you," I said while pouring myself tea.

"Don't' swear in vain," she chided. Of course, I was supposed to call her last night. It was around ten p.m. in Tehran, and she would go to sleep very soon.

"Let me tell you something, *bacham,*" she started. I brought the cup to my lips, letting the hot tea burn the tip of my lips before taking a tiny sip.

"From today, the world is going to change. You are going to change. And, at first, it will be so difficult. You will want to give up because everything will seem hopeless, but there is a life for you beyond your pain, and I promise you it will be worth it." She was referring to my lack of direction. She always knew how I struggled with finding my way without me ever telling her.

"I know," I said, not wanting to discuss my future. I mindlessly opened the fridge, looking for a banana, but noticed the

Dijon mustard instead. Milad always hid snacks behind the mustard because no one actually used it. *How old is this? Two years, maybe more.*

Bingo! You are so predictable, kid! I only tore a tiny chunk off the cookie so he wouldn't kill me. I plopped it in my mouth, savoring the sweetness.

"*Gushkon!*" my grandma scolded, snapping me out of my indulgence.

"I am listening." *What was she saying?*

"It's not present yet, but it will come. You will feel alone in the world, and I will not be there to guide you, but the path is laid, and there is nothing we can do to change that."

"I know, Mamani," I said, accustomed to the nature of her rants, never fully understanding where they would lead.

"Remember that your father is just a man, but he is still a good father. And tell your brother to pry himself away from those video games, or he'll turn square-eyed."

Everything my grandma said stemmed from the depths of her heart, leaving no room for arguments, so I always refrained from disagreeing with her.

ELEVEN

Adam

Nestled in the vast expanse of the desert west of Cairo, my father's learning facility stood as a hidden oasis amid the barren landscape. The solid structure rose proudly from the desert sands. Approaching the facility, I walked the path lined with palm trees and into the courtyard, landscaped with vibrant flowers and lush greenery.

Without the ability to aďhār, discovering our quarters was nearly impossible. Of course, you couldn't appear directly inside because of the wards. Dūshevs, who hadn't mastered teleportation yet, were either escorted by one of us or drove the six hours through the desert themselves.

Except for the silent passage of nomadic Bedouins on their endless journeys, no one passed our oasis. The Bedouins seemed to possess an unspoken knowledge of us. Their paths never veered toward the warded facility, for stories and whispers carried far and deep in these distant reaches.

Within the walls, corridors extended like a labyrinth. Sunlight filtered through stained-glass windows, casting colors onto the polished marble floors. The air carried a subtle scent of aged books and the accumulated wisdom of years inscribed on the bones of this place.

As I ventured deeper into the corridors, the sound of footsteps mingled with hushed whispers of the women working for my father. In this household, hierarchy held great importance, with my father positioned at the apex of the social order, followed by the high and mighty elders, then the Dūshevs, the apprentices, and finally, the housekeepers.

The elders held a tight grip on the knowledge they didn't want to share with the rest of us. Despite a few of them being younger than me, they considered themselves vastly superior. They took pleasure in our limited know-how and reveled in their self-appointed authority.

I had just arrived at our grounds, looking to speak to my father, only to find him with Edgar and Karam. Elias had had his evaluation by the elders, but I wasn't there for that.

"Father, can I speak to you?" I asked, wanting Edgar and Karam to get lost, but I couldn't exactly say that.

"Is this concerning Aldridge?" my father asked, not looking up from his book.

"Surely, you are not here about your squabbles with Aldridge," Edgar said. *Squabbles!* He was testing me, but I wouldn't stoop to his level. Initially, I didn't want to tell them about Aldridge. I wanted to handle him by myself, but it wasn't worth risking Maya's safety for, so I had to bite my tongue.

"I just want to be rid of him," I said, looking at my father, ignoring Edgar's mocking gaze. "So, if you will take his soul off my hands." My father looked up at that.

"Tell me, Adam, how did you exactly come to meet this Maya girl?" he inquired. His piercing gaze unnerved me because nothing slipped past him. I hadn't told my father her name, but hiding things from him never worked because he would unearth all our secrets through meditation. Of course, I had no intention of hiding things from my father. He always knew what was best for us. With his abilities, my father always seemed to possess knowledge before we confided in him. I realized he likely knew more about Maya than I did. My father's meditation techniques was reserved for the elders, a sacrifice I had gladly made if it meant not having a child of my own. Except this rule didn't apply to my eldest brother, Joseph, who was also taught this meditation technique, destined to take my father's place one day.

"We crossed paths a few times, and eventually, we got to talking," I said. The best lies were always sprinkled with truth. I was scared that the idea of Maya would give my father ideas for the future.

"No, Adam. I want you to recount the exact day you first laid eyes on her and how it made you feel," he pressed further.

"I didn't feel any sort of way," I replied, attempting to brush off any significance regarding Maya.

"Then, why did you pursue her?" His skepticism forced me to think on my feet.

"Why are you obsessing over the girl when I'm asking you to take Aldridge's soul from me?" I countered.

"Aldridge will come around, and you two will get along just fine. Remember, you went a decade not speaking to your brothers," he said with such indifference as if it was the same thing. As if my issues with Aldridge were of no concern to him now that Aldridge wasn't bothering my father anymore. My father was right. I did go years without speaking to anyone. I traveled the world before becoming a Dūshev and taking souls for my father. In the beginning, I just wanted to live life independently. I didn't want to rely on my father's money, even though he didn't hand out cash without the labor. It was a job like any other, with the pay above average, but the mental toll was also more significant.

During those years, I fell in love many times, but two encounters left marks on my back. One I met in Malaysia, the other in France. Each, in their own way, shaped me to be the man I am. The first one lived near the veined rivers of Beluran, Sabah. The day I met her, she was washing clothes all by herself. The secluded village was untouched by the currents of change. Life there was uncomplicated, grounded in traditions that endured the test of time. I loved the simplicity of basking in a paradise of inner peace. When I lived there, I had no worries; an eternity of life was ahead of me. Day after day, we shared stolen moments under the rising sun in our secret meeting spot before the village was fully awake. Ultimately, it had to stop. Bound by cultural obligations, she was promised to another, and I understood. Her culture didn't allow their women to marry outside of the tribe. So, I let her go and moved on. Truthfully, for an entirely different reason. A reason I both wouldn't and wasn't allowed to share with anyone. That facade held firm until Maya came into my life, turning everything upside down.

I continued traveling and ate my way through the world. Years passed, and my journey led me to France. Passing through Saint-Sylvestre, Nice, I met a confident French woman with sharp edges, disheveled waves, and uncombed bangs. A woman who was unafraid to defy conventions. The black dress, red lips, and killer stare told me she was trouble. I was drawn to her like a moth to a flame. My heart surrendered from the moment our eyes met.

She effortlessly toyed with my emotions, a predator reveling in her mastery. Compared to her being thirty-three, I was a kid who didn't know better. She was an art dealer's daughter with the confidence of a shark. Aware of her beauty, she could have any man, yet she chose me.

She took me home the first night I met her. I thought it would be a one-night thing, but she wanted more. She wanted to keep me around to satisfy her needs. She wanted love, attention, words of affirmation, and worship, and I willingly obliged. I poured my heart out to her and told her how I felt, how I wanted to spend my life with her, and how she meant everything to me. I wanted to marry her. In fact, I asked her just two months in. She refused me. She said I had to be patient with her, and I was. Because I understood. I would have given her the moon if she had asked, and never in a million years did I think it would end. Soon after, she dumped me for a rich old man.

You are young, Adam, and I need a real man. She broke my heart with her soft French accent. I was devastated for years, and I decided to never love again. Even if it meant never speaking to a woman again. I stopped traveling and went back to Egypt. I had to be with my family, my father in particular. He knew I needed the time away to be fully present as a Dūshev. Things were different back then. My father didn't care about us having girlfriends or forcing the growth of the family tree. Within a year, he reinforced our family values in me, bringing me back into alignment with my true purpose. Perhaps he was giving the same leniency to Aldridge, who hardly deserved it. I thought he had finally understood that Aldridge was not the golden boy he used to be, since he had ordered us to take his soul if we encountered him. Of course, no one told me keeping another Dūshev's soul was a very overwhelming feeling, like there was too much energy inside me, trying to break free.

"I hope you don't expect me to hold on to his soul forever," I said, dialing back my irritation. I had to give him the benefit of the doubt.

He shook his head. "Of course not. Now, tell me about your healing powers," he pressed on. He didn't wait for me to answer because he already knew and wanted to see my reaction.

"Not only is such a gift rare, but it also speaks volumes that you acted on instinct. That's why I must understand the connection between the two of you. Have you considered impregnating her?" My father always seized the opportunity to secure another grandchild. If he wanted something, he didn't ask before taking it.

"God, no." I sighed. Instantly rejecting the notion. Even before Maya, I had made it abundantly clear that I would never grant him a grandchild. If I ever truly fell in love, why would I want her to die because of a son I didn't know or care for?

"Ground your energy, Adam. It was a simple question. No need to be defensive. I'm merely ensuring that you do not procreate with the wrong woman," he said.

Caught off guard, I struggled to find the words. "Wait, w—" I stammered. I had always assumed he wanted me to have a child.

"Adam, we have discussed this. Your soul was split during labor. It's not uncommon among people, but we are not people. You know that!" he said, shaking his head in contemplation. My father had unintentionally revealed where he thought the other half of my soul was. He believed Maya had the other half of my soul. It was scaring him, which, in turn, scared me.

My father had told me about my split soul, but it never concerned me. I never felt like I was less than any of my brothers. I was just as good, if not better. I was unbothered because, unlike Daniel and Elias, who each possessed half a soul, I wasn't lacking in any area regarding my powers.

"I made a mistake," he muttered.

Our discussions on my split soul were always elusive, with him only providing vague explanations. It seemed inconsequential, yet he never missed an opportunity to remind me throughout the years. Then again, my father was always on edge when he discovered my involvement with someone new. To him, every woman I met was potentially carrying the other half of my soul. The question was, what was so terrible about the two halves of my soul uniting?

I found Elias waiting for me right outside. Since Elias couldn't adhār, he would be flying home, but his flight was most likely tomorrow morning. Elias didn't like flying during the night because it messed with his schedule. He had already gotten his evaluation from the elders, but testing my abilities to train him was unnecessary and offensive. I was one of the best masters they had, and they knew that.

Elias motioned us outside, and just by the look in his eyes, I knew something was terribly wrong.

"I think they know about the girl," he said, looking nervously around. "Because your father told my father that he wanted to talk to you, and when my father asked if it was because of *her*—your father nodded."

"They spoke in front of you?" I asked, wondering if they were planting seeds.

"Obviously not!" He rolled his eyes. "I just don't understand why they would care. You've met her, what, a month ago?" he said.

We had more than just met. I knew we were so much more than that, but Elias didn't have to know the severity.

"I might have to stay here for a few days to feel things out. I promised Maya Aldridge wouldn't be a problem," I said. "Now I have to worry about them, too." I gestured toward the doors.

"Aldridge—" He was taken aback. "She knows about us?"

"It's not a big deal." I forgot I never actually told him what happened with her and Aldridge. I wasn't trying to hide anything, and when we went looking for Aldridge, he automatically assumed it was the same old bullshit.

"Not a big deal? You are well aware that's not true!"

"Look, Elias, a lot of shit happened. Long story short, Aldridge kidnapped her to get to me."

"What?" he whispered.

"She saw everything—I couldn't get out of it," I said.

"When things like this happen, we let the elders decide what to do next. You know the protocol."

"My father already knows all this and much more, it seems." It was hard to hide when my father decided to keep an eye on his offspring. Idris and Aldridge were the only ones who had managed to stay under the radar. Somehow, they could avoid my father's prying, but I wasn't going to fuss around it. I needed her to be far away from all this, and the decision that I had just made would probably bother Elias, but he had no say in this. I hoped for a positive reaction, even though I knew it wasn't what I would get.

"I'm going to ask Maya to move in with us." I had a feeling this was the only way I could keep my sanity; she had to be close to me at all times.

He rolled his eyes. "Whatever. Just keep me out of it," he said.

Maya was a distraction, temptation in its purest form, and if I wasn't occupied with this mess with my father, I would give in to that temptation.

The elders had gathered for dinner. They had switched the dining area to a bigger room with more art on the walls. I couldn't remember what this room had been before, but how could one ever keep track when so many of them were left unused? The place was so big that, sometimes, I was tempted to adhār around. My father didn't like that, so he had many places warded, even within the facility. That didn't keep me from walking straight through the door, though.

"Adam, have a seat if you're staying for supper," my father said. I hesitated for a second. Sometimes, I didn't feel welcome in my own home. The room was tense; there was something they weren't keen on sharing with me. I didn't know what my father was plotting. He liked to keep his deck face down, but I was impatient and had to find out why they were being secretive.

It was painfully silent; only the chink of plates and cutlery sounded between us until I couldn't take it anymore. "Father, I think I have the right to know if there is an issue regarding me."

"Please, don't flatter yourself. Not everything is about you," Herman said. Herman was one of the elders, sitting next to my father.

"Although," my father interjected, "your brothers disagree with me on a certain matter. Perhaps it would be best if she carried your child after all." Did he not insist moments ago that I should never?

"I think it's fair to say that it's my decision only. Besides, I would have to be in love with her. And I am not—I just met her."

"Who told you such lies? She can carry your child regardless," Darius said.

My father was the one who told me that and didn't intervene to correct my elder brother, Darius.

"She will not live long. You might as well," Nashir said from behind me. Nashir was one of the ladies who cleaned up after us. She was an old, wrinkly lady with a hunchback. Her skin was as pale as the dead, her nails long and yellow, and her gray hair was in a tiny, firm bun. She always walked a little too slowly to eavesdrop. She usually mumbled in undetectable dialect when she walked by like a snake. Even her voice made me squirm.

"Perhaps you need to hear it from the help. She predicts the future based on our current choices," Herman said. He lied through his teeth, thinking I was an idiot.

"She will be no use for you when she's dead, Adam. At least let her carry our legacy," Herman continued. They poked and teased one after another, and my father stood by. I did my best to ignore the urge to flip over the entire table on their heads, but that didn't last very long.

"Stop lying to me!" My voice was louder than I had anticipated.

"This is the intensity of twin flame connections," my father said to the elders, looking amused. Did he think I had no control over my own emotions? It fired up something primal inside of me, something I couldn't restrain. "She does not exist for your entertainment or for breeding!" My hands were shaking, and my vision blurred. They hadn't exactly threatened me, but their intentions were clear. The words flew out of my mouth before I could stop myself. "I will protect her from the lot of you, and I will have the head of anyone who touches her!"

"Sir . . ." Nashir interrupted again.

"Enough, you can leave." My father looked at her. My boiling blood turned cold. *Fuck! What did I just do?* "Wait—" I followed Nashir out.

"Adam," my father called after me. I had to hear what she was about to say before my father dismissed her. I would know if she lied or tried to brainwash me.

"Spill it," I said as I caught up with her. She looked calm. Like she had been waiting for this moment her entire life. "By being near her, you are taking her soul. You might as well let your future son have the soul," she said.

"How original—and how easy you offered me the lie." I smiled. She returned the simple gesture in the most horrific way. "Are you willing to risk it?" she asked.

"I'll take my chances. Thank you very much."

My family had a reputation for taking matters into their own hands. I couldn't trust them, not regarding this. I went back to speak with my father. Although he would have plenty to say, I knew he would see reason. It was best to listen and nod most of the time. My father liked obedience.

"I'm asking you nicely, Father. Let me have this experience and learn from it," I said.

"I have done everything in my power to keep us safe, and I will not let you ruin us. Do you understand?" He was far angrier than I had anticipated, and I really didn't understand why.

"What are you talking about?"

"It seems like, no matter what I do, our fate is set in stone," he muttered, looking into the wall without being present. "A child might be our only solution."

It wasn't an option to leave her alone anymore. I was too deep in, and I didn't want out. I had to lead them on, lead my father on. Something I hadn't done before, let him believe I was considering doing things his way.

"I'm sorry I have offended you. Please give me time to weigh my options, and I will get back to you." That pleased him, and he gave me an accepting nod.

When I left my father, I picked up my phone and called Maya. She picked up on the first beep.

"What are you doing—are you busy?"

"No. I'm not doing anything. Why?"

"Can we meet?" I didn't want to say too much over the phone. Better to speak to her in person.

"You can come over here if you want because I just poured myself a cup of tea," she said. "No one is home."

"Are you sure?" I didn't want to intrude, but I had a sinking feeling and really needed to see her.

"Of course," she assured me. "I'll meet you upstairs."

I adhāred to her house, arriving in front of her bedroom door before she had reached the stairs. I heard her soft steps approaching, and suddenly, everything clicked into place. Perhaps my father was right, perhaps not, but I didn't care. All I knew was that her energy made me more myself than anything else. Her presence put me in a trance. Waiting there, seconds before seeing her, I realized I was falling in love with her, so much so that it terrified me to leave her alone. I couldn't leave her unprotected. I pulled her into my arms and hugged her as soon as she was close enough. She was mine; she belonged to me, but it felt like I had stolen her from someone else, and it was driving me crazy. When I was close to her, I wanted nothing else, but at times, I felt a barrier between us that I couldn't explain—we were two yolks in each of our own membrane.

"Is there something wrong?" she asked. She didn't know what feelings I had suddenly recognized within myself.

"Everything is perfect." *As long as you are in my arms.* Her hair was behind her ear; she pulled a chunk out and flipped it to the other side so her hair parted from the left. She did that a lot. She didn't think she looked good with her hair tucked behind her ears and often flipped it from one side to the other. In reality, it didn't make much of a difference.

I kissed her softly and pulled back to look at her again. "I just missed you. That's it." Every time I touched her, something magic happened. We interlaced. I wanted to slip my hand under her shirt and stroke her bare skin, and just thinking about it gave me the wildest urge to pin her down and ravish her.

"Do you have a crush on me or something?" she mocked, fire in her eyes.

"I hope you understand that we are more than just together, and no one else can have you."

Every atom in my body craved her. I wanted to pick her up, throw her on the bed, and play her string by string like a cello. She hummed a reply, and her body seemed to surrender to me. She let me stroke her skin and bury my face in her hair. I dug my teeth into her shoulder and turned it into a kiss. Then I trailed kisses along her neck and to her ear. If I didn't stop now, I wouldn't be able to control myself.

"I want you to move in with me." Maybe I was being foolish. Perhaps this wasn't such a good idea, but I had to say it before I forgot why I came here to begin with. The taste of her skin was still on my tongue.

"What!" She pulled away and frowned. "Where is this coming from? Is it Aldridge again? I thought your father handled that." She put the lies into my mouth, making it painfully easy. I didn't want to worry her more than necessary and tell her that my whole family was a threat.

"Yes, and you'll be safer with me," I said.

"Adam, I can't just move in with you. It's a huge step."

"You don't want to. I can tell—It's moving too fast. I'm sorry. I thought we were on the same page." If I wanted to keep her safe, I had to do everything in my power to convince her. Even if it meant this.

"Don't say that. We are on the same page!" She reached for my face. "I mean, we can try . . . I guess."

"Can we try from today?" I could almost hear the wheels turning in her mind. She would have to explain all this to her father so that it wouldn't look like a rushed decision.

"Okay," she relented and let out a breath.

"I love you," I said out loud for the first time because I truly believed I did.

١٢

TWELVE

Maya

I woke up alone in Adam's bed. I was there the whole weekend and told my father I had been at Alie's the entire time. Of course, my father knew about Adam, but I wasn't sure if I wanted to tell him how serious it had gotten. Still, it was so odd that he didn't question me. He hadn't even called me once while I was gone. He would usually call and ask if I was having a good time or needed anything.

Adam wanted me here because he felt it was safer. He said no one could teleport inside this house except him. Other Dūshevs could teleport out of here once they walked in but could never directly teleport inside. I couldn't see the point of that protection system when their front door was permanently unlocked.

He had gotten very protective over the last two days. It was like something had changed—well, something *had* changed. He said he loved me and didn't notice that I dodged them. He probably didn't even realize what he had said. Perhaps they came out as a reflex. I didn't say it back, and he wasn't waiting for it, either. What if I said it and my words shattered everything? What if this feeling wasn't even love, and I said it and ruined what we already had? Maybe we were moving too fast, but so what? I liked being around him, and people in their twenties made worse decisions than this. I could always move back in with my dad if I wanted to.

My phone started vibrating, and I panicked for a second because I thought it was my dad and had manifested his call, but it was just Milad.

"What if I was sleeping!" I snapped at him.

"Are you still at your boyfriend's house, or did you go home?"

"What—no, I'm at Alie's."

"Sure." Milad dismissed my lie. "I need you to do something for me."

"What do you want?"

"I need you to go into my room, find my old laptop in one of my drawers, flip it over, and remove the battery. I've written a string of words on the battery. I need you to call me and tell me what they are. It's very important."

"Right now?" I said. "Can't you call Dad?" Milad had been at a tech camp this whole weekend, and of course he forgot something for his computer when he needed it the most.

"He's not picking up, and I need it right now. So please, please, please, just hurry."

"I'll send you a picture when I find it," I said and got up from the bed.

"No!" he practically yelled. "Absolutely under no circumstances do you take a picture of it! Please, just call me when you are home."

"Okay. Relax," I said and hung up.

I needed to go home for that password before going to work. I had an early shift. Alyssa decided a Monday was the best day of all days to take inventory. The store would be closed while we counted and registered everything into the system. It would probably take all day because of the mess in the basement.

I went to the bathroom, washed my face, and brushed my teeth. Unlike the rest of their house, which looked like it was decorated by dead people, Adams' bathroom was big and clinical white, with a decent mirror. I stood there, staring at my reflection way too long before I decided to lick my forefinger and mark it with an X. Adam lived with his nephew Elias, and I had only met Elias a handful of times. He was the roommate who didn't bother you unless you bothered him. Adam and Elias were both early risers—as in very early. So, they were both out of bed long before my alarm went off at seven. Adam and I talked about the moving-in-together part, which honestly scared me. Still, I promised him I would start spending more time at his house and gradually move in.

I arrived at my house and checked the mailbox out of habit before going in. Both locks on our front door were locked— which was odd. Because my brother hadn't been home, either, since Friday, I suspected my dad had brought his girlfriend over. I snuck inside and tried to be as quiet as possible. The kitchen and living room were empty, so I went upstairs instead of being dramatic. He was probably sleeping while I fabricated stories about his secret girlfriend.

When I finally found the tiny business card with the list of random words, I called Milad to read them out loud for him because—god forbid—I took a picture of it.

"And you're sure you read them in order?" my brother pressed.

"The numbered order you wrote them in. Are we done now?"

"Who are you talking to?" My father had come into the room. Apparently, I hadn't been as quiet as I thought I was.

"Milad," I said. "He wanted a password. Did I wake you?"

"I'm going to bed again. Please keep it down." He sounded unusually grumpy.

I went into my room and dumped all the clothes I had had with me onto the bed. I changed into a clean outfit, quickly put some product in my hair to tame the frizz, and lit an incense stick, even though I was literally minutes away from going out—my room needed a cleanse, too. I didn't get much farther than my father's bedroom before a feeling tugged at my gut. I looked at his door, wondering if he had always closed his bedroom door at night.

Without warning, I opened his door before I could talk some sense into myself, and boy, did it pay off. "No!" my father shouted, but it was too late. She was dressed in her favorite lace bra, pulling up her jeans as I opened the door. I couldn't believe what I had seen. I didn't want to believe it, but she was right in front of me, and I couldn't unsee her.

"It's not what you think," Dissie said.

"You're disgusting!"

"Maya, honey, let me explain," my dad said.

"She was my friend!" I choked up.

"Maya!" he said and tried to reach for me.

"Don't fucking touch me!" I slipped away from his hand, rushed into my room, and slammed the door. I kind of expected him to barge in after me, but he was too busy getting her out of the house. "What the fuck!" I said to myself and started pulling clean clothes and necessities out of my drawers. I had to get out of there as fast as possible.

How could she do this to me? Has she not already slept with everyone in this fucking town? Aren't they enough? He is fucking his daughter's friend. What the fuck is wrong with him? Fuck!

The whole thing made me sick. I hated him so much; I hated him for taking my friend from me, for ruining my life, for everything that had turned my life upside down. I couldn't tell my mom; she would take Milad and then his life would turn upside down. He was so happy here with his friends he wouldn't like moving to Salt Lake City. *Fuck!*

On the bright side, I could stay with Adam as long as I wanted. It was so reassuring having him and having a place to go; I don't know what I would have done without him.

١٣

THIRTEEN

Adam

I had another soul to track down and collect from someone whose life was soon to be over. Dūshevs had about a month to collect a soul. In case I was busy with Elias, it was acceptable to postpone it, but I wanted these things to be over with as soon as possible. I couldn't say I enjoyed it very much. All aspects of being a Dūshev took a toll on me; I wasn't meant for this life. I wasn't sure if I ever had a choice of becoming a Dūshev. Some of my brothers seemed to have that choice. My father gave us the impression that we could walk away at any given moment. But it didn't seem that way. When I decided to accept the title and become a Dūshev, I had no clue what it entailed. I was so young and eager to make my father proud.

Even adʹhāring was exhausting; traveling long distances weakened us. When I was first learning, I lied and told my father I knew how to adʹhār when I didn't. I desperately sought his validation; I wanted him to think I was better than everyone else.

Show me, my father had said when I claimed this. One of his housekeepers had entered the room, and he wanted her to watch, to make a spectacle of me. I wasn't prepared to demonstrate to him, let alone have the help watch my every breath. I thought I could say I had mastered the skill and that he would take my word for it, but I wasn't backing down. I closed my eyes and imagined my body disappearing. I slowly lost the sense of my limbs, like they had never been there. Even gravity wasn't the same. I wasn't floating, but I wasn't standing, either. Suddenly, I had ceased to exist for the time being. I did not live when I was in the void. I did not breathe, see, hear, or feel. I felt nothing until I landed on the opposite side of the room. The sensation of the cold wind from the air-conditioning stroking my skin came back, the pounding soreness from being on my feet all day, and the drop of nervous sweat sliding down my temple. All at once, I was present again. The scariest part was time because I didn't know what day it was or where I was in the first few seconds when I reappeared. My father was not fooled; he knew it was my first time. Eventually, I learned the right way. I understood there were no shortcuts to being a part of this family, this order, or a Dūshev.

My next victim was in Copenhagen, Denmark. I always traveled to the location a day ahead to ground myself. The streets were empty after eight. Hospitality wasn't a huge thing there; in general, they didn't enjoy company very often or even small talk, for that matter. They were private people who stayed home, labeling it *hygge* to admire their designer furniture.

The neighborhood I was collecting from was a developing ghetto. I had a look around the area and went back to my hotel, which was nearby—more an inn than a hotel. At maximum, twenty rooms and low-quality breakfast but lovely staff.

At the brink of dawn, I walked to the residential complex and stood outside their door for ten minutes to ensure I didn't hear sounds from inside. Nothing, so I adhāred to the other side of the door and took cautious steps. Parents and three kids in a two-bedroom flat. Only one son with a wasting soul. The two other boys were probably just a few years younger. I didn't have to look through their personal belongings or look for an ID to find him; I could feel it. His soul was on the edge, barely gripping his shell.

He opened his eyes as if woken by my presence. This didn't happen every time I took a soul, but it made everything a lot harder when it did. There was no time to waste. So, I put a hand on his chest and shut his air supply with my powers. The way I forced his soul out was so brutal I never wanted to do it again. The icy soul crawled through my body and stopped in the center of my chest. His eyes didn't show white as they should have; he stared at me, horrified, unable to move, until the soul left his body. His raised chest fell back on the bed, and he closed his eyes. Even if he was to survive the night, it would've been over soon. The experience was terrible, the worst I ever had with a soul. His eyes were sad and hopeless. I took it all away, every breath and every memory. I wish I could have taken his pain, too, but there was nothing I could do. Sometimes, I thought I was the only one of my brothers who struggled so much with souls. It seemed like it because no one else complained.

Elias wasn't home. It was late at night, and he wasn't in his room. I went to the kitchen to get a snack before going to bed next to Maya. Ever since she had moved in, I had felt a weight lift off my shoulders. Something about her presence completed me, and I couldn't pinpoint what it was exactly. Regardless, it was nice knowing she lived under my roof and slept in my bed every night. The fridge wasn't very exciting. A banana and a handful of almonds had to do. I shoved them in my mouth and poured myself a glass of water to flush them down.

Upstairs, Maya slept so quietly. A short moment, and I would join her. I only needed to brush my teeth; they were soaked in my sugary saliva. I was so tired that my reality seemed to blur together. Either I had adhāred to the bathroom or autopiloted myself upstairs without realizing it because, one moment, I was in the kitchen, and the next, I was spitting the remaining toothpaste from my mouth. I wetted the toothbrush again and put it back in my mouth. Somehow, I couldn't get it right, like an invisible barrier held back every stroke with the toothbrush. I heard Maya gasp from the bedroom. I thought the running water had woken her but realized I was gravely mistaken when I entered the bedroom. I couldn't see who, but a Dūshev stood beside her, his hand above her chest, taking her soul. I leaped, landing on top of him on the floor. The Dūshev vanished beneath me, his face distorted in the dark, a lost memory. I stopped it from happening, stopped her soul from leaving her body. Perhaps it wasn't too late. Maya opened her eyes, chest falling back down on the bed, and groaned like she was in pain. Even though I rushed, my movements were so slow. I rushed to her, and it still felt like it took me minutes to reach her. As I held her face, I closed my eyes and tried to fix whatever the Dūshev had broken inside her. *I can do this. I have done this before. But how!* She took a deep breath and didn't stop. Her lungs were an endless black hole. Her mouth wide open more than before, she took everything in. Her heartbeat sounded like bongo drums, getting louder and louder. Her chest rose again. *This can't be happening.*

"Maya!" I yelled, but her heart stopped. I screamed her name again and again until everything went dark, and I realized that it wasn't real. It was all a dream, but the bongos continued playing inside my head.

"Sir?" No! Someone was knocking at the door of my room.

"Is everything alright?" he asked.

"Shit!" I looked at my phone. *Shit!* I had slept through my alarm. Check-out was fifteen minutes ago. "Yes, I'm sorry. I'll be out in two minutes."

I was drenched in sweat, and the sheet stuck to my skin. I washed my face, went out of there, and checked out. I used the restroom in the lobby to adʼhār straight to Egypt. It was closer than home and the only place I could manage without further ado. I didn't see my father. I was beaten from all the long-distance adʼhāring and soul-taking combined, so I asked for a room and slept for another five hours 'til they woke me again at dinnertime. After the last time I was here, we hadn't really spoken. In my family, we usually pretended the last fight never took place and acted civil.

"How are you feeling?" my father asked. "You seem exhausted." My father could always read the emotions in my eyes. I was exhausted. So much more than usual. Even lifting the spoon was hard.

"I don't know what's going on, but it's getting harder and harder to take souls," I confessed to him.

"Aside from your own, there are two souls in your core, correct?" he asked.

"Three. One is Aldridge's." I reminded him.

"I'll take care of that." This was my father's way of apologizing for pushing me too hard. He walked up to me, reached for my chest, and pulled Aldridge's soul out of my core. I was finally free and a thousand pounds lighter. I didn't know what my father planned to do with it, and I didn't care. I was just glad to be rid of it.

"Three days from now, soulless twins will be born. Transfer the souls, and you will be off duty for a while. I don't want you to exhaust yourself."

"How long?"

"As long as you need, my son," my father said. "But until then, you cannot adhār or use any powers. Two at the same time can be very demanding."

I stayed with my father and the elders without interacting too much with the rest of them. I minded my own business like I was on vacation at a resort. Every day, we had dinner together, and that day was no exception.

"Adam, after you have delivered the two souls tonight, would you mind coming back here? I need your opinion on Theodor's technique," Edgar asked.

Theodor had the same powers as Elias. Of course, they weren't from the same mother, but Edgar fathered both. Theodor was younger and had just started practicing his evaporating skills. His father, Edgar, had been a master before, but he didn't have a long list of apprentices before his son. Now, he wanted to go back to teaching. Apparently, being an elder wasn't enough.

"Sure, I'll come back right after," I said.

Edgar and I never got along very well, but it had nothing to do with his son. I didn't mind helping Theodor become a better Dūshev. It wasn't his fault that his father was a stubborn moron who didn't let him be taught by more competent masters.

Later that evening, the twins were born in El Maadi Private Hospital. I stole a doctor's smock and walked in as though I belonged. It was late, and only hushed conversations and occasional beep of monitors could be heard from behind the half-closed doors. The sterile scent of disinfectant hung lightly in the air of the corridor I entered. A nurse rushed past me, paying me no attention. I entered a room where the premature newborns were treated for jaundice with light therapy. They lay in open bassinets, wearing only diapers and eye patches. Their souls were strong and vibrant, outshouting the two soulless ones.

Giving a soul was no easy task, either. Not only did my body resist letting go of the soul, but the infant was like a warded force field. My right hand hovered over his chest when I forced it out of me; it stung my entire arm. I felt his weak heartbeat and heard every tiny breath.

My father had always told me to be extra careful with infants. They felt the soul force its way into the neural pathways to merge with the body, which wasn't the most pleasant feeling.

I took a step closer to examine his twin and prepared myself for round two. When I was done, I felt so utterly empty. It was what I wanted; I wanted to be free, and I was. At least for the time being, I didn't have to take another soul, kill another person, and fuck up another family. And best of all, I didn't have to carry the heavy burden of Aldridge's soul. After getting rid of it, I realized how much it affected my well-being. My short temper and anger outbursts probably came from him and his soul. I couldn't remember a time when I had felt so frustrated and overstimulated as I had when his soul was with me.

I kept my promise and found Edgar and his son practicing early in the morning. They were in our courtyard near the fountain, where they had lined up containers with water on the lip of the fountain. I didn't know how hard he was on the boy, but I expected much more than what I saw.

"Ah. Just in time, Adam," Edgar said. "Come and see how far my son has come. It's his first year only." Theodor held a cup, looking at it, trembling and teeth grinding. Nothing happened for a while until, finally, the water evaporated.

Edgar clapped with excitement. "Did you see that, Adam?" he asked enthusiastically. It was kind of pathetic. I nodded, walked closer to the table before him, and picked up a full cup. "Is this just water?" I said and took a sip.

"What did you expect?" Theodor asked with an attitude resembling his father's.

"The apprentice should be able to do more than evaporate tap water from a cup after the first year. Have you tried soaked garments? Or almond milk, for instance," I said and drank more of the water in my hand. Apparently, my question hit a nerve. Theodor stepped in front of me.

"Am I not good enough for you, Mr. Know-It-All?"

"During the first year, Elias was evaporating water regardless of its whereabouts," I said. "Soaked mud, sand, even clothes." I glanced at Edgar. He said nothing because he knew how hard I disciplined Elias, and regardless of how Edgar felt about me, he always told his son how proud he was of his progress.

When Theodor looked at his father, I threw the remaining water at his shirt and face and adhāred twenty feet back. I had both my feet planted firmly on the ground, ready to be attacked by Theodor. *One, two* . . . Theodor leaped with all the rage of the world. As if his father had prepared him for one of my lessons, he was almost waiting to be provoked. Theodor would have landed on top of me if I hadn't moved out of his way. Instead, he lay face down on the ground.

"You need to learn how to dry your hair and clothes by the end of—" The words bunched up in my throat, and my world suddenly stopped. I saw a vision of Maya gripping the towel that wrapped around her body, water dripping from her hair. This was my first hallucination. I had never had those. The last time I adʰāred in the blind because I felt her needing me, it was just a hunch that took me to her. Not only could I see her this time, but I could somehow feel her soul was in danger.

١٤

FOURTEEN

Maya

Adam had been away for a few days, and I hadn't heard a word from him since he left. He was probably taking souls, but he didn't give me a clear statement of what he was doing or where he went—not that it was any of my business. It was all very new, and I didn't know how to position myself. Would I have cared to ask if I lived at home? Would I have noticed? It only bothered me because I felt so isolated here. I lost my best friend and the roof over my head all in one day. All week, I had this pit in my stomach telling me that something was wrong, that something terrible was about to happen, and I felt like I was counting down the seconds until the bomb exploded.

When Adam wasn't there, and I wasn't busy with work, I didn't know what to do with myself except lock myself up in his room—well, not exactly lock, but still. Elias rarely talked to me, making me feel like I wasn't welcome in this house. This wasn't what I had imagined when I said yes to moving in with Adam, not that I had a choice. I wanted to go back home but couldn't stomach the thought. The feeling of betrayal was still an open wound in my gut. I really thought I had a best friend who I could share everything with, a father who cared for me and a boyfriend who . . . *What are you even thinking? You are no one's first priority.*

I was taking a shower, the warm water cascading down my body, filling the bathroom with steam. I heard the distant sound of voices from downstairs and wondered if Adam was back. He usually didn't use the front door, and I could have sworn I heard the front door slam. With a twist, I turned off the water, holding my breath. Soft footsteps climbed up the stairs. Each creak of the staircase echoed in my ears. Wrapping myself in a towel, I left the bathroom to change, but the bedroom door swung open before I reached the dresser. The burst of air from the sudden entrance sent a shiver down my spine, and the towel slipped slightly, reminding me of my vulnerable state. I quickly regained focus and tightened my grip on the towel.

"Adam! Have you missed me?" the guy said as he walked in. Heat rose from my skin, and I got lightheaded. He was one of them. "Get out of my room," I said with a high-pitched voice. I sounded more scared than I thought I would. Elias came in right behind him, grabbing him by the shoulders.

"Is Adam hittin' that?" he asked Elias, pointing at me with his head. Elias didn't even look at me. Instead, he tried pulling him away. I could tell he was embarrassed.

Adam appeared and sent a jolt through the room. A wave of relief washed over me, and the room seemed to exhale with me. His gaze shifted from me to them in a fleeting exchange of unspoken words before he slammed the door behind them. Turning toward me, Adam closed the distance with purposeful steps. A silent understanding passed between us before his arms enveloped me. He felt the slight trembling of my body, sensing the echoes of fear I couldn't shake. His embrace tightened, pulling me closer. A rush of heat flooded my cheeks due to the awareness coursing through me—the stark realization of how naked I was.

"Who was that?"

"Elias's twin brother, Daniel—I swear I could have killed the idiot." He shook his head. "He's an idiot for barging in like that." Adam pulled away, and I saw the wet mark my hair left on his shirt. His mouth turned slightly upward. "What?" Something was different about him. *Something is missing.*

"Nothing," he said, adjusting the waistband of his pants. My eyes followed his hands as he casually tried to hide the length of him. I bit the inner parts of my lips.

"You just need to ask, and I'll give it to you." He had caught me staring, and I was absolutely mortified. It wasn't the first time the opportunity lay bare—literally, and he still hadn't made a move. Maybe he was trying to be a gentleman, but whatever it was, his restraint was driving me crazy.

"I bet you would. Now, turn around. I need to change."

He arched an eyebrow and leaned up against the closed door. Men were so easy to trick. Did he really think I would give him the option if I didn't want him to watch me undress? Everything was on my terms, whether he knew it or not.

"Fine. Suit yourself." I turned around to walk toward the dresser. Initially, I was going to wear a T-shirt and a pair of jeans, but that was before I knew he was coming home. Because he could barely contain himself, I let the towel unravel and drop to the floor. I could have sworn I heard him swallow through his clenched jaw, but I didn't look back. I picked out the silky black dress I had just bought and put it on. It was very short, loosely draping from left to right like water. It barely covered my breasts and was wildly inappropriate for this time of day.

"You're not gonna wear underwear?" he said. I looked back at him as if just realizing he was there. There was nothing in his eyes that revealed what he was thinking.

"No." I had planned to, but I changed my mind when he asked. *I will torture you for leaving me alone in this house.*

And as if he shook off a thought, he teleported into the bathroom. You would think it was too hard for him to walk past me and into the bathroom. *KO, baby.*

"You okay?" I said, taunting him.

"Just taking a quick shower." The water started running.

I left the dress on but put a knitted sweater on top of it. This house was too damn cold for me. On the dresser, one of his books had fallen from the shelf. It was an old version of *Alice in Wonderland* with the white rabbit on the cover. I couldn't remember ever seeing this book on his shelves, but it was beautiful. I put it back on the shelf with the rest of his collection and put on some socks for extra warmth.

Adam came out of the shower and looked relieved when he saw the sweater but made no comment on it. We went downstairs to eat with Elias and his brother. Elias put the scrambled eggs and bacon on the table and sat next to Daniel. As I made myself tea, Adam filled a plate for himself and remembered that I didn't eat pork and only served me eggs and mushrooms.

"So, Daniel, is it?"

Daniel smirked. "He told you everything, I'm assuming?" Elias looked at his brother in anticipation or dread; I couldn't tell. Adam didn't bother interjecting. His hand found my knee and drew lazy circles on it. Either he didn't care, or he was distracting himself, holding back his irritation.

"Nothing about you, no." I shrugged. "I guess you're not that important." I was in the mood to play, but Daniel just scoffed and reached for the salt instead of picking a fight with me. His fork fell under the table, so he pushed back his chair and went on his knees. Adam's hand immediately released my knee and reached for the hem of my dress. I knew there was no way Daniel would glimpse anything under my dress. Still, I crossed my legs on instinct.

Daniel got back up with a cocky grin on his face. "Please, Adam. I'm a gentleman. I would never put my head between anyone's legs without asking first." Elias stopped chewing like he knew all hell was about to break loose.

"Watch your mouth," Adam said, not breaking eye contact with Daniel. Daniel scoffed again. We finished eating in awkward silence. I refused to get up and be embarrassed. Finally, Daniel and Elias got up; Elias cleared the table and went after Daniel into the living room. I turned my body to Adam and took a sip of my tea. He avoided my gaze and kept playing with his food.

"Something is different about you—did you change your cologne or something?" I couldn't pinpoint what was different, but something was definitely off.

"Are you going to make me beg?" he said, still not looking at me.

"Beg for what?"

"For you to put on some underwear so I don't lose my mind."

"I'm not sure I know what you mean." I took the last sip of my tea and got up from my seat.

He watched me carefully. "You're gonna be the end of me," he said, following me like a puppy into the shared bedroom. As soon as we entered the room, he pinned me against the door.

"Okay! If you insist. I'll put on some underwear."

He put his hands around my neck like he wanted to strangle me, but his touch was gentle, and I kind of wished it wasn't. His thumb moved from my lip down to my chin and along my jaw. "Oh, we're past that." His knee parted my legs. I was still wearing the dress, but that was hardly a barrier.

"The things I could do to you." His voice was one octave lower than before. I didn't know if he did this to prove himself because Daniel got to his head, but I didn't care. I wanted him.

"You're all talk," I said, or he would never make a move.

His shirt came off, and then my sweater disappeared while I tried to unbutton his pants. He stopped me by the second button, took my hand, and led my fingers between my legs, guiding every move, sending chills up my spine. His fingers intertwined with mine, and he suddenly pushed them in. I arched my back, and a moan slipped through me.

"What was that?" he whispered in my ear. He did it again, and my head tipped back with a thud against the door, laying my neck open for him. His tongue was on my collarbone, licking all the way to the hollow of my throat, biting me, scratching his teeth along my breasts. He pulled my fingers out, grabbed my chin, and made me watch as he licked them clean. Somehow, we managed to get to the bed while tearing at each other's clothes.

"I will split you in half," he purred, and I couldn't think of anything I wanted more. Time slowed down when his skin touched mine. Seconds and minutes blurred together before he thrust himself into me in one hard push that made my eyes water. I felt windblown, out of breath, or something else entirely. All I knew was I had this urge to give him my all. I had been waiting for Adam my whole life. Whatever he wanted from me, he could have. Everything else was a fog from that point; I couldn't remember anything past the first thrust. My mind left my body, and something fundamentally changed within me; being with him felt like shedding skin—I was light as a feather, but the pit in my stomach was still there. I was lying sideways when he took my hand to his mouth and kissed it repeatedly before placing it on his chest and covering it with his own. His heart was beating really fast—like he wanted to tell me he loved me again, but he didn't do that. Suddenly, his touch felt like a stranger's, and I couldn't shake the feeling that I had made a huge mistake. I had wanted to sleep with him, had wanted him for so long, so why did I feel so out of place?

١٥

FIFTEEN

MAYA

I hadn't expected the day to come so soon. I had talked to her a week ago, and she was fine. My mom called and told me that Grandma had passed the night before. She was gone, really gone, and I hadn't seen her for two years. I wished I called her more often. I wished I had told her I loved her, but it was too late, and it hurt so much to think about it.

I hadn't eaten since I got the call from my mom, and I was starting to get dizzy. While preparing to pack, I started fumbling with my things, stumbling over my stuff like a toddler. *I can't deal with this right now. Get your shit together! We are not fainting again!* I had to sit down for a second to regain my balance. My head started spinning, and I had to grab the chair to avoid falling over. I decided it would be best to grab something to eat before I actually fainted, but when I was walking down the stairs, I realized something was not right. My feet felt swollen and had lost their sensibility. I was sweating, and my fingertips tickled. At first, the room started spinning. Then the air turned into massive waves, pushing me from right to left with every breath I took. Every time I closed my eyes, it felt like I was on a ship minutes before vomiting. My body gave up. The world turned black, and sounds died away. I wasn't sure how often my head bumped into something hard before I felt my back touch the mattress. The transition from displeasure to comfort was distorted, but I liked the feeling of the soft comforter on top of me. The sounds leaked into my silent mind as I heard Adam say my name; his voice sounded like it came from under water. I managed to open my eyes for a second to look at him.

"How are you feeling?"

"My grandma is dead," I said. "She died last night in her sleep—of a heart attack. She could have survived if they had gotten her to the hospital." The realization hit me. Why hadn't they managed to save her? Who was responsible for this?

"I'm sorry," Adam said, wiping tears from my face. "Please, don't cry."

I couldn't stop. I was silent, but the tears kept pouring out of me. "Please, stop crying," he kept saying, making soothing circles on my back.

"I'm sorry—I can't make it stop."

"Have you had anything to eat?" I shook my head. I had forgotten to eat or drink, and the combination of dehydration, lack of food, and the grief of my grandmother's death had made me collapse. Adam went downstairs to make me something to eat. While he was downstairs, I packed the rest of my stuff and started looking for flight tickets. There was no way I was missing the funeral.

Adam came back with a sandwich and looked at the bag I had filled to the brim. It was the bare minimum: my sleeping mask, black scarves, a light trench coat, everything black I owned, and the necessary toiletries.

"When is the funeral?" he asked as he offered me the sandwich and put his arm around me.

"They're trying to push it to Tuesday so that we all have a chance to fly in." Milad also wanted to come, but both our parents said he couldn't go because of school. Even though Milad was fifteen, that kind of funeral wasn't a place for him. I had already been exposed to it when I was ten, which was no ordinary thing. It was brutal and traumatic, not a place for him.

"Have you found any tickets?" He said and leaned over to look at my screen. The tab was down, so he couldn't see where I was going. I had a feeling he had no clue I was going to Iran.

"No, all the flights have such long layovers, but I don't think I have a choice."

"Why?" He frowned. "Where is the funeral taking place?" I don't know why, but I was scared of telling him.

"Tehran," I said.

"Tehran, Iran!" There it was, the shock in his eyes that I was anticipating. His eyes were about to pop out of the sockets.

"Why do you look like that?" It kind of made me defensive. I understood when others felt that way, but Iran was like any other country with its own set of laws. He, of all people, should have known better. It wasn't a foreign place for me, but he made it sound like I would get kidnapped and die.

I booked a ticket for the following day. My flight had a layover in New York and an even longer one in Doha. I had no other choice; it was the only thing available if I wanted to go as soon as possible.

I made Adam promise he wouldn't show up in Iran no matter what. We could talk on the phone, but other than that, my family wouldn't understand, especially my uncles. Some of them were on the religious side. It wasn't the norm to have a boyfriend, let alone bring him to a funeral. My mom asked me to keep my American ways on the low to avoid conflict. I appreciated that she never pushed their ways on us and let us decide for ourselves. In return, I wouldn't make her look bad. Whatever we did was directly reflected on our parents, so my mom would get a lot of shit for letting us be Americanized, since my father, obviously, couldn't be blamed. Not to mention, I was the only one in my family who didn't go to college. All my cousins were either in college or had degrees already—and not all fields were praised equally; my cousin Ashkan studied microbiology and was seen as lesser than his sister, who was a dentist. I would like to think I was a resourceful person, but I was at the bottom of that list. In Iran, my only value was my American passport, which could get me married off to a rich guy in Iran. I didn't know what to do with my life or if I wanted to go to college. Frankly, I didn't want to do anything. Nothing seemed exciting. There was absolutely no job or career I wanted to do for the rest of my life. And it left me feeling like a malfunctioning member of the family. I wish I had a goal or a dream I wanted to pursue; life would be so much easier if I did.

After checking in my luggage at the airport, Adam and I found a bench to sit on. I didn't want to go yet because I would start crying as soon as he was out of sight. I had been holding the tears back. I wasn't ready for the pain that would come with it. I leaned my head on his chest with his arm around me. I was snuggling my hand into the sleeve of his other arm—trying to feel the touch of his skin as much as possible before having to let go.

We hugged for at least ten minutes before we let go of each other.

"Feels like you're never coming back," he said, kissing me again.

"You know that's not true."

"Call me when you land."

"I will," I said and kissed him one last time.

As soon as the flight took off, I started crying as if my tears were bottomless. I couldn't control them, even when someone sat next to me; it was a child who didn't pay much attention to me because he was playing a game on his device. No matter what I did, tears kept streaming down. I did my best to hide and stare out of the window. The pain was ripping me apart; it hurt so much that I started questioning whether it was physical or not because my hands started hurting like hell. It began slowly with my fingers and continued to my wrist, but lately, nothing had been normal about me. The last week had been weird for me. It's like my body anticipated something horrible and was coping with it before I got the call from my mother. I slept about fifteen hours and woke up each morning with a massive head-ache. My mind and body had changed into something I couldn't recognize. Sometimes, my body would go completely numb for hours, and I had to pretend I was tired because I didn't want Adam to notice. I even went to a doctor, who took my blood and found nothing. Then I went to a specialist. She couldn't tell me anything useful. They did a bunch of tests on me, and the cardiologist took an EKG test of my heart, but there was nothing. That's why I thought it was my body's way of knowing about my grandma's death before it had happened.

Worldwide, people had a funny picture of what Iran was supposed to look like and how women had to dress there. It was widely known that women in Iran were required to wear headscarves due to the Islamic regime. Still, only people who visited knew what that meant for the average Iranian woman. The Iranian woman was not at all what people would imagine. They didn't all wear long black burkas and covered up everything—just like in any other part of the world, spirituality was a spectrum. To the world, Iranians were portrayed as oppressed women without a voice. If only they knew how loudly they expressed themselves.

Sure, the headscarf was a huge part of it, but for most, it hardly covered the hair. That was not to say we didn't have women who covered fully; we did, and they, too, were proud.

The modern Iranian woman had a flower-printed scarf and a matching trench coat called a *manteau*—a borrowed French word for coat. Many women wore full glam makeup because it was perceived as lazy, not to be high maintenance. The more you did, the better, it seemed.

I had barely landed, and already, they had introduced me to about fifty family members I had never met before. The whole family met at my grandfather's house. My mom was there, too. She hugged me, and I let her, but we didn't speak. Things had changed since the last time I had visited. My cousins had grown so much and seemed very different and standoffish. I thought I could find solace with them, but the girls were distant. I had nine cousins from my mother's side; four were girls, and all four were from different places around the world. Except for one, my male cousins still lived in Iran.

My cousins were preparing to leave for the ceremony, so I decided to get ready, too, because I was afraid they would go without me. I was walking toward the bathroom when I heard my mom arguing with her sister.

"I did everything to keep her away from your kind. You're not about to ruin that," my mom whisper-yelled.

"This is our legacy and a test she has to pass. You cannot deny her the right to be a part of it," my aunt, Shirin, said.

I wanted to stay and hear what they were discussing, but someone came, and I had to move along. When I got back out, it was time to leave, and I never got the context I desperately needed.

Two minibuses came to pick us up, ready to take us on a somber ride to the cemetery. We approached the sprawling expanse of *Beheshte Zahra*—Zahra's Paradise. The cemetery stretched out before us, a vast, almost surreal landscape of remembrance. The cemetery was meticulously designed and was so massive that it had roads and shops. Easily the size of a small town. Guards stood sentinel at every second or third corner, guiding mourners through the maze of memories. I was once told that there were over one million graves in there. Despite its size, Zahra's Paradise was tightly packed with graves. They seemed to lean in close, almost huddling together. Few bore the typical headstones; instead, most featured smooth marble slabs, their surfaces etched with heartfelt inscriptions. A select few graves stood out with towering gravestones adorned with intricately engraved images of the departed, their smiles etched in stone for all eternity.

The funereal customs were worlds apart from what I knew back home. The older women in the crowd gave themselves entirely to their grief, their wails echoing through the cemetery. It was more than mere crying; some of them crumbled to the grass, needing the support of others to stay on their feet. One woman even collapsed entirely while the rest pierced the air with their cries. From what I had seen in Iran before, this was the norm. These reactions came when they were about to start the ceremony. There were unique traditions regarding how to bury people in Iran. Practices that followed Islamic traditions. They didn't use any caskets. The deceased was wrapped in a white sheet, almost like a mummy. Then she went straight to the grave, just like that. The white sheet was used as a sign of purity and respect. People weren't supposed to see the dead person. Nothing was shown. I was glad they didn't show her face. I wouldn't have been able to hold it together if I had seen her. I wanted to preserve her memory. She was a joyful and beautiful woman with the most heartwarming smile, and I didn't want to forget that. I had to step away for a moment, seeking a second of peace from the overwhelming emotions that engulfed me. Everything had become intensely real, and the irrevocable truth that she was no longer with us was harder than I imagined.

After the ceremony, we went to a mosque, where people prayed for her. Outside the mosque, tables and chairs were lined up for dinner. Some people only came for the food, but it was a huge part of the tradition, a way of giving back to the community. So, many of our neighbors were invited, neighbors who might not have been the most fortunate. We ate so she could eat with us. The only thing I hoped for was that she was at peace. My beliefs about the afterlife were based on nothing, and though I prayed she went to heaven, I struggled to accept the concept that seemed almost too idyllic to be true.

١٦

SIXTEEN

Maya

I finally felt like I belonged in Iran. My cousins started loosening up and including me when going out. I finally mustered the courage to go to the cemetery alone and visit my grandma's grave. I went a few times, once on a Friday when traffic was crazy and the cemetery packed. I wasn't making that mistake again. On the highway leading to the cemetery, children of all ages with tired smiles and tiny hands sold fragrant flowers—mostly *Gol Mohammadi* and bottles of rose water glistening in the sun. The tradition was to wash the grave with water first, then cleanse it with rose water, and finally, pluck the rose petals and cover the plot with them. Beside each grave, mourners kneeled, their hands wiping the marble plots as they lovingly washed away the dust with rose water and gently blanketed the resting place with petals.

When I returned to the house, my cousin Sepideh called me into one of the bedrooms.

"We were going up north to visit *Khale* Leyla, pack a few things for a couple of days," she said.

"Who's going?"

"*Khaleha*—the aunts. Well, expect your mother." I wondered why my mother wasn't going, but it was honestly a relief. I was always so tense around her.

My grandmother's sister, Leyla, was at the funeral, but I didn't get to say hello. I met her once when I was ten, but I didn't know her well. She lived in a city eight hours from Tehran by train. We could've flown, but tickets were hard to come by. So, instead, we got on the last train of the day. At midnight, to be precise, because my aunt didn't want to be on a crowded train. The train was probably the oldest in history. It made bumpy noises every single second, and because of that, the trip felt much longer than it should have. Five hours in, the train stopped so people could go outside and pray the morning prayer, and when they were done, they got a plastic cup with hot tea to go. It was a very aesthetic experience, like stepping into a wormhole and crossing time. I didn't want to complain about the weather in Iran because, this year, we hadn't seen the sun much back home, but sitting on the train with no air-conditioning and it being a bazillion degrees outside, I wanted to throw myself out of the window.

When we arrived, I immediately noticed the difference in the morning air. Tehran's pollution was awful. Here, the air was pleasantly fresh. The city wasn't as crowded, and it was less noisy. A minibus picked us up shortly after getting off the train. I met the rest of the family who couldn't attend the funeral. Our family was so big that even I got confused. Eleven women lived in that house on a daily.

"Can I ask you something?" I said to Sepideh.

"Of course."

"This might sound stupid, but why is everyone wearing scarves inside the house? There are no men around. Is it a mourning thing?"

"Oh, no, not at all. They are veiling."

"Yeah, I see that, but why?"

"Didn't your mom go over veiling with you? It isn't for religious reasons. Outside, we wear scarves because we have to. Inside, we veil for protection."

It made no sense to me, even though it sounded straightforward. If I asked again, she would think I was a brick wall.

My grandmother's sister, Leyla, was out when we arrived because she had to get special herbs for the night. We were doing another funeral ceremony with the women closest to my grandmother. We were all still wearing black because the custom was that you wore black for forty days. I wasn't quite sure about the rules, but I had come prepared. After dinner, Leyla went to the kitchen and burned something in a mini frying pan. The pan was small and was covered with a metal net. It turned out to be the herbs she got from the market. She walked around and spread the smoke to every corner of the house, then over everyone's heads until it filled the house like fog. It made a funny rustling sound. She said a bunch of weird stuff when waving the little pan. Her eyes looked upward, and her voice became hoarse as she spoke. Then the rustling stopped, and the smoke disappeared. The round and sharp scent of the herbs still covered every inch of the room. It was a familiar scent, but I couldn't remember if my grandma used to burn it for us or not. When Leyla went back into the kitchen, I looked at my cousin Lara.

"What is that?"

"Esphand—it's something everybody uses here. People burn it to bring good fortune and ward off the evil eye," she said. "Your mom never did that for you?"

I felt a little embarrassed to admit that either I didn't remember or that my mom left before I learned about our culture.

Later that day, Leyla wanted us all to get ready to go out. Four cars came and took us for a two-hour ride outside the city. We drove to the mountains and hiked the rest of the way up to where the cars couldn't go. A breathtaking view unfolded before my eyes: the city's lights shimmered like a radiant carpet under our feet, the sky a velvet background for the descending sun. Far below us, the city appeared to be ablaze, as if the entire planet was in a conflagration of red and orange flames. Wisps of clouds gracefully veiled the darkening sky, deepening in hue with each fleeting moment.

The aunts found a clearing and started a bonfire. One of them sprinkled herbs and stones between the branches and the wood. Everything about it was bizarre. It looked nothing like a bonfire I had seen before. It didn't have the standard orange flames. It was more of a reddish color, but I figured it was probably caused by some of the things they had mixed with the wood. Everybody gathered and held each other's hands; they took mine, too. Leyla spoke in Farsi. She wasn't next to me, so

I didn't hear everything, but I caught some of her sentences. Translated from formal written Farsi, it sounded like she was saying, *We offer you the fire, burning steady and pure. Shall it combine and grow with the strength of all Sāhers and repel foreign magic.*

I usually didn't understand prayers, but this one was simple enough. Still, I didn't know why the word *Jadu*—magic was mentioned during a prayer ceremony. The fire was almost double in size when it suddenly went out. It happened in a split-second, like when one blows out a candle, and then they all let go of each other's hands.

"What happened?"

"Why didn't it work?"

"Did we do something wrong?" They all spoke at the same time, like crossed wires.

"*Entekhabesh nakardan*—they didn't choose her," Leyla said.

We were supposed to stay at Leyla's for a few days, but they decided to return to Tehran the next day. They all pretended the day prior didn't happen and moved on like it was the most ordinary thing ever. I couldn't help but feel left out. Either there was a language barrier or a cultural one because I had no idea what I had witnessed.

Our trip back to Tehran was during the day, so the train was full of sweaty, smelly people. Fresh air barely got through the tiny windows, even though the train was speeding. It was like the air didn't work the same in Iran; it didn't move. Sepideh and I got to sit together, allowing me to ask her some questions. Sepideh might actually have known what went on.

"Who was supposed to be chosen last night?"

"One of us, clearly," she said with a blank expression.

"No, Leyla was talking about someone specific."

"If you know, then why are you asking?" She sounded frustrated but then her mask clicked back into place.

"Because I wasn't filled in. I don't know shit," I said. "Can't you just pretend to sympathize for a second?"

"I'm sorry, you're right, but you should speak to your mother about this, and you weren't chosen. So, now, you can move on. We all went through it, and no one told me what to do after," Sepideh said.

I had no idea what she was talking about, but I had to keep her going. "What did you do?"

"Nothing dramatic. I just broke up with him. What did your mom say you should do?" she said. *Broke up with who?*

"We don't talk," I said.

"Wait! When you say you don't know shit, what do you mean? Were you never taught about us? The Sāhers!" She lowered her voice when she said *Sāhers*. There it was, that word again. What did it mean? I couldn't ask her and look ignorant.

I shook my head.

"I'm sorry. I can't help you with that. You need to talk to your mother," she said with disbelief. I had no idea what my mom was hiding from me, but I had to find out. I couldn't believe I was being deliberately left out just because I hadn't spoken to her. Was she punishing me for being a brat? She could have stayed if she really wanted to. She tried to keep me far away from them, but it worked its way into my life anyway.

At worst, I thought my family spoke to the dead and played with tarot cards. The previous night's ceremony looked like something from a cult; perhaps I wasn't good enough to participate. Why did grandma not teach me? She could have told me about it over the phone. She was always going on and on about our legacy and duty. Why wasn't she more clear in her delivery?

This was why I always felt out of touch with reality.

The moment we arrived at the house in Tehran, I raced inside to find my mother. She was sitting in the kitchen with some family members, drinking tea.

"We need to talk," I said. She put down the tea and got up right away. We went into an empty bedroom, where she closed the door.

"You don't have to do anything they say, Maya. This is the exact reason why I have been absent from your life. I don't want you to get involved. There is no such thing as a chosen one."

"Relax, I wasn't chosen to do anything, but why did you keep this from me? What the hell is a Sāher?" I said.

She made praying hands, looked up, and mumbled *Khoda-ro shokr*—thank God. I didn't realize she had become religious ever since they divorced.

"You need to tell me everything."

"Maya, listen to me. You do not want to mix with these people. They are doing the devil's work," she said.

"These people are your family. Why are you so paranoid?"

"*Azizam, Harameh*—My dear, it's a sin."

"If you don't tell me, I'll find out by myself and make sure to become the chosen one!" I said.

"*Azizam*, listen to me. I will speak to you in your language so that you don't think I am forcing anything on you. I didn't tell you because I don't believe anyone should fulfill the prophecy. Not you or any of your cousins. You are children and very easily manipulated. My sisters will do anything to make it happen. They think someone has to be chosen, and thank the lord it wasn't you. That means the devil didn't get you, and you still have your soul. Now, the only way you can protect yourself is by staying far away from him and his kind."

"What?" I had no other words left. Was she talking about Adam, or was I connecting the dots out of sheer panic?

"You don't know their kind, Maya. They cannot be trusted. Even if he seems to be in love with you. It's better if you save yourself and get out while you can."

"It's not—" I couldn't finish my sentence because I didn't know what to say. She shook her head. I was glad I didn't confirm anything. She didn't need to know about Adam. I was just being paranoid, just like my mother. *This isn't what I think it is. I'm being delusional. Breathe in . . . Breathe out . . .*

"I'm not discussing this with you," I said. She had no right; she hadn't been a parent for so long, and she couldn't come and pretend to be one now. I let the frustration overtake me, and I left.

I was so curious about it all. I couldn't be in my own skin, and since my mother wouldn't tell me anything, I figured I could do some good old-fashioned research. I went down to the biggest library near me in Tehran, and I brought a friend. I needed her to translate for me because I couldn't read Farsi. Naimeh was a girl who lived in the same neighborhood as my grandmother but had moved to a better area. We still kept in touch on the internet. She didn't know my cousins, and that's why she was perfect for the task. I didn't want the word to spread about this. I wanted her to help me without anyone knowing. Before the library, Naimeh and I wanted to catch up a little. I hadn't seen her since the last time I was here. We always used to go to cafes and talk about boys. This time, we opted for a walk with an ice-cold honeydew melon juice. When we got to the library, I asked the librarian for some books on mythology and Persian magic. Naimeh knew about my unexpected request but didn't know the actual reason behind my research. She thought I was doing research because I had switched majors in college, not knowing I never actually went.

The lady walked us through the beautiful maze of books, her footsteps echoing softly against the shiny marble floor. As we ventured deeper into the library, I couldn't resist the urge to trail my fingers along the bookshelves, their surfaces meticulously carved with intricate leafed branches and cherry blossoms. Each corridor seemed to be whispering secrets from the pages of the books that had been living on the shelves for generations. The librarian pulled three books from different shelves and said it was the only material she had. They couldn't be taken home, only looked in at the library. We turned a few pages in the first book, and the wispy scent of age rose from the pages.

I made her flip through the pages for hours and read lots of absurd mythology. One of the books was a complete waste of time and had nothing about the Sāhers. Instead, it was about how Christian Persians used the bible as a spell book. The two other books were actually what I was looking for. They were quite difficult to understand, even for her, because they were written like classic Persian poetry. If you knew anything about Persian poetry, you would know it was an art just reciting it. People took classes just to be able to understand and recite them. We had spent hours reading and skipping pages that seemed irrelevant. Things were explained in so much detail you wouldn't know where to start or what to believe. There were all sorts of spells, formulas, rituals, and even directions on preparing yourself to practice magic. Because that's what it was: magic. Sāhers were witches practicing old Persian Pagan traditions. Traditions that were considered sinful. Although the rules were bendable, people here were more accepting of weird ideologies. They believed that magic existed, but it was strictly forbidden to practice or—as my mother put it—*the devil's work.*

So many Persian holiday traditions, such as *Yalda*—the winter solstice—were pagan traditions passing as Persian culture. In fact, Iran was one of the few countries that still celebrated *Nowruz*—the new year in spring, which corresponds with the spring equinox. It's a tradition for us to set up an altar with seven symbolic things whose names start with S. Not all altars were decorated the same. Most people had gold coins, garlic, sweet pudding, sumac, an apple, a dish of wheatgrass, and vinegar. As a tradition, Iranians jumped over fire because it was believed to cleanse you. The spring equinox was in the sign of Aries, so it made sense in more than one way. Those traditions were far from Islamic but still practiced and enjoyed throughout the country.

The books mentioned Pagan traditions and holidays lightly, but it wasn't the main topic. There were more pages dedicated to meditation and the art of getting rid of the mind from the body. The out-of-body experience had a very extensive chapter for itself.

A lot of thought had gone into these spells. It was nothing like what I imagined. You had to gather everything you needed, such as colored candles and incense with various smells. Then you would need to build an altar to put the collected items. If anything moved, the spell could, potentially, be ruined. Many rituals and spells corresponded with the moon phases, the elements, and whatnot. Before any spell-casting, there were things to take into consideration. You would wash your body under running water to purify yourself, which resembled the act of ablution in Islam. The tools you needed also had to be cleansed; that was done with incense smoke. Even candles had to be anointed; the candle had to be rubbed in oil from the middle of the candle and to the ends and never from one side to another. And finally, you could cast a circle, whatever that meant.

When I thought of spells, I imagined they had their effect right away. The books shattered that picture. Some spells had to be repeated more than once to work. Some of them every day for a week, some once a week, and others, you had to continue performing 'til you saw the results.

The book was full of spells to bless people with good luck or success but also spells to break up a married couple or harm an enemy. To be quite honest, I thought it was satire at first. I couldn't believe they had written all those things down and meant it.

The last book was a story about witchcraft as a way of life. It transported me into a world where witches had walked this earth long before anyone called themselves Iranians. These witches, the Sāhers, were not newcomers to this land; they were its original inhabitants, bound to this land by ancient rituals. In these stories, there was no mention of men; the mothers carried the weight of tradition, passing down their heritage to their daughters. Husbands remained blissfully unaware of the arcane rites and rituals performed in their homes and at their temples. Every secret temple was consecrated to fire, which they believed was the purest element. Therefore, tending to the eternal flame in the temples was one of the most honorable obligations of the Sāhers. It was unclear if the temples had been destroyed in battles or buried in history, but as the eternal flames went out one by one, so did the strength of each Sāher.

Still, their belief remained strong; it wasn't about choosing which deity to worship or what path to follow. The Sāhers' duty was to maintain the balance of nature and defend it against those who sought to disrupt it. It wasn't a battle waged against rival gods or creeds but against those who dared to tip the scales, defying the natural order of good and evil. The deities didn't want sacrifices; they only asked for good thoughts and deeds. I found myself ensnared in a world where witchcraft thrived.

The book recounted battles in which the Sāhers had fought, battles they had always lost. It was told as a form of prophecy about nine harrowing battles in total, eight of which would end with many injured and dead. Even with this knowledge of impending doom, the Sāhers remained determined, living by the rule: no retreat, no surrender, and were driven by an unwavering belief in the promise of a final victorious end.

Among all the battles, the last one stood out. In the year 1287, on a moonless night, the Sāhers and their leader Apranik, known formally as the daughter of the eldest, faced a group of young men led by the spirit of Ahriman. These men had the ability to bend the elements in unnatural ways and were unlike any mortal men; their powers stemmed from dark sources. The clash of magic unfolded like a dance of light and darkness, with the Sāhers weaving intricate protection spells while their opponents summoned the very darkness to do their bidding. Sparks flew as the men hurled bolts of lightning and waves of smoke and shadows that threatened to engulf everything in their path. Despite the Sāhers' unwavering resolve, the odds were stacked against them. In the end, the night bore witness to a tragedy, and only one battle remained. My thoughts drifted to Adam and his family. *It could very well be them.*

Naimeh was utterly mesmerized by the contents of the last book. She kept reading without pausing, and I had to stop her because I caught her reacting to something. She made a *huh* sound and crossed her legs.

"What is it?"

"For argument's sake, let's say everything this book says is true. That means the next—and presumably last—battle will be this year," she said.

"That can't be right." The battles described occurred between the 11th and 14th centuries.

"Obviously not *real* real. It's mythology, but if it were to be true, they would have to find a worthy leader before the 18th of Mordad this year to ensure fulfilling the prophecy," Naimeh said. I was beginning to think it was the same prophecy my mother was talking about and that my family was looking for someone to lead them into the final battle. Thank God I wasn't actually chosen. Because if this wasn't fiction, and I had guessed correctly, the last battle was my family against his. *No. I'm being delusional. What is wrong with you!*

"What does it say about their leader? Anything specific?" *Let's refute the theory.*

"It reads, 'Lie beneath the scion born past spring equinox, recline, for the Goddess Ishtar, her powers shall entwine,'" Naimeh said. "I don't know how else to translate it."

But she didn't need to because I understood. The grains formed a desert. The accuracy was uncanny. I couldn't make this up if I wanted to. If *lie beneath* meant sleeping with, and Adam was the scion, then I could potentially be the chosen one, even though Leyla said I wasn't. I had to hold my breath to keep my shit together because I had already slept with Adam. What if I couldn't take it back? *Fuck me!*

Perhaps I was overanalyzing a myth, but what if Adam was preparing for it all this time? What if his whole family was in a war against mine and he knew of my heritage, so he targeted me? I shook off the thought because I would drive myself mad if I kept thinking about it. I was suddenly very eager to go back home. I had to go home and make sure it wasn't true and that Adam wasn't a part of this upcoming war. I had no idea if there was an ounce of truth in those pages, but I wasn't going to sit around and wait for it to happen.

IV

SEVENTEEN

I called Adam yesterday and told him I was arriving late. He said he would pick me up from the airport, but he didn't answer his phone when I called. Maybe he had forgotten, so I got a cab instead.

I missed my friends, and I missed Dissie the most, but she wasn't a friend of mine anymore. So, instead, I called Alie on the ride. It had been a long time since I last talked to her; I wanted to hear about other people's everyday problems instead of my crazy worries. Alie had put me on speaker and told me Lena was seeing someone.

"While you were gone, I kinda hooked up with . . ." She got quiet for a second. "Elias."

"What? How?"

"It's a long story, but we're kinda dating now." I had no idea how they even found each other. He wasn't exactly the type who was hanging around town. He was always working out, even without Adam to push him.

Pulling up the street where Adam lived, I saw a lot of cars parked end to end. Loud music was blasting from the house. The sound of the growling stereo was so intense I couldn't believe no one had called the cops yet. People I didn't know stood both outside and inside, no one I recognized. I got my bags out of the trunk and walked toward the house. People looked at me like I didn't belong, and maybe I didn't. The smell of beer and cigarettes was scratching my nose. There was vomit soaked into the carpet in the corner of the living room and on the stairs. People stepped on it and didn't even notice.

"I'm sorry." I stopped a girl. "Have you seen Adam or Elias?"

She looked confused. "Who?"

I called both of them, but my calls didn't even go through. I called Lena to ask if she knew where Elias was; she didn't but told me not to worry. Of course, I hadn't told her about the party, or she might have felt differently. People were walking in and out of every room of the house. I passed the toilets and heard moaning. The scene was taken out of a picture of a frat party. Two girls were fooling around with a guy in our bedroom. *Is that . . .*

"Get the hell out of my bed!" I said and turned around like a kid who had accidentally switched to adult Cinemax. The girls giggled and got dressed.

"Oh, it's you." Daniel's voice sounded.

"You're disgusting! This is my bed," I said.

"Relax, I'm not even naked yet," he said, walking past me.

"What are you doing?"

"Having a party . . ." He stated the obvious as if I were an idiot.

"I rolled my eyes. "Do they know you're having a party here?"

"Do you see them?" he said, pulling his T-shirt over his head.

"They are gonna kill you when they get back. You know that, right!" He huffed a response before I closed the door in his face. I took a long shower and tried to fall asleep to the noise from the party. Luckily, I had the earplugs the airline gave us, which helped a lot. I was knocked out as soon as I put my head on the pillow and covered myself with the blanket. I think I had slept for a few hours when I could have sworn the bedroom door had opened. I dozed off again and didn't move until I felt Adam crawling in bed behind me. His hand went across my back. Another moment passed before I heard Adam bark something at the top of his lungs. His voice didn't come from behind me, but it startled me so much that I got up and turned around. I caught a glimpse of Daniel's silhouette before he teleported. I hadn't fully realized what was going on. Was Daniel really lying beside me in bed?

Across the room, Adam was boiling; he wasn't looking at me or even happy to see me after such a long time apart. Instead, he took his phone and called someone.

"If I see your damn brother one more time, I WILL kill him! I'm not kidding this time, Elias. Get him out of my way," Adam said, hung up, and looked at me.

"Has Dan ever been inappropriate with you before?" He snapped at me, still fuming. *What is going on . . .*

"No." I got up from the bed, and I was about to fall apart. The bones under my skin were suddenly made of jelly. I had missed him so much, and Daniel had ruined our moment in seconds. It could have been so magical.

I still managed to take the last two steps to hug him. Reluctantly, he hugged me back, and it felt like a betrayal, but I was where I was supposed to be—with him. His scent was around me; his hair smelled of rain and bark.

Adam pulled away. "How did Daniel end up in my bed?"

"I'm just as clueless as you, Adam," I said. *Does he think something is going on?* "I was sleeping and felt him crawl in bed with me." Adam's eyebrows arched. "I thought it was you, so I slept through it." It felt like I had to defend myself.

"I tried calling you," I said.

"I'm sorry. We were training. I thought you were coming back tomorrow. I don't know how I missed it." He looked at me for a second, wanting to say something, but he had a change of heart. Instead, he went in to take a shower. Something was off, but I didn't want to press on it. I looked at my phone and saw it was eight in the morning, and even though I had slept seven hours, I was exhausted. I didn't want to go back to bed now that Adam was up and ready, so I got up, put on a summer dress, and started styling my hair. Meanwhile, Adam had gotten out, but he didn't say much. He was acting weird, sitting on the edge of the bed, looking into the air. So, I put the flat iron down and walked over to him. "What's wrong? Why are you quiet?"

"Nothing," he said.

I stood between his legs and cupped his face. "What are you thinking about?" He looked at me with a frown on his face. "Has he touched you before?"

"No."

He got up and pulled away from my hands. "I just don't understand how he felt so comfortable lying next to you like it was no big deal." His tone shifted.

"I want you to think twice about what you're saying, Adam." I unplugged the flat iron and threw it into the drawer. I didn't care if it would burn the house down. I didn't know how to express my frustration and anger without starting to cry. I couldn't believe the accusation in his tone. Besides, it was pretty clear Daniel had done this to get under his skin. And here I was, trying to look cute for him, when all he did was accuse me of cheating. I left the room, not wanting to look at his stupid face. I wanted to cry, wanted to cry so badly, but there was nowhere to hide, and I didn't want to bump into Elias while I was on the verge of tears. Moving in with him was the most stupid idea I had ever had, and now I had nowhere to go. I didn't want to be the kind of girl who called her friends at the slightest inconvenience. So, instead, I went to the downstairs bathroom and cried in silence until I was done.

Lena was always around Elias. Their relationship went from nothing to something in an instant. They were obsessed with each other, spent every hour together, and even finished each other's sentences. She often said she wanted to come over and hang out, but instead, she spent the whole day with Elias. I felt resentment building up, so I spent more time at Alie's house to avoid Lena. I didn't have much else to do if I wasn't at work. I had forgotten how much time I had spent with Dissie. Adam wasn't around much. He wasn't even stateside most of the time, but I managed to avoid both Elias and Lena.

The day before, Adam came back from Egypt but not for me or for Independence Day. He came back because of the charity fundraiser scheduled for later that evening. He was going to perform one of his recent poems. It was an annual thing that Sean's family hosted at their house and invitation only for the high-society types. This year was the first time I was invited—through Alie, of course, now that she dated Sean. We barely knew Sean; he was nice to Alie, and that was all that mattered.

I had found a black dress in a vintage shop that fit like a glove but not so tight I couldn't move. It had an open back, which I loved in dresses because it revealed just enough.

Sean bought Alie an expensive dress his cousin had picked. He wanted her to look extra glamorous in front of his mother. She was unapologetically judgmental when it came to how Alie presented herself at this event. The event wasn't until eight, so I went to Alie's parents' house. They were having their version of an Indian-American barbeque for the Fourth of July.

After the barbeque at Alie's, we went downtown to catch the parade. More people than expected had shown up with their flags and clapping hats. We could barely stand and watch because kids pushed us from every side possible. The teenagers were doing a terrible job hiding the fact that they were drinking alcohol from soda bottles.

Someone had made homemade fireworks, and the cops had no control of it. This guy ran out of an alley, and an explosion went off before I could blink. It was so powerful that I jumped forward. Luckily, no one got hurt; these kids never thought of the consequences of their actions. There were a lot of families pulling their kids away from the parade. Everything got intense in a short period of time. I don't know how I lost Lena and Alie. I tried calling them, but they didn't pick up. The noises and smell of fireworks made my head spin. I wasn't feeling very well and was sure going to pass out. My legs felt loose, sight blurry, and the voices around me were unclear. I managed to take myself to a public restroom and lock myself in there before causing a scene. I slowly sat on the floor and let my mind fade away and my body melt into the wall.

I only woke up again because my phone was ringing. I realized I had been passed out for two hours. "Hello," I said, with a throaty voice I couldn't conceal.

"Have you seen my black tie?" Adam asked.

"Um . . . I think it's in your sock drawer."

"Hang on," he said.

"Adam, can you come and get me? I'm not feeling so good."

"Why, where are you?"

"I'm downtown, across the street from Mino's."

"Alright. I'll be there soon."

He picked me up not long after and didn't bother asking me what happened or if I was okay. When I leaned my head on the car window, it vibrated and bumped more than usual. I only had two drinks before the parade, but it felt like I was poisoned. I mixed the drinks myself. Nothing was in them besides what I had opened myself. It was a brand-new bottle of vodka, and usually, it took more than four drinks before I would even feel tipsy. This was a very unusual reaction to alcohol.

"Are you okay?" he finally asked like it was an obligation.

"I don't feel so good."

"It can't be that bad. I would have felt it," he said. "I always know when something is wrong."

"I've been passed out on the floor of a public restroom for nearly two hours. I'm pretty sure you stopped feeling things." I snapped. The thought had occupied my mind for days. I turned my head to the window again. Something had shifted between us. Maybe I had gotten a bit moody, but I wasn't the only one. Whatever magic we had between us wasn't there anymore, and it was killing me. I knew the honeymoon phase was short. I just didn't know it would be this short. Did he stop caring about me? Was I not what he expected in a girlfriend? Was I unreasonable to want this much attention from him?

As soon as we got home, I ate some protein cookies. I had to get my shit together and be presentable. I didn't want to miss the event. Maybe sparks would appear in his eyes if he saw how pretty I looked in that dress. The final look in the mirror didn't show what was really there. The real Maya wasn't standing there. I even fooled myself with the façade. The makeup, the perfect hair, and the beautiful black dress concealed the desperate girl who tried to get her boyfriend back. I was putting on the second earring when Adam teleported to the room. I never got used to him jumping in and out, and dropped the earring on the floor. It rolled all the way to his feet. He picked up the earring, walked closer, and handed it to me.

"Do you have Sean's phone number?"

"Um—yeah, look through my phone," I said.

He took my phone from the charger, found the number, and put it back on the bed.

"Thank you. I'll wait for you downstairs," he said.

I would be lying if I said I didn't care what he thought of me. If he even liked how I looked in a formal dress. He used to kiss me when I did something extra for him, but it was almost like he didn't notice the difference.

"You're stunning, by the way," he then said before closing the door. *You're stunning, by the way.* My heart dropped in relief to hear that he still cared. His reaction wasn't like it used to be, but I took whatever I got. *You're stunning, by the way. You're stunning, by the way. You're stunning, by the way. You're stunning, by the way. You're stunning, by the way.*

We drove to Sean's house, not really speaking. He didn't even put a hand on my thigh like he used to. He was calm and focused on driving, dwelling on his thoughts.

We arrived at their mansion—that's what it was; it looked like a palace. Sean's family lived like royalty. Their home had an overwhelming excess of everything; all the rooms were adorned in a romantic style. As we passed through the set of French shuttered doors, I was immediately engulfed by the scent of blooming flowers enveloping the air, similar to stepping into a florist's shop. Chandeliers dangled overhead, dripping in crystals, catching and refracting the muted light that mimicked the French baroque era's ambiance when electricity had not been invented. The gathering was rich and sophisticated, paired with champagne, wine, and hors d'oeuvres. I felt like a child in the midst of an adult soiree, too timid to exchange my soda for a flute of champagne. I could legally drink, but it felt wrong.

I stood behind as Adam said hello to some of his friends, who were completely immersed in his conversation. Alie walked up to me; she wasn't enjoying herself at all. She felt that Sean's mother was ignoring her all night. To me, it seemed like she was super busy with her guests. Sure, she had a lot of help, but people were pulling her in thousands of directions, asking her all sorts of questions about everything imaginable. Alie, of course, thought she was purposely ignoring her because she wasn't worthy of their family, which wasn't true. Sean was very tentative and came to check up on her moments later.

Adam was still busy talking to his friends, caught up in the moment with Sean's brothers and father, and I didn't want to pull him away because it would be obscene to do around old people. I desperately tried to talk to strangers and socialize, but these people were so hard to crack. I didn't have anything in common with them. I escaped a table whose topic headed toward *the importance of the republican party in our country*. Politics wasn't my scene at all; I barely got the basics.

I was staring at an expensive-looking oil painting in their hallway when I noticed a guy walking toward me from the corner of my eye. "This painting is exquisite," he said. I smiled politely.

"Of course, it's nothing compared to you." I almost vomited in my mouth. He was way too old for me, at least forty, and certainly looked the part.

"My boyfriend said the same thing. I'm trying to see if he's right." I nodded toward Adam.

"I see." At least Adam worked as armor against creepy old men.

Not long after, Adam took center stage before the eager, standing crowd. I loved watching him perform; it was the sexiest thing on earth, igniting all my senses. As he began to speak, it was as though he transported himself and everyone in the room to a different realm with his poetry. His words carried the weight of his passion, and you could practically taste the shift in the air. His magnetic presence lingered when he finished, and applause erupted and carried on long after he gracefully stepped off the stage. Sean's father and his friends swarmed around him like hungry vultures. Everyone wanted a piece of him, and it almost made me cry. I felt so out of place and awkward. This was definitely not my scene. I went outside to get some fresh air, and their garden unfolded before me. Beautiful hedges were meticulously shaped, and the towering trees had branches reaching for the sky. They rustled softly in the gentle breeze. At the heart of the garden was a man-made pond, so picture-perfect it almost seemed unreal, with a wooden bridge spanning its width.

I sat on a bench and wondered if it was time to let go of Adam. I could work more hours and get my own place. I had a good chunk set aside. I didn't have to depend on him to put a roof over my head. Maybe he just felt bad for me and didn't want to throw me out of his house. Maybe I had overstayed my welcome. It was probably also time I figured out what I wanted to do with my life.

Adam came out of their house and sat next to me. He didn't say anything. For a while, we just sat there in the breeze.

"I thought you had gone home without me," he said.

"Why would I ever?" I said. I felt prickling in my eyes, but I didn't look at him. He took my hand, pulled me up, and said, "If you were forced to dance in hell, I would carve out the inferno through my shell." Tears escaped my eyes. He knew it was my favorite poem and used to recite it for me. Perhaps it wasn't over between us. Perhaps we just needed time.

He leaned in and kissed me, and the butterflies and the tickling toes all came back. It was a perfect kiss. Nothing could take that away from me. A memory I would preserve in my heart forever; something I could always go back to.

"Never doubt what we have," he said. And although it was what I wanted to hear, it didn't sit right with me.

EIGHTEEN

Adam

I had been distracted by all the things occupying my mind, but I liked to think I noticed details. There were a lot of things that concerned me. Maya was changing. She had always been the type of person who didn't want to show any weaknesses. I could tell she cried a lot because her eyes were puffy, but when I asked her, she said nothing was wrong. She would talk to me when she was ready; I just had to give her the space she needed. She didn't want to admit it, but her daily routines had changed, and I suspected it had something to do with her overall health. She had fainted at the parade and claimed it was nothing. She slept almost all day, and when she wasn't sleeping, she drank lots of coffee. Suddenly, her favorite beverage choice. It went from coffee with milk to all-black coffee—four to five cups daily. I kept telling her to eat more food and get some vitamins, but she wouldn't listen or see a doctor, and I didn't want to force her either.

That day, we were going out for dinner. Maya was getting ready in our room, with the door ajar. I caught her standing and gazing at the mirror as I walked by. She was ready to go but kept taking deep breaths. She was struggling with her high heels. She tried to walk with them but kept twisting her ankle slightly. She could barely stand but forced herself to wear them.

At the restaurant, Maya obviously couldn't keep up the act of being fine and wanted to go home after the main course. That got us into an argument, and I snapped at her.

"You just won't admit that you're sick!"

"I'm sick of being called a liar," she countered.

"I can tell you are about to collapse. Why are you being so stubborn?"

"I'm fine. I just want to go home. You don't have to go with me," she said. "I can get a cab."

She got up and walked away without saying a word. Obviously, I wasn't going to let her go home by herself. I wanted to yell at her and ask her whose home she was going to, but that would be below the belt. I just wanted her to wake up and stop being irrational. To prove me wrong, when we got home, she made herself a cup of coffee so she wouldn't fall asleep. I was starting to think there was more than just coffee in her cup. Maybe she was addicted to drugs and took them in her coffee. I didn't know why I hadn't thought of it earlier.

"Can I have some of your coffee?" I asked.

"Sure." She handed me the mug. It didn't taste any different from regular black coffee without sugar. Frankly, my patience was running thin because I didn't know how to help her, and it was getting the best of me.

Even though I was worried about Maya, I had to pay my father a visit. He would become suspicious if I didn't entertain him and his ideas. My father asked everyone except for apprentices to show up at the facilities. Word got out that it had something to do with our exposure. Samuel, my older brother, thought he was the reason. He messed around with a lot of women, and sometimes, he couldn't help himself and would try to impress them with his powers.

My father asked us to gather in the evaluation room. All who qualified to aďhār were required to be there. Someone had been spotted aďhāring by a high-ranking government official, and my father was not happy about it. The elders were sitting at the long table like a panel of judges. My father got to his feet, and the whispering dulled to nothing.

"I have asked you to come here today because Dūshev matters have traveled beyond these walls," my father said. "We are being watched, and every move we make can put us at risk. Nashir has brought it to my attention that there is a war coming. A war that can end us all if we are not careful." *Wait what?*

"I thought this was about something else," I whispered to Samuel. He elbowed me to shut up. I wasn't sure if this was a political thing between the humans and us or something entirely different.

"At least it has nothing to do with you," I said to Samuel. Skandar turned around and scowled.

"Let me make it clear to everyone. You might have already met a witch from this coven without knowing it," my father said. I didn't hear what he said before that, but it was probably important because his tone had shifted. "Don't let their charm fool you. They are deliberately looking to find a weak spot to infiltrate and destroy this family. They must be stopped, whatever it takes."

Witches. I rolled my eyes and looked at Samuel; he fidgeted with his watch. Everyone else was looking at my father, listening attentively. Skandar raised his hand. I leaned toward Samuel and whispered, "I didn't realize we were in school again." Samuel chuckled.

"What exactly should we pay attention to?" Skandar asked.

"Siren-type women trying to seduce you," Edgar said. *Oh, they're serious!*

No one had ever met one of these witches, not even my father. Still, he was absolutely sure of his words. He never doubted Nashir's predictions and assured us she had our best interest. Some of my brothers and nephews were pretty gullible, too. They dedicated their lives to the elders, never second-guessed orders, and would do anything for my father. Even fight a war if necessary. I liked to think myself capable of critical thinking. I respected my father and his expectations of us. Still, I believed Nashir was brainwashing my father. I didn't expect him to involve all of us.

My father cleared the meeting after a long, unnecessary speech about our sacred family that we had all heard before. Although they did make sure to tell us to stay for a few days. They wanted to delegate our assignments and change schedules.

I wasn't taking souls anymore, but my father still wanted me here. Later that evening, I got a chance to catch him after dinner and wanted to mess with his brain. Get him off track, maybe get him off my back.

"Father, I have some concerns about Maya," I said. "I think she's pregnant." She most definitely wasn't.

"Are you certain?" he asked. He was either afraid to show his excitement, or he didn't believe me altogether. This was something I could never take back. I had to know if it pleased him.

"I'm positive."

He grabbed onto my shoulders and pulled me toward him. I don't remember the last time my father embraced me. "That is wonderful news. You will not regret this, son." An ache rose in my throat, knowing I would never make my father this happy.

"A few things are changing about her, though . . . Remember when I told you I felt it when she needed me and that I could heal her injuries? That's all gone now. Why do you think that is?" If I mixed truths within my lies, maybe I could get some helpful information from my father.

"I would assume the soul has possibly shifted to the fetus," he said. "I'm sure there is nothing to worry about." Then he went on and on about all the great things about becoming a father. Trying to convince me of the benefits of being an elder. The privileges and all that followed. I still remained hesitant regarding the matter to maintain character. I wouldn't want him to think I was playing him because I didn't think I was.

١٩

NINETEEN

MAYA

I woke up at St. Claire Hospital. Turns out I had been unresponsive for two days—or in a coma, for lack of a better word. It was such a weird experience, waking up feeling like you had just woken up from a good night's sleep. I hadn't been in an accident or anything. I was on my way out of my dad's place after dropping off Milad. Apparently, I had collapsed behind the wheel. Luckily, the car was in park. Milad didn't panic; he called Dad, and they brought me here. Of course, I couldn't remember any of that and was filled in by the nurses. Anything that happened in the weeks up to that point was blurry. I was told by the third nurse that they had already called my dad and that he was on his way. She talked me through everything and made sure I wasn't freaking out. Then, following protocol, she asked the same questions the two other nurses did before her. I wasn't in any pain, and I just wanted to get it over with.

"Can you tell me your name, sweetheart?" she said.

"Maya Ara Forest."

"And when is your birthday?"

"January eighth," I said.

"Perfect. The doctor will be here soon to brief you. Oh! There she is." She handed the doctor some papers and left the room.

"Maya Forest"—she looked at me like I was a kindergartner—"I'm sorry, but we haven't been able to diagnose you.

It looks like nothing is wrong with you, but we would like to run some—" Her pager went off. She looked at it for a second and looked back at me. "Tests."

"Alright," I said.

"I'll put it down here. The nurse will be back with you as soon as she gets the chance."

"Thank you so much." I leaned back and smiled at her before she left. Making sure it didn't look like I was about to bolt out of the door. I waited a few seconds before getting up, changing into my clothes, and tying my hair up in a high bun to hide the mess. There was no way in hell I was staying here or waiting for my father to pick me up.

It had taken me a few days before my memory recovered to what it was. I didn't have to take the nurse's words for it. I actually remembered. Not that I was going to admit to it. My dad was blowing up my phone when I got home from the hospital. Initially, I didn't want to pick up, but he texted me, saying he would call the cops if I didn't. He just wanted to ensure I was okay, and I didn't want any drama. Even Elias interrogated me when I first got back. I didn't expect him to be remotely interested in where I was going. He had no idea what had happened and was very suspicious. Adam hadn't been home, and I guess he had been too afraid to ask him where I was, since he was left in *charge*. He threatened to tell Adam I had disappeared for two days, even though I told him I was visiting my mom. He didn't believe me, so I started screaming at him.

"Then, I must be cheating on Adam!" That shut him up. Some guys were just naturally scared of hysterical women, which worked in my favor. If Adam wanted to know what I was doing when he was not home, he could ask me himself. Not that I would tell him. It would worry him that I had fainted again, and there was literally nothing wrong with me.

Usually, when Adam teleported home, he would come straight to our room, but when I was brushing my teeth later that night, I heard him talking to someone on the phone from downstairs. He was saying he wouldn't be back before next month. He said he was staying home 'til the first of August, which was more than I ever got from him.

I quickly checked my face in the mirror before walking down to meet him. He was still speaking on the phone but reached his arm out to hug me.

"Missed you," I said.

He kissed the side of my head. "Alright, see you then," he said and hung up. He kissed me again, this time on the lips. "Where have you been?" He let go of me, waiting for an answer. "Elias told me you were gone for a few days."

"I went to Portland to visit my mom," I said. *Where the hell did I get Portland from?*

"Oh."

"Ever since my grandmother passed, we have stayed in touch." The lies just rolled off the tongue.

"That's nice. And speaking of—you never told me about the funeral or Iran. You were gone for a couple of weeks, after all," he said, leading me into the kitchen.

"Um. The funeral was . . . sad—I don't know what to tell you. I was with my family most of the time." I shifted. I didn't realize it would make me feel so uncomfortable talking about the funeral.

"What's your family like? Who are you closest to?"

"My cousins, I guess, but I like my aunts as well," I said.

"How about uncles? Are they not nice?"

"I guess." *Why are you so awkward!* "I mean, they're nice and everything, but I have nothing in common with the men in my family, and we never talk."

"Tell me a crazy family story, something odd or embarrassing. What makes them unique?"

This conversation was going nowhere, and I couldn't figure out why he was making small talk, as if he was getting to know me.

"We're quite boring," I said, thinking of the Sāhers. Was that really what we were? Or was I desperately trying to be a part of something bigger to escape my mundane life?

"There must be something interesting about them," he said. "Every family has some weird uncle or aunt."

"Well, my mother's cousin is kind of the freak of the bunch. She thinks she can see the future by reading tarot cards depicting devils and angels," I said. Something was on his mind, so I threw him the bone. She did read cards and predicted the future but never important stuff.

"So, none of your aunts are witches," he said and faked a smile. Goose bumps rose on my arms.

"Yeah, and no fairies, either," I said, suppressing a frown. Maybe he knew about the Sāhers. He must have heard about them; they all must have. They had been around for centuries; of course they knew of each other. The conversation died down, and Adam went back to being on his phone. Though, this time, I was grateful. I wasn't sure I could answer more of his questions without raising suspicion.

٢٠

TWENTY

Adam

I had to leave in the middle of the night. I got up and left without waking Maya. She would make those sad puppy-dog eyes, asking me not to leave. I didn't have that luxury; I had to return to the elders, even though I didn't want to. The past two weeks with Maya had been easy. I think we both tried not snapping at each other. She was always down and expected more of me than I could offer. I wanted to be there for her—I really did, but my father had expectations for us, and I couldn't deny him. My father wanted to teach us his meditation technique. A technique my brother Joseph had mastered long ago. Joseph was my father's first son, and supposedly, he was very knowledgeable. He would be the one teaching us one of the techniques. He had learned his skills from a closed practice. Like my father and the elders, Joseph believed we were all in danger of extinction. This was no joke to them, and we were all to take it seriously. I just couldn't help but wonder if my father used this as an excuse for something else. I had another theory; he always seemed obsessed with having more grandchildren and expanding the family. Perhaps everything played a part in a bigger scheme. I didn't mind learning a new technique, so that was why I went.

Being back in Egypt this time was a whole different experience. I was in tune with my powers, sensitive to my family's presence, and very intuitive. It was nice to be back, and it was nice to see my brothers in a different light; we were all there to learn, and it was like being a kid again. And if, by any chance, my father was right, and we had to fight, I would be proud to be on the front lines and stand up for my family.

My brother Joseph spent most of his time meditating alone in a small room. When he wasn't doing that, he preached about his way of life. Listening to him felt like school all over again. We sat on yoga mats in the evaluation room, waiting for him to give us instructions on how to breathe correctly—because that was a thing, apparently.

"Join me and close your eyes. Breathe in . . . Be comforta-ble . . . Breathe out. Don't let life park in your mind . . . Breathe in . . . Let the thoughts pass like traffic . . . Breathe out . . . You are drenched in oil, and every thought slides off. Every drop of water is rejected," Joseph said as he walked in between us like in a maze. "Breathe in . . . and out."

"Now, I know we've been eager to let in the thoughts. So, let them in." He paused for thirty seconds. "They weren't important, were they?" he said.

"Many of you will not be able to get there yet, but remem-ber, practice makes perfect."

After the session, I wanted to ask him how long it would take until we would actually start learning anything, but before I got to say a word, he started preaching again. You couldn't get a word in with this guy.

"Adam, the things I learned weren't given to me by our father. Not everyone can master my skills. The spirits will not provide you with the energies and powers if you are not patient. I have sensed that patience is not your strength," he said.

He knew nothing about me. I was more than competent, but there was no point in proving him wrong. He claimed to do amazing things with meditation. He thought his powers could protect him from any form of attack. The meditation would act as a shield against any supernatural power. My ego got the better of me, and I started planning to challenge him. I wanted to see more of his so-called self-defense powers.

During dinner, I watched his every move. He was slurping the hot lentil soup from his spoon when I began to pull the air out of him. He started coughing a little before I turned up the volume, and he began gasping for air.

"Enough, Adam!" my father demanded. I don't know how he guessed it. It could have been Kristian; he liked to mess around too.

"Fine! I'm sorry," I said and released Joseph from the pain. "I thought you could protect yourself from anything?"

"Well, I wasn't prepared for an attack at the dinner table," he said.

"You're right, my apologies. Your enemies will wait for you to prepare yourself."

"It would be nice to know what all this is about either way," Ethan said.

"I didn't come here to waste my time, either. I have a thesis to write and a thousand books on standby to read," Fidel piggybacked off of Ethan. I had created a domino effect, and Joseph was just sitting there, embarrassed, in his own mess. It was my intention to cause the chaos I created, and it was worth it. The guys and I were upset and felt we were wasting our time.

"You all will stay for your own sake. This is a matter of our family's distinction. I do not take it lightly," my father said, shutting everyone up. Joseph sat proudly, even though I had just proven him wrong. He probably still thought it was a valuable skill to learn, even though you had to be prepared before an attack.

For the next couple of days, we kept practicing and meditating. He was even harder on us, who doubted him. Clearly, he had a thing with his ego, too. After a while, he warmed up to us and wasn't as miserable to be around. Samuel and I wanted to get on his good side so he wouldn't see it coming when we messed with him again. Frankly, we were just bored by his teaching style. I had asked him if he wanted to test his theory and see if he could handle an attack when he was prepared, but I didn't tell him we had something more fun in mind. I wanted to know if he could take more than one person. Samuel and I would both attack him at the same time. Samuel's gift was to paralyze people with his mind. He could do that by stopping the electrical impulses from the brain down to the different parts of the body. It was something Samuel had perfected over the years. Technically, I would be able to do the same with a lot of practice, but I wasn't much for precision work. I like the more significant impact that made my opponent scream.

We went to a specific spot in the desert to experiment with Joseph. The desert was one of the most convenient places because of its barrenness. Joseph said to pay attention to when he started to levitate; that's when he would be ready for the attack.

Everyone was focused on Joseph, and it wasn't long before he actually began to rise from the sand. When he rose above the ground, I signaled Samuel to attack. We both gave him all we had. I wanted him to understand there was nothing he could do to escape what I had in store for him and how ridiculous he sounded for saying this was a helpful skill.

The power I produced with my mind and body was so intense I had to roar it out of me. Never before had I felt so strong or capable. It was a deadly force if done more than once. If Joseph wasn't prepared or very weak, I could kill him.

But shortly after Samuel hit him with the first round, he was lying on the ground. I couldn't stop. I had to finish it and let the others take care of Samuel. As my power spanned through the air, breaking the sound waves, my head started hurting like I had never experienced before. The excruciating pain hit the back of my head, making my skull burn. It felt like acid was corroding every inch of my brain. My whole body hurt; my skin was scorching, my blood boiling, my nerve endings sizzling. I tried to scream the pain away, but nothing helped. It took my breath and strength away. It turned out that my powers had backfired and hit me instead of Joseph. The attack was so powerful that it pushed me ten feet from where I stood. Everything went black. My lungs were empty, and my arms and legs lay motionless. When it finally stopped, I opened my eyes and got back on my feet, heaving from the pain. Samuel had gotten up as well. "It's like I paralyzed myself," Samuel said. "I've never tried anything like it." His powers backfired as well.

"I must say I'm impressed. It worked better than expected," I said to Joseph. I had to give it to him. It was certainly something.

"It is a powerful gift to master," Joseph said proudly.

"It's more than just a shield. It works like a mirror. This could be the perfect weapon," Samuel said. "If we were taught to do this, no one would dare attack us."

Although the technique had flaws, Samuel was right. It could come in handy. Still, three things about it didn't work. First, the shield couldn't be used during a surprise attack because you wouldn't have the time to meditate. Second, there was the long wait from the meditational stage to levitation. A few seconds in a fight could mean the difference between life and death. And third, the biggest problem was the shield could only be kept up for a short period.

Nevertheless, it was an educational tryout for me. I learned something about my powers that I didn't know before. If I knew I caused that much pain, I couldn't send shock waves left and right. Perhaps there was more to learn from the elders and Joseph, after all. In the end, my father wanted what was best for us.

٢١

TWENTY-ONE

Elias

Lena slept over last night and woke up with me this morning, even though it was early. My mornings consisted of waking up at seven, jogging, showering, and finally, eating breakfast. After that, my day would actually begin. Adam and I would work on perfecting my powers on Tuesdays, Thursdays, and Sundays. On Mondays and Wednesdays, I worked out at the gym. Since he had been gone a lot, I practiced by myself. I liked it better when Adam was there. He pushed me harder than I would ever push myself. It wasn't that bad; I enjoyed walking through the five-mile road, evaporating everything on my way, but it wasn't the same without him pushing me and getting on my nerves. It wasn't a challenge anymore, at least not with the rain. I had become quite good. Lena didn't know about us; I didn't want her to. Not now, not ever. I didn't see a reason to tell her. When we started dating, I thought she was just another girl, but she always proved me wrong. We could sit in complete silence for hours and just be in each other's presence. Ever since I met her, my life slowed down to her pace.

I took my gym bag and walked downstairs. Lena was bored but didn't want to work out with me. She wanted to wait for Maya to get up. Maya went to bed very late last night. I caught her watching TV when I was down for water at 4 a.m. I had hardly gotten into my car when I heard Lena scream, and I ran back inside. She was in Maya's room, curled up in the corner, crying, with her hands covering her mouth as she looked at the bed Maya was sleeping in.

I slowly removed the blanket that covered Maya to see her expressionless, pale face. Her eyes were closed, her lips tinted blue, and there was no pulse, but her body was still warm.

The sun was burning my back through the window. I felt the sweat bead on my forehead. Lena was hyperventilating, still sitting in the same spot. "Call an ambulance!" I said. She fumbled with her phone but got through eventually.

"I need an am-ambulance. My friend is not breathing," she said.

I carried Maya down from the bed and tried to give her CPR. I didn't know if I was any good at it, but I kept going—I had to. I felt the anxiety locking me in, trapping me in a cage. I had no idea how to handle a situation like this.

After what felt like hours, the paramedics barged in and took over. They used a defibrillator on her, and after a few tries, they found a weak pulse. They put her on a stretcher within seconds and carried her out to the ambulance. I had called Adam about sixteen times while driving behind the ambulance. It kept going straight to voicemail. I even called my father but only got a hold of Nashir, who said Adam wasn't in Egypt. It was always like that. When we really needed him, he was impossible to track down.

Lena called her entire contact list and told them to come. Maya's father and little brother were the first to arrive. The kid cried like hell. I felt so bad for him. He almost couldn't breathe. Lena held him by his shoulders, trying to comfort him. Maya's father was dazed, staring at the closed doors where the doctors were working on Maya. I wouldn't know what to do if she didn't make it. How would I tell Adam that the one job he gave me I couldn't keep? My hands were tied. I couldn't control her health, but how would I tell him I failed? I was so scared of how he would react if anything happened to her.

My fears came to life when the doctor came out and declared her dead—August 9 at 11:11.

We found out Maya was admitted to the hospital a month before. They never discharged her but couldn't force her to stay since there was technically nothing wrong with her. Her father and Milad knew she was sick. She did everything to keep it a secret from the rest of us. I'm sure Adam didn't know because he would have never left her alone if he had known.

You would think it got easier to deal with death because we lived as long as we did, but it didn't, at least not for me. Some of my uncles had learned to become numb to it, but for me, it only got harder to accept that we were all alone. No girlfriend, wife, or friend could stay with us forever. Only our family was able to remain by our side. Our only option was to choose how we wanted our relationships to end. Either we waited it out, or we left before time caught on. Perhaps that was why *Jedo* pressed for us to have children if we could. He must have felt true loneliness, being as old as he was.

TWENTY-TWO

Adam

I was growing tired of the endless meditation and the company of Joseph. I was ready to go home; the lessons were getting repetitive, and I wasn't learning anything useful. I would have dinner with them, then go back home. My father wanted me to stay longer and made excuses for why they needed me there and how the family was above all. I knew that and valued our family more than he knew, but I had to get my feet back on the ground and remember I had a life outside of his walls. I hadn't planned on staying there for so long, and when I lost my phone a few days before, I realized how bored I was without it. This wasn't my first time losing my phone or keys at the facility. I always seemed to misplace my stuff.

When I got home, I was surprised to find the house empty. I checked all the rooms, but nobody was home, and since I didn't have a phone, I had to pick up one of my old phones to call Maya. It took forever to charge. When it did, I immediately dialed her number. I heard the phone ringing from under her pillow, sending a shiver down my spine. *Something is off.* She usually didn't get out of bed that early and wouldn't leave the house without it. Elias didn't answer his phone the first hundred times I had called. He finally called me back after a few minutes.

"Elias?"

"Where the hell have you been?" he said.

"What's going on?"

"You need to come to the cemetery, the one close to the mall. Park next to the florist, and I'll meet you there," he said and hung up. I wanted to aḍhār there, but there would be too many people around. *What's next to the florist? A pet shop or something—what is he doing there? Did he say come to the cemetery or next to it?* It took a good ten minutes to get there. I got out of the car and walked toward the florist; Elias wasn't there. Then I crossed the street and waited by the cemetery entrance. I could see an ongoing ceremony from afar when I realized Elias had parted from the crowd and was walking toward me. I met him halfway and recognized some of the people attending: Alie, Lena, Dissie, Sean, and a few other familiar faces. *Has someone close to us died?*

"I'm so sorry," he said, stopping me with a hand on my shoulder.

"Who's dead?"

"Maya is dead, Adam! I called you, called home! Where the hell have you been?"

"What?" The words didn't register. Every inch of my body trembled, my lungs shutting down, my vision failing me. I only saw the casket before me, its polished wood gleaming under the pale sunlight filtering through the clouds. The crowded path was unclear, their faces blurring into a sea of grief-stricken strangers I could no longer put names on.

"I'm so sorry," Elias said as he tried to stop me. His hand was firm on my shoulder, but I pushed him away with a swift, almost involuntary motion, far enough away that he wouldn't bother me. I think he flew backward, his shocked expression fading. I didn't look and didn't care. It didn't matter if they found out what we were. It didn't matter if I had to confront them all. Nothing mattered if it was true. I was blinded with great rage and wanted to take it out on someone. I wanted revenge, but I didn't know who to blame.

The casket was closed, sitting on a metal frame, ready to go down into the cold soil. I couldn't let it happen. I couldn't let her go down there. I had to see her, touch her, to believe it. Maybe I could heal her, bring her back from the abyss that had claimed her.

Without thinking, I broke the casket open, my hands fumbling and desperate. The wood splintered under the force of my touch as I tossed away the pieces. My grief-stricken frenzy and the sound of cracking wood echoed in my ears. Pieces of the lid scattered around me. When I saw that the casket was empty, I lost it. I flipped it over, my hands trembling with a mix of relief and frustration. People spread out, gasping in horror at my actions. I couldn't blame them. There were no limits to what I would do to find the truth.

"Where is she? Where is Maya?" I yelled and grabbed the pastor or whatever he was. He was stunned, his face pale, and he didn't speak until I shook him again, my hands rough and desperate. "Answer me!"

People backed away, fear etched on their faces, but her father came toward me, his eyes filled with a blend of anger and confusion, but it didn't matter because his daughter wasn't there. Maya wasn't inside the casket. Had they cremated her? Who approved it?

"I swear I have no idea. She was there when I sealed it," the guy stammered.

I let him go, my mind racing. I walked past Maya's father, his eyes wide with shock, his fists clenched at his sides. He looked perplexed, unsure whether he wanted to murder me for causing a scene or was confused over where his daughter was.

I marched over to Elias instead. *He must have answers!*

"What the hell is going on, Elias? Where is she?" I demanded, my voice a low growl.

"I don't know where she is, but she died three days ago, and you were nowhere to be found!"

"Why didn't you call me as soon as you found her? You could have called the elders to reach me. Why didn't you do anything?" Police sirens were coming from a distance. This didn't look good for me: a Black man losing his shit at a funeral.

"Did you even listen to me?! I did call! I called my father. Nashir picked up and said you weren't there. I did what I could in your absence," he yelled back, his frustration matching mine. I was left speechless when I heard his final words. The things they said and did to keep me away from her. The way my phone conveniently disappeared. It was all a big lie. Nashir had been playing me all along, and I bought it. They had all been in on this. It was their big plan to separate us, and they had succeeded.

I walked away from the scene and left Elias to do the explaining. Either way, the police had more pressing matters: Maya's body was missing. My world shattered into a million pieces, the truth sinking in like a stone in the pit of my stomach. The sense of betrayal was overwhelming, but a fierce determination for revenge ignited within me amidst the storm of emotions. I would tear down the whole facility and make those responsible pay for their manipulation. When I was far enough away, I aďhāred back to Egypt.

I found Nashir in the kitchen with all the other employees. She panicked when she saw me. She knew exactly why I came back. I wanted to rip her to shreds and slash her throat so she could never tell another lie. I wanted her to feel my pain and to put her on fire—make her scream her lungs empty and bleed through her pores. I tore up every bit of her brain with my powers and made her feel the acid burn across every inch of her scalp. She was on her knees, screaming, begging me to stop. I gave her blows of lightning in small doses. I wanted the ache to last as long as possible.

My brothers were called down to the kitchen, their footsteps echoing the urgency of the situation. They wanted to control the chaos that had consumed me, but I felt unstoppable, more vital than ever. All my focus was on Nashir, and my need for answers was eclipsing any rational thought. They tried to restrain me, but every attempt to get in my way was met with resistance. I harnessed the very air in the room, suffocating any opposition.

Samuel, in his desperation, tried to paralyze me and halt the terror I had unleashed. His powers, usually flawless, failed against my determination. I felt his futile attempts like mere pinpricks at my feet, nothing more than a minor inconvenience. Samuel adhāred, likely off to fetch the elders or my father.

"What did you do to her?" I demanded, granting her respite from the torment.

"You did that!" she shrieked through choked sobs, her words a bitter reminder of the choices I had made.

"You chose to stay with her. You absorbed her soul because it was rightfully yours. You were warned. You can't blame anyone but yourself!" Nashir had been right all along. She had warned me from the very beginning, predicting Maya's fate, should I have continued to be with her.

I adhāred to the desolate heart of the desert, the same place where we had trained with Joseph. Under the vast expanse of the night sky, my knees buckled beneath me, and I collapsed to the sand, the weight of her words crushing me. The dam holding back my tears finally broke, and I wept until I could no longer. I curled up in the darkness, my anguish echoing the silence of the barren landscape.

My father found me shortly after, his stern presence casting a long shadow over my despair.

"Will you look at yourself, Adam! You know how these things work," he chided, with a blend of disappointment and understanding.

"There was no corpse," I whispered, my voice barely audible over the voices in my head. *She might be alive. There was no body. They could be wrong. It could have been someone else.*

"Even if she is still alive, you know it's inevitable. You have her soul. Search within yourself. Deep down, you know you are finally complete because of her. She was your twin flame."

"I can give it back. I just need to find her," I pleaded, my words desperate, clinging to a fragile hope.

"It doesn't work that way, son. You can't re-split it," he said, mirroring the heaviness in my heart.

"I refuse to accept it!" I protested defiantly against the cruel hand fate had dealt me. "It could work." I didn't want to believe it. We couldn't end like this, separated by the whims of destiny. Yet, as the truth settled in the depths of me, I knew that our story had reached its devastating conclusion, leaving me with a void that nothing could fill.

WAKE UP . . .

I could feel my heartbeat again. It started slowly, a faint thud on the edge of death. As if life itself was cautiously tiptoeing back into my veins, I sensed the movement in my bloodstream, the rush of blood through my heart and out to my veins, reaching the tips of my fingers before receding back again. My windpipe felt dry, but the gentle flow of oxygen came to me, a lifeline reconnecting me to the world, each breath a miracle and each heartbeat a testament to my resilience. The sensitivity returned to my body, and I felt the reassuring presence of my limbs, the awareness of my own existence. One by one, the senses gradually revealed themselves, like a symphony tuning its instruments before a grand performance.

Amidst the haze, I heard talking, distant whispers that echoed in the corners of my consciousness. My mind couldn't yet put the words together. The syllables seemed to float in the air, disconnected and incomprehensible. With a conscious effort, I finally opened my eyes, blinking away the remnants of darkness. My vision, once blurred and distant, had transformed into a richer, more vibrant reality. The blur that had clouded my sight was gone, replaced by a world of vivid colors and sharp contrasts. Every detail, previously overlooked, now stood out with clarity. All those years, when my eyes had colored outside the lines, I had been blind to the intricacies of life. Now, I could truly see! The blobs sharpened and solidified into distinct figures, each contour defined and every hue saturated.

My eyes met someone else's, a pair of eyes filled with a mixture of relief and apprehension. I didn't recognize her right away; it took me a few moments to put a name to her face. Then, like assembling puzzle pieces, fragments of my memory returned with a rush, and I realized the face belonged to my cousin Sepideh.

"It's time, Maya," she said, her voice soft but resolute, carrying a weight of responsibility and expectation. With those words, reality crashed back over me, and I understood the gravity of the moment.

٢٣

TWENTY-THREE

Maya

In the hazy moments right after waking, my mind was a blank canvas. It felt like I had been plunged into a bottomless void, a room enveloped in darkness where my memories were nothing but shadows. I couldn't remember the last thing I had done before I got here. Confusion reigned as I struggled to piece together my reality. As I got to my senses and was back to a decent level of comprehension, my family told me I had been in a coma for the second time. Since the doctors couldn't diagnose me, my father shipped me off to Iran to see a specialist. *Where is this specialist now?* I wondered. When my aunt Shirin told me all this, it sounded like she had rehearsed in the mirror, like she was trying too hard to convince me. Her strained attempts at reassurance left a lingering doubt in me. Deep down, an unsettling feeling gnawed at my core, but I wasn't going to question her. I knew something was off, and I couldn't trust her.

When I had a moment to myself, I decided to shower and clear my head. When the heat of the water hit my skin, I released the deep breath. At that moment, beneath the soothing patter of the water, the tension that had gripped my body began to dissolve, trickling away like sand slipping through my fingers. *I have come back from the dead!* I realized. I was dead. I was actually dead. My memory started returning as I closed my eyes and let the sound of water drown me.

Images flipped through my mind until they became a clear vision of the day the shadows left my body. The day I gave him everything I had and expected nothing in return. A deep sense of betrayal settled over me. *Foolish girl! Wake up!*

My mind was a tumultuous sea, tossing between authentic memories and fabricated illusions. I found myself back in the library, the faint scent of aged paper lingering in the air, the motion of my fingers tracing the curves of the carved cherry flowers on the wooden shelves. Naimeh's delicate fingers turning the pages in front of me. Every sentence she read played before my eyes like a movie.

The Sāhers weren't supposed to fight them; only I did. My quest played out in great detail. The goal was to destroy them but not in the way I thought. A version of myself traveled from place to place to hunt down the four eldest sons. I tricked, manipulated, and seduced them until they were dirt under my nails. I couldn't kill them; instead, the ritual required me to obtain a drop of their blood to rub between my fingers before they dealt me the killing blow. Each time, I would become more powerful, and I would do that until I had the blood of all four sons. In the final part of the ritual, I had to find a chalice to drink the blood out of. The ritual would be complete only when the last drop of blood touched my tongue.

The stories about the Persian witches from that library were about my family. They were weaving a prophecy that had haunted the Sāhers for centuries. My mother's words echoed; there was never chosen one, just a desperate desire for someone to fulfill the prophecy, regardless of who they were. The weakest of us would release her soul to a Dūshev. Sepideh had tried to tell me that my cousins had all been involved with one of Adam's brothers, trying to fulfill their duty. I looked down at the book Naimeh was holding. The Farsi text stood out clearly, and I remembered the war I was supposed to lead. It was as if I could feel the smooth texture of the paper under her touch, my senses deceiving me, blurring the line between reality and imagination.

Then I attended my own funeral as a guest. The warmth of the afternoon sun caressed my skin as I stood in the quiet park. Closed casket, my friends in mourning, my father still as a ghost, and Milad. *Milad.* It was like a punch in the gut to watch him cry. I could almost taste the saltiness of his tears, a bitter reminder of my mistakes. It was my fault, all my fault. If I hadn't left him. If I hadn't been so stupid. *It hurts. Let me take your pain, Milad. Please, let me take your pain. Wake up!*

Adam made his grief look real for someone who took my soul—always the performer, taking the audience by storm. I guess he was always made for the stage. The distant sound of applause echoed in my ears, a haunting reminder of his theatrical facade. *How long have you planned for this? Taking my soul, leaving me gutted?*

A knock on the bathroom door reverberated through the air, jolting me back to reality with a start.

"Maya!" Sepideh's words were laced with concern.

"I'm fine." I clutched the edge of the sink, my fingers pressing into the cool ceramic, grounding me in the present moment. *What the hell was that!*

I felt much better when I ate the food they left me in the kitchen: a plate of rice and a stew called Ghalye Meygu—Meygu being the shrimp part, but this one was strictly with the herbs, similar to Ghormeh sabzi. *Holy fuck! This is good.* I had never had anything like it. Persian dishes were usually on the tangy side, but this was also a little spicy, and it made a huge difference.

Sepideh and Shirin had come to sit with me. I didn't say much because there was nothing to be said. Not after all the things I saw in my vision. I didn't trust them because it seemed everyone had their own agenda for me. Why else would they lie to me?

"Where is my dad now?" I asked.

"He had to go back because his visa expired, and Milad had to go back to school," Shirin said. *First lie.*

"Where is my phone?"

"He didn't bring your phone, not as far as I know," she continued. *Second lie.* Was she really going to pretend I never died? That everything back home was left normal?

"I need to make some calls." I wanted to talk to my brother—and Adam. Would he even care? What good would come out of telling him I was still alive when it was all his fault? Was he looking for me? Coming for me?

"Don't worry about that just yet. We have a lot of things ahead of us," she said and left the kitchen. That was the first honest thing that came out of her mouth. I looked at Sepideh. She seemed so uneasy.

"What's going on with you?" *I'm giving you a chance here . . .*

"What do you mean?" she said.

"You seem nervous. Whose house is this? I haven't been here before."

She hesitated. "It's Shirin's house. You have been here before."

"I need to talk to Milad. Can you give me your phone, please?" I said.

"You can't!" she burst out.

"Get me a phone. I need to talk to him right now!" Whether she was upholding their lies or not, I didn't care. I just needed my brother to be okay. There was no need to traumatize him without reason.

"We don't have cellphones here, just a house phone that only works domestically. Look, Maya"—she sighed—"this will be a weird time in your life, but eventually, they will tell you the truth. You shouldn't question them or demand things. Otherwise, they're going to be rough on you. Just go with the flow."

I appreciated that she was trying to be honest with me. However, I still found it funny that they thought they could take advantage of me. They thought I was utterly clueless. How on earth did they expect to keep me here and not tell me anything? I had free will, and they could not force me to stay or to participate in anything. Although I knew nothing good came from rebellion when it came to my family, therefore I had to play this right.

"Alright, walk with me," I said and got up.

"Where are we going?" she asked but followed me like a child does her mother.

"We're getting some fresh air," I said. Shirin was giving Sepideh the look, as in, *make sure she doesn't run away.* I almost laughed. I took a scarf hanging from a chair.

"The spirits whisper in my ears, and so all of you must hear it, too. Get the word out. Blood will be spilled. Gather the ones who are ready to fight, who are not afraid to look death in the eye," I said to Shirin, making it sound more dramatic than it was. I had to be convincing. "And one more thing—stop lying to me." She looked at me curiously but didn't object.

When we got outside and walked down the street, I stopped and looked around, trying to recognize my surroundings. I had never been to this neighborhood.

"What are you looking for?" Sepideh asked.

"Nothing, I'm just getting acquainted with the area. I need to know what I'm dealing with," I said, mostly to myself. *Maybe you shouldn't have said that out loud. Stupid!*

"Whatever you need, I'm here for you. You don't have to acquire anything yourself." I turned to her and wanted to bite her head off. Her words triggered something inside me.

"Really! Whatever I need? Great. Give me the truth and leave out nothing."

"Um."

She was about to say something, but I cut her off. "Let me stop you right there. You have one opportunity to get on my good side because, soon, everyone will try to get a piece of me, and I'll be damned if I let anyone touch me or my power again. Do you understand?"

I didn't know what I had said or what I meant, but Sepideh nodded, understanding the weight of my words. They wanted the prophecy to come true. They wanted the chosen one, the leader of the Sāhers, and I would show them a leader. Sepideh took out a pack of cigarettes from her pocket and put one between her lips while fumbling with the lighter.

I am not a sacrificial lamb. No, you are not. You are wanted here.

When I last came to Iran, I was clueless, or perhaps I truly wasn't ready for the truth. I had no idea what kind of power I could manifest from within me or the magic I had access to. Even though I had no experience whatsoever, I felt it at my fingertips. For someone who never practiced mindfulness, I was so much more intuitive and learned how to access a higher level of meditation through water, either under the shower or in the tub, with my head below the surface. During each session, I learned something new about the prophecy and my part in it at large. Sometimes, it was so overwhelming that I got migraines after, but they were tolerable. I just wanted to know more and see more. It felt like a superpower I was hiding from everyone around me.

I had told them I remembered what had happened, that I knew I had died, and understood my duty. It was easy to slip on the mask, to pretend I was someone strong, capable of what they expected of me. But in the end, I would not let them make a fool of me. I felt so lonely here. I missed Milad and even my father. Who would take care of Milad if all my father did was provide him food on the table? My brother was still young and needed guidance. I felt so guilty for being here and playing along with their games. I had no expectation of my mother. Whether she knew I was alive or not, I didn't think she would take responsibility for any of her children. It was hard to admit, but I missed Adam. I had thought he, of all people, wouldn't buy the charade of my supposed death. I had thought he would look for me, but maybe he truly didn't care.

Leyla was in my peripheral at all times. I thought about running, but something was urging me to stay, to learn the truth. Leyla tried to bond with me by telling me stories about our closed practices. She was the only one telling me the truth, trying to convince me that I was meant to die to be born as a Sāher. Perhaps she was right. *This is your destiny. You are the chosen one. You are needed here. You belong here.*

The prophecy was written in so many variations that I didn't know which one to believe. Leyla insisted on one particular wording of the prophecy: *She who forcefully bears the soul of our enemy must release it to the thirteenth son on the thirty-third day of Nowruz with the blessing of Goddess Ishtar. She will sacrifice our blood and flesh to retrieve what is rightfully ours and bring order to nature.*

Which was scarily accurate to what had happened. Except for the part about forcefully bearing the soul of our enemy, I did *release* my soul to the thirteenth son. Adam had told me he was the thirteenth of his brothers. In a way, he had tried to warn me or test me to see if I would flinch at the mention of the prophecy. Of course, I didn't because I had no clue about the path that had been laid for me. Although all roads lead to Rome—the Sāher, whose soul was taken, would be the one to end it all. I was the only one who could end this, the only one whose blood would bond with the Dūshevs and slowly eliminate them. In my visions, I had seen it all. All the things I was supposed to do, all the work I had to put in. And for what reward? None at all. Going after the Dūshevs was not child's play. How could I possibly forget what they were capable of or how strong they were?

Even though it felt like betrayal, I didn't want to kill Adam and his entire family. Sure, I was angry, but I wasn't a lunatic.

"I do want to apologize for whatever Dissie had to do to you," Leyla said.

"What do you mean?" The question came before I could stop myself. I had no clue what she was talking about.

"Dissie moved to Mist Creek because you were our last hope, and everyone else had failed. She is a distant relative and initially planned to get Aldridge close to you even though we weren't sure of their birth order—as I said, we were desperate. That didn't work out, so instead, she seduced your easy target of a father." Her features were regretful. I hadn't expected Dissie to be at this level of a spy. I thought she liked to have fun and took it too far. It turned out it was never personal between us. She didn't care how. She just needed to get the job done, no matter the consequences.

"You were chosen for a reason, Maya. And I am so grateful that you became the one. Know that you are worthy, that you are wanted and needed here. You will lead us to greatness." Although I still didn't fully trust her, Leyla's words settled in me.

"Aldridge didn't fail to take my soul. I pretended to be fine to protect Dissie because I thought she was my friend until she started sleeping with my father," I said, wanting to confuse her. "I was already soulless by the time I moved in with Adam. I just didn't have anywhere else to go." I paused for dramatic effect. "I can still remember how it felt when Aldridge sucked the last piece of life out of me and drained my body." I didn't care about Aldridge or the other Dūshevs; I didn't care if they all died, as long as his name was out of the equation. I would deal with Adam myself because I had to know the truth.

I was going nuts without contact with the outside world, but I couldn't complain because I was fulfilling a prophecy, fulfilling *my duty*. There was still no sign of Adam. I was truly forgotten by everyone I knew. At least I had the books and my imagination to keep me company. My mind was never quiet; I was never alone inside my head. Sometimes, I wondered if the dialogue inside my head was mine or if I had spiritual downloads of sorts.

Leyla had given me four huge books she wanted me to read. As if she somehow knew I had suddenly gained the ability to read Farsi, I had, but I wasn't about to tell her that. I don't know how it happened, but once I figured out I could actually read, I snuck into the room they used as a study and library and read through anything I could get my hands on before anyone came looking for me. I read so fast that it almost felt like my fingers couldn't turn the pages fast enough. I'd read about hexes, potions, and even love spells. The books seemed a bit out there, but I figured if there was any truth to them, I had better learn some protection spells and incantations. I devoured anything I could find on the subject and learned to protect, glamour, veil, and disguise myself through all means necessary. My family had gotten used to me hanging out in the study. *I like the scent of old books*, I had told them, but whenever I heard them coming, I would put back the book I was reading and pretend I was doing something else.

My cousin Lara had pretended she was looking for a specific book while following Leyla to the study so she could watch her scold me.

"You have to understand that you have a purpose now," Leyla was saying. I hadn't paid much attention to her since she started rambling. "Have you been studying the material I gave you?" she asked, picking up the book she had left me. "This isn't a vacation, Maya!"

I could feel my blood boiling. "Do you think I'm enjoying myself?" *Trapped in a house with people ready to sacrifice me.* I got up from my chair. "If I am supposed to lead Sāhers, maybe you should start listening to me for a change and stop telling me what to do." I motioned to the book in her hand.

Without touching it, the book was smacked out of her hand and hit the shelf beside Lara. I could have sworn I didn't even brush it. I went to pick up the book, still amazed by what had happened.

"That's your powers kicking in," Lara said. *So, it is true. I actually have powers. Yes. As long as you stay on your path.*

Both left and didn't bother me for the rest of the evening. Maybe that was the trick: acting out so they would leave me alone while I figured a way out of this mess. While I was alone, I tried to do that thing again. I tried moving objects with my mind, but it never worked again, no matter how frustrated I had gotten.

٢٤

TWENTY-FOUR

MAYA

I had discussed the journey with Leyla. Still, she insisted on a huge clash between the strongest supernatural powers in the world. I tried telling her that was not how the battle would play out, but she wouldn't believe me until I finally found it in one of the books I had skimmed. Of course, I was sure of this because of my visions, but I had also seen it somewhere in a book, and that was a much more convincing reason. She couldn't believe her own eyes when I showed her the book, claiming the text had changed overnight. In the end, it didn't matter. Even though I only had to bring one person on my quest to find the first four sons, the rest of them would still need to prepare for retaliation. The Dūshevs would fight tooth and nail to keep things as they were.

Leyla called us in for a group session and started chanting aloud. After introducing the Sāhers to all the changes, some were visibly upset, having difficulty accepting the new course of action. I was sure they had an especially hard time with me as a leader. To them, I was inexperienced, had no traditional education in the practices, and was only twenty-one years old. I noticed the ones who gave themselves to the ritual. They had a rhythm to their breathing like they were synchronizing with the words. My cousin Lara stood up and walked away, while Leyla was still chanting. Two more followed her out of the room, but Leyla didn't stop.

Next to me, my aunt Shiva's turquoise stone ring started glowing through the black veins of the stone. It followed the same rhythm as their breaths. Everyone seemed to have a piece of jewelry with a turquoise stone. Sepideh had a necklace, and even though it was hidden under her shirt, I could see it glowing.

Leyla finished, looked at me, and pointed at a shelf with her eyes. I walked up to the display cabinet that went from wall to wall. The only thing that caught my eye was a little bronze box with a beautifully carved lid. Inside was a turquoise stone pulsing, emitting a gentle, ethereal glow, waiting to be claimed. As soon as I saw it, I knew it was mine. A tingling sensation coursed through my fingertips as my fingers brushed its surface, sending shivers down my spine. I felt an immediate connection, an inexplicable pull, as if the stone and I shared an unspoken bond, leaving me electrified and eager to claim its mysterious power. The room became pitch black, plunging into a deep, velvety darkness so thick it seemed to envelop me completely. The temperature plummeted, biting at my skin and sending shivers rippling through my body. I could feel the frigid air settling around me, tangible and icy. *What the hell is happening! Wake up! Wake up! Wake up!*

With my first step, I heard the unmistakable sound of snow crunching beneath the weight of my feet. The sound crisp in the silent blackness. As I cautiously moved forward, the inky void slowly yielded, gradually revealing a different world before my eyes. A breathtaking snowy landscape stretched out, pristine and serene. Each snowflake sparkled like a diamond in the pale light, and the trees, adorned with a delicate frosting, stood tall and majestic. In the distance, rugged mountains reached for the sky, their peaks crowned with glistening snow.

Out of nowhere, a guy was thrown across my view into a pile of snow. He started laughing and got himself up. "Do you always have to show off when we meet up?" he said while looking at me. I had never met him before and didn't know how I even got here.

"Who are you?" I asked. He kept on smiling and just stood there without answering me. Then a girl walked past me toward the guy without looking in my direction.

"You need to be reminded that I'm as strong as you," she said. *Is that . . .*

"I just need one touch," she said and kissed him. He grabbed the back of her neck and kept going at her like I wasn't there until she pulled away and hurtled him into the snow. You would think he didn't weigh a thing. An involuntary scream came out of me when she turned around and looked right at me—it was my cousin Seema. Her face was a little distorted, but it was definitely her. And he . . . he looked so familiar, with his dimpled cheeks and the slant of his eyes. *Oh my god! He must be Adam's brother!*

The darkness returned swiftly, swallowing everything as soon as I became aware of what I had seen. I watched in eerie silence as it blanketed the trees and mountains like a suffocating black cloud, obscuring the world in an impenetrable shroud. I jolted awake, my heart pounding in my chest, only to find myself lying on a hard surface. As my senses adjusted to my surroundings, I realized I was back in the room with my family. Surrounded by them all, even the ones who had walked out.

"It felt so real," I said as soon as I opened my eyes. It wasn't my intention; I didn't want them to know what I saw.

"What did you see?" Leyla asked.

"Nothing in particular. I just saw myself standing in the desert. The weird thing was that I could feel the hot sand under my feet. It felt so real," I said.

Either Seema was still involved with a Dūshev, or I saw a snippet from her past. She might not have wanted this war to happen, either. Maybe she could help me prevent things, but I couldn't ask her just yet.

"The Firuzeh belonged to my sister," Leyla said. *Mamani.* "Now it belongs to you. And it will continue enhancing your powers as long as you wear it. You should start veiling."

What I had learned was I could veil in many ways. Sometimes, I wore a hoodie or a cap; other days, I used a scarf for veiling to please them. I wasn't sure if they approved of my alternative methods. It was somewhat unorthodox for Sāhers not to veil with a scarf.

For once, I was sitting on the couch, doing nothing, when the doorbell rang. My aunt opened the door for her. It was Dissie. She had dyed her hair back to brown, which, somehow, made her look so much hotter. How was it even possible to be this beautiful. The scarf on her head, a forest green, matched her vivid emerald eyes.

"What the hell is she doing here?" I said so she could hear me. I was still mad at her and wanted her to know her place.

"Didn't anyone tell her?" she said and raised her hand, pointing at me. "I had to do what I did, Maya. How else would Adam have taken your soul? We needed the forced proximity."

"He didn't take her soul. Aldridge did," Shirin cut in.

"Way before you started screwing my dad," I said.

"A lot of things from the books changed," Shiva said. "I'll fill you in."

In the following days, Dissie apologized profusely, trying to explain how she never intended to hurt me. That our friendship meant more than any man ever could. I almost threw up in my mouth when she spoke of *men* in the same sentence as my father. I pretended to forgive her because it was *necessary* for the prophecy.

Somehow, she still felt like the only one I could trust because she was honest from the moment she stepped inside this house. She would never truly be my friend again, but I needed allies, and my cousins were all acting different.

When Dissie and I were finally alone, she told me how, sometimes, Milad would cry in his room and how much she wanted to tell him I wasn't dead but couldn't. I almost broke down in front of her. If they knew how much it affected me, they might not have trusted me on my own.

"There is a spell that makes them all forget," Dissie said. "It takes the pain away, too." She touched my arm, and I tried not to flinch. I had already read about the spell in one of the books, but it didn't occur to me that it was something I would need. The one I found was a potion you poured on the front door of the last place you called home, and everybody you knew would forget you existed. It only worked on ordinary people, not the supernatural ones. For the Dūshevs, there was a separate potion.

"You know you have to go back and do the same," Dissie said. I nodded, even though I had no idea. I didn't want my brother to forget about me—or Adam, even after what he did. *Am I really doing this?* I knew it was for the best that my friends and family forgot about me. I wanted my brother to live his life to the fullest, and he couldn't do that grieving. *This is for him.* It seemed like there was not much left of mine anyway. As far as I had read, I wouldn't be able to live that long, even after finishing the work set out for me, and frankly, I didn't care.

٢٥

TWENTY-FIVE

I woke up daily, stomach twisting, aching for air, thinking it was a nightmare. I didn't know what way was up anymore; I was barely functioning. I had fallen in love with her before I was man enough to admit it. Deep down, I must have known why I made excuses to glance at her from across the street. Why Proctor became my favorite place to be. Trying not to forget how she would suppress her smile when I flirted with her before we were anything and merely getting to know each other. Trying not to forget her voice or the face she made when she mocked me about correcting Nabokov. The nights she fell asleep in my arms while I recited my poems. Poems that had meant nothing until they did. Until I found out I was writing them for her, all of them for her—before her voice started to echo in the wind and whisper to my soul. I didn't know what a huge part of my life was missing all those years. And now, who was I now? I started drinking tea because of her. I wanted to fill her absence with whatever I could.

The elders wanted to mess with my head again. They wanted to see if I was stable enough to teach Elias, especially his father, Edgar. It was time for another evaluation. I was only in Egypt for Elias; I hadn't been there since the last time, when I had almost killed Nashir. She deserved it, though. She misled me; they all did. Even my father, I was disappointed with. He was hiding things from me; never being completely truthful. I didn't interact with anyone. It didn't need to be more complicated than it already was. I was standing outside in our garden while they evaluated Elias. Smoking one cigarette after the other didn't make time go faster. I promised to quit smoking for good, but it took off the pressure and helped with my anxiety and fear of being alone. I felt like a silly, pathetic human. Deep down, I didn't think she was dead. I could still hear her voice in my head, and I kept telling myself she wasn't gone.

"Adam. Hey, Adam," my brother called.

I turned around and caught Samuel aḍhāring from the front door, landing in front of me.

"You okay?" he asked.

"I'm fine."

"Look, I would have said I'm sorry for your loss, but I'm not," he said.

"Okay?" I said, wondering what kind of condolence that was.

"You won't believe what I overheard last night . . . I had gone down to the kitchen in the middle of the night, when everyone was sleeping, because I was hungry. You know that door from the kitchen that leads to the hallway where the housekeepers have their rooms? They stood there, your father and Nashir. I heard Nashir say, "He can never know she is still alive." Can you believe it?"

"What." His words echoed in my head; I was struggling to make sense. *She is still alive! Maya is still alive!*

"I know! You have to think before you act now because we don't know for sure what they were talking about, but who else do we know died recently!" Samuel always had my back. He was the only one I trusted. There was nothing he would gain from lying to me. Even though I wasn't fond of staying in Egypt, I would get valuable information by just hanging around, like Samuel did most of the time. I would have to go back and forth to work with Elias, but it would be worth it in the end.

It was uncommon for the elders not to assess Elias immediately unless he had done terribly. I was sure Elias was more than qualified; they were just messing with me, trying to get to my head. The elders sat quietly, scrutinizing me, not even showing the barest hint of sympathy toward Elias.

"How many hours a day do you practice with him?" my father asked me.

"Not every day. A few hours, three days a week. I know it's not much, but he doesn't need more. He is extremely skilled," I said, finding myself wanting to defend Elias. I couldn't believe they were questioning his abilities. Edgar and Herman exchanged glances, their faces etched with concern. Elias's father stood from his seat and walked toward Elias, his eyes filled with worry.

"Is he pushing you too hard, son?" he said, gently placing his hands on Elias's shoulders. "It's okay. You can tell us. He has no authority here," Herman interjected, his voice soft and reassuring.

"What!" I said and scoffed because I couldn't believe what I was hearing.

"Are you kidding me? If anything, I think Adam has been lazy," Elias said, bemused. Edgar stepped back, waiting for me to explain. I shrugged, trying to maintain my composure.

"As I said, he is competent and even ready to kill."

"You're a huge fan, I see," Elias said to me, a smirk playing on his lips. I bumped my shoulders into him so he would trip. He shoved me back.

"Ready to kill! You must be out of your mind!" Herman said, interrupting our banter, heat rising to his face.

"Do you want to give it a go, my lord?" I retorted with a hint of challenge in my tone. Elias looked at me, amused. We were both trying not to laugh despite the seriousness of the situation. I only mocked Herman because he thought so highly of himself. My father, ever observant, remained silent, his gaze flickering between us.

"Explain to me how Elias finished this level in just a few months when it should take years?" Herman's frustration was palpable.

"So, what you're saying is that I am qualified for the last level?" Elias asked.

"That's impossible. We've never done that before," Edgar said in disbelief, looking at my father for an explanation.

"Unless Lena is pregnant," my father said, his eyes narrowing as he glanced at Elias. He was always one step ahead, considering every possibility. We all turned our heads to look at Elias. "That would certainly have greased the wheels," my father continued, walking up to Elias, his gaze piercing.

"You stay away from her!" Elias said, his voice a low warning, a new level of seriousness in his eyes. He then adhāred before our eyes. My jaw dropped in shock, and clearly, theirs did, too. I couldn't help but laugh a little when they looked at me. I didn't know he could adhār yet. Since when was he so secretive?

"Huh! What do you know! Well, there you go, a grandchild," I said. My father gave me a warning look, making me freeze in my spot.

"I had no idea," I said. "I promise I am just as surprised. I'm sure he is just being protective of her and the fetus." My father gave a single nod and dismissed everyone except me and Edgar.

"Make sure he doesn't do anything foolish and let him understand that we only want what's best for him. Edgar will visit you soon enough," my father said and dismissed me, too. I adhāred back home to Mist Creek to see if he got here in one try. Unless this wasn't his first time adhāring. When I got there, Elias was freaking out. He had already started packing his bags, planning to run away with Lena.

"It's not like that, Elias. This is what my father wants for all of us. He is very proud of you for becoming a father this early on. It just means that you won't be needing me anymore."

"So, I'm done?" he said. "Just like that?"

I smiled. "I always knew you were too skilled for your own good." It ended before we expected, but considering my plans for the next few months, it was perfect timing. I had to find the truth, no matter what it was.

I returned to Egypt shortly after and didn't let anyone know I had taken one of the guest rooms. I just threw my bags in there and went back to the elders. Now that Elias didn't need me, I could focus on getting some answers from my father. I walked into the elders' meeting room and found my father alone.

"Father, I need to speak to you." He gestured me to sit and closed the book he was reading.

"I have reason to believe that Maya is still alive. The disappearance of her body is still a mystery and—"

"There is no mystery, my son. Cadavers get mixed up all the time. She is probably in another grave by mistake. You must let it go." His words were a blow to the gut. He was being rational, of course.

"If there is a chance she is still out there, don't you think I should be looking for her?" I pleaded.

"Death is not easy to deal with. I understand your pain. I have lived it countless of times," he said.

"But she is pregnant with my child. Don't you think that it's important?"

"Unfortunately, even if she was alive, she wouldn't be pregnant. You have her soul, my son. You must know that. You must feel it deep down. Don't tell me you have been blinded into oblivion."

"No," I whispered. "I have not."

"Resilience will come to you in time, my son." I knew he was right, that he only wanted me to get through this pain, but the seed of doubt had been sown, and no matter what I did, I couldn't shake the feeling that she was still out there.

"Dinner is ready, sir." Nashir had walked in soundlessly, not sparing me a glance.

My father had invited my brothers to Egypt for another meeting. Samuel told me this dinner was scheduled a while ago, but I wasn't asked for some reason. Now that I was here, the elders would pretend it was a mistake that I was excluded. My father wanted to share something, and I was not missing out. Edgar was usually the one organizing these meetings, and he hated my guts.

"A great battle is ahead of us," my father started.

"Are we still obsessing over those witches?" I whispered to Samuel. He gave me a nod and looked at my father.

"Although most of you have volunteered to fight, I am afraid I will need most of you in rotation to protect the chambers," my father continued. It made me think of all the stories he used to tell me as a child. We once had a massive marvelous collection of treasures in a chamber under the Red Sea near Yemen that could only be accessed through a tunnel. Somehow, the treasures were discovered by explorers, and everything they *found* ended up at the British Museum and with the royal family. We later discovered that the English had only emptied the first chamber, and the rest was actually with someone else. It wasn't much: a chest hidden inside of a wall, protected with a spell. It was the chest with the turquoise gemstones. The people who had taken the chest had left a note in Arabic: *Coming is the fall.* We never really figured out what that meant, but my father took it as a warning sign because only practitioners could cross wards like the ones my father had used. My father was convinced they were stolen by those same witches. He believed they used them as talismans, and with black magic, they had turned the stones against the Dūshevs. My father has been searching for the turquoise stones ever since.

"Even when you're not actively engaged in a battle or guarding the chambers, you must remain vigilant," my father warned. "If you encounter a woman you believe to be a witch, approach her carefully. The stone emits a unique energy that only we can sense."

"What do we do then, steal the stone and run?" I asked.

"Isn't it obvious, Adam?" Edgar said mockingly. "You kill them."

"Unfortunately, we cannot take any risks. Never doubt that feeling or hesitate to kill them because they will not spare you. Furthermore, never remove the gemstone before their last breath, as it remains bound to them until the moment of death," my father said.

"Today, all of you will get information about your positions and duties for this coming year. No one is allowed to share this information because it can jeopardize our chances of victory and, most importantly, our lives," Edgar said.

"Each of you will have a private meeting with me and memorize the general and individual information," my father said.

"Memorize! I can't do that. I have the memory of a goldfish," Abraham exclaimed.

"You'll manage," Edgar assured him.

My brothers were called in to speak with my father one by one until, at last, I was called in.

"Finally!" I said, but my father's stern gaze silenced any further outbursts.

"Adam, patience is a virtue you need to cultivate." His voice was like steel. "By now, you should understand that every decision has a purpose. I won't require your services until the year's end, perhaps even longer."

I clenched my fists, trying to hide my frustration. "I have nothing else to do. Now I am being excluded?"

"Are you questioning my authority?" His eyes bore into mine, challenging me to defy him.

"Of course not," I replied, swallowing my pride. This should have made me happy. I was finally free to do what I pleased. So what if I wasn't asked to do any important tasks? For the time being, he wanted me to take a break. The majority of us were just supposed to lie low and wait for him to give us instructions.

٢٦

TWENTY-SIX

Maya

I worked on what I thought was important, which was my shadow work. Every day, I would wake up, meditate, read, and practice my spell work. I discovered the ability to manipulate the world around me. I didn't have complete control over the power, but I felt the energy coursing through my fingertips, tangible yet ethereal. I could move and lift objects without a touch. They were yielding to my unspoken commands, even though I still had to use my hand like a wand. *Powers you can access, only if you stay true to your path.*

My cousins had been trained and taught in our pagan ways long before they were tested with a Dūshev. They were already practicing Sāhers by the time they had met one. I, on the other hand, had no clue. So, no wonder I was the weakest link and offered my soul like a sacrificial lamb; I never stood a chance.

The sun bore down on us, its rays burning through my clothes as I trudged toward the obstacle course. Each step sent jolts of protest through muscles I never knew existed, making my legs feel like lead. I had never worked out a day in my life, but that didn't stop Leyla from putting us through endurance drills every morning. Sweat drenched my clothes, clinging to my skin like a second layer. My throat burned with each gasp of air, the taste of iron lingering on my tongue. I clung to the hope that this ordeal was shaping me into something stronger for whatever challenges lay ahead. I was in such bad shape that I was always the last to finish, and my cousins were seriously beginning to doubt how I would survive this. I didn't blame them, but this wouldn't be a war where combat was necessary. Leyla, on the other hand, treated our physical training with a level of intensity that bordered on obsession, even though the thought of us engaging in combat seemed ludicrous. Despite the impossibility of us ever challenging someone like a Dūshev, she insisted that mastering our physical forms was essential. She thought it would come in handy if it came down to it. I thought it was a waste of time—a feeble attempt to match the powers of the Dūshevs, powers beyond human strength.

"You're dragging your feet, Maya!" Lara shouted. She was far ahead of me, and I hadn't even tried to match her pace.

I glanced upward, my eyes tracing the clouds that were building up above my head. *Clouds . . . Where did the sun go?* The hushed forest surrounded me, its trees shifting in the breeze. The weather was in a bizarre dance that morphed from sunny to windy to high humidity and a slight drizzle. The wind swirled, tousling my hair, while the drizzle kissed my skin. Each breath I took tasted of the dampness I hated so much. I enjoyed running barefoot, but why I had decided to do it, I couldn't remember. It wasn't exactly helping, since I was still much slower than them. I had already lost the first test by letting go of my soul to Adam; I couldn't also be the absolute worst at everything else. As I got closer to our house, I heard a girl sneezing behind me. I turned around and saw the drizzle crystallizing and beginning to look more like snowflakes. Each flake, a unique crystalline entity, hung, suspended in the air, adrift in a slow-motion descent. My skin prickled, goose bumps rising like constellations on my arms as the snowflakes gently dotted my skin. The path I had just come from blurred and changed in seconds and was covered with a beautiful sheet of snow. The surreal shift played tricks on my senses, distorting reality before my eyes and almost making me forget why I had turned around. Seema was standing there with . . . *with that guy. The Dūshev!*

"You brought him to our house, our safe place?" I yelled at her. She didn't turn her head. Instead, she looked at me from the corner of her eye.

"Seema, are you kidding me?" I said. I was utterly shocked as I turned my head back to our house and saw nothing, nothing at all. Only a snow-covered hill with a trail going up. I was completely disoriented and couldn't believe my eyes. When I looked back at them, I saw him taking her hand and kissing it. Time seemed to stretch and warp around them.

"Is it true that this ring means everything to you and your family?" he asked her.

"Who told you that?" she said.

"This tale is as old as time," he mused.

"Well, it is very important to us because we harness our powers from it," she told him. He examined the ring. "But don't worry about all that. I will never let them get to you. It's always going to be you before them," she said.

"As long as we can be together," he said.

He was playing her so hard, and she had no clue. I felt so betrayed, even though I literally would trust Adam with the same information. I walked toward them, snow melting under my feet. The line between reality and imagination blurred. The figures of my cousin and the Dūshev shrouded in the falling snowflakes seemed more like hallucinations. And then, with a gasp, I was yanked back to consciousness and found myself jolted awake from the dream. With a pounding heart, I realized that what I had experienced was not just a dream but a glimpse of a vision. It was 3:33 a.m., and I had only slept three hours before waking up from this lucid dream. I could never go back to sleep with all those images in my head. I was beginning to think that these dreams or visions were something to look out for. How I had access to them was still a mystery, though. How on earth would we have an honest chance of survival if Seema handed them everything on a silver platter? I spent all night lying in bed, thinking without coming up with a good answer to any of it.

I spent most of my time thinking about who I could trust in this family and how to deal with the Dūshevs. Could I even escape my faith and be free, or was I bound by this? And if my dreams were any indications of the truth, then the Dūshevs knew of our gemstones. The Firuzeh I was carrying was not just funneling my power. It was so much more than that. I read a lot about the origins of the Firuzeh in our books and even experimented with it. The Firuzeh itself wasn't the most durable stone in the world. These, in particular, were really fragile and connected to the wearer. Therefore, we had to be extra careful not to lose them. *If the Dūshevs get a hold of your Firuzeh . . .* I never thought I would feel this way about Adam or his family, but I learned that Dūshevs didn't take souls to help people. This whole practice of taking and giving souls benefited them. *They're selfish.* Without it, they wouldn't live as long as they did. All that about souls not fitting a body was a lie. *Lies. Lies. Lies,* crafted by Adam's father. *They have been tugging at the balance of nature for a long time, and if they're not stopped . . .*

Dūshevs were practitioners able to align their powers with nature, but that wasn't enough for them, so they found a way to become stronger by acting like temporary vessels for souls. *Selfish!* I wasn't sure if Adam would continue to take souls if he had known the truth.

I tried to think of ways to carry my Firuzeh. I had kept it in my pocket or in my bra ever since I first got it. I decided that my powers were too valuable to risk losing. I wasn't ready to lose the abilities I had just gained access to by relying on a piece of jewelry. Since my Firuzeh was relatively big, I figured it wouldn't hurt to turn it into a few pieces of jewelry instead of depending on one piece. I could end up losing all my powers by breaking the stone, but I couldn't ignore the voice in my head that kept saying, *Break it, break it, break it.* Then the voice changed, and I heard Adam's voice inside my head. *Alone.* I thought I was making it up until I heard his voice again. *Maybe?* I shook it off from my head because I didn't have time to start wondering where it came from. Ever since I was brought here, I hadn't given much thought to my stance on Adam. His existence had slowly drifted away from my mind. It was probably something Leyla had made sure of. There was a spell over me to distort my perception of the Dūshevs—I knew that. I wasn't stupid, and I had read enough about spell work to recognize one put on me. I felt it covering every inch of my skin like grime, but I pretended not to. The lengths they would go to make sure I didn't betray them was astonishing. In the same house, under the same roof, someone was still hung up on her test of a boyfriend. Of course, they couldn't control or alter my perception of Adam and the Dūshevs. I was going to get rid of all their influence one way or another. I wasn't going to be anyone's pawn anymore—not even Adam's. *Maybe?*

On my way out of the study, I heard Dissie whispering. I couldn't make out what she was saying, but the door to her room wasn't closed, so I pushed it open and stepped inside.

"Okay, I'll meet you there," she whispered, looking through the blinds, being oddly paranoid.

The door didn't creak, so she hadn't heard me enter.

"Who are you talking to, Dissie?"

"Maya—" She leaped out of her spot when she saw me. I walked one step closer and reached for the phone. I could tell she was nervous, but she still handed it to me without question.

"Please don't tell Leyla I brought a phone with me," she said.

"Leyla? Hmph." *She should worry about you!* Maybe the power had gotten to my head, but was I not supposed to be the leader of the Sāhers. *You are . . .*

"You should be more scared of me," I told her and unlocked the phone. There were a bunch of missed calls from random numbers. No one was coded in. Dissie took an insecure breath. I glanced back at her; her eyes were wide open. I didn't care enough to pry into her personal life. If I was supposed to know anything, there was a big chance I would see it in a vision, so it didn't matter what she was hiding. I handed her the phone back and saw relief wash over her body. *I could call my brother—and cause him more harm, more pain.*

"Go and meet whoever you want to meet." *No! Don't let her go.* "But say your goodbyes and come back without a phone." *One less. One less. One less.* "Because if I have to cut off all my ties, then so should all of you. This isn't something to be gambled with."

"Thank you, Maya. I always knew I could trust you," she said.

I turned and left her by herself. Her room was suffocating me, and I had difficulty telling the difference between my thoughts and energies trying to occupy space in my head. I went to my room and wrapped a scarf tightly around my head. Sometimes, the tighter I wrapped the scarf, the better I could focus on what I was doing and saying, but the harder it was wrapped, the faster I got a headache. There had to be another way of veiling. I was clearly doing something wrong because my cousins wore the veil loosely draped around them, but that wasn't working for me.

We had a marble staircase at the house's main entrance that would work as a chopping block for my Firuzeh. Outside, I found a rock large enough to use as a hammer and wrapped the Firuzeh in a towel so it wouldn't go everywhere. It didn't take more than two hits, and it broke into five pieces. I didn't feel any different. It didn't seem to change anything when I broke it, which was a good sign. *I hope.*

In the time I had spent here, I had gained the trust of Leyla, not so much my aunt Shirin. She still had an eye on me wherever I went, but because I didn't want to seem inconspicuous, I made it look like I was asking for permission whenever I wanted to go out.

"Leyla, can you please call Ashrafi for me? I need to go to the *Bazar.*" The last time I went, Shirin had asked Sepideh to go with me. I trusted Sepideh, but I wanted to go by myself.

"What do you need?" Shirin asked. *None of your damn business.*

"I will get my Firuzeh set in gold," I answered her with a smile.

"It's best to set it in silver, like the rest of us. It has been so for generations." She thought she could tell me what to do because I hadn't been taught by my mother. *What kind of mother neglects her child? What kind of mother doesn't come to see you after a sacrifice of your life?*

"Maybe we need to change things if we want a different outcome, no?"

"There is no need to delay Maya," Leyla said. "If gold is what calls to her, she will set the Firuzeh in gold."

Shirin huffed off, leaving me alone with Leyla.

"Thank you," I said.

Ashrafi was our designated driver. He would always take us to the weirdest places, ask no questions, then take us home again. I asked him to take me to the gold market, and he told me about a jeweler he knew and trusted. He parked a few blocks from the place and said he would wait until I returned.

"Tell him Ashrafi sent you," he said as I closed the door.

The whole street was only jewelry stores. It was the primary gold market specializing in gold, precious stones, and fine jewelry. The street was a dazzling maze of narrow alleys and lanes lined with shop windows glittering with gold. I browsed the different stores and bought a few things for my little endeavor. Before the main street, in a small alley, was this hollowed space in the stone wall where an old lady was sitting with a tray of sand. She also had a cup with a few coins in it. She used her left pinky to doodle in the sand. When she noticed me staring, she stopped moving. I smiled and walked away, realizing I was being rude. Ashrafi had said the store was shop number sixty-six called Mahnaz Tala and would be next to a bank.

The man inside the shop didn't seem very approachable.

"I was told you could set my stones in gold." I showed him my Firuzeh.

"These broken pieces. It won't look nice. I have plenty of beautiful rings with Firuzeh."

"*Aghaye Ashrafi* said you were the best at customizing pieces from scratch."

"Hold on a minute," he said, dialing a number on his phone. "*Salam Aghaye Ashrafi, khaste nabashi,*" he said and went into the back. Persian pleasantries were so extra—*May you not be weary.*

When the shopkeeper came back, his smile reached his ears.

"You should've told me Ashrafi sent you," he said. I didn't like that. Only by namedropping Ashrafi could I get a smile out of him. "How can I help you?"

"I have these four pieces of Firuzeh I want to be hidden inside a golden sphere or egg, whatever shape is easiest. I want to wear them as pendants in my hoops, necklace, and bracelet." The fifth was a clast and could easily be embedded in the clockwork of the wristwatch I had just bought down the street.

"So, you won't be able to see the stones?" he asked, probably thinking it was an odd request.

"Alright. Shouldn't take too long. Come back in a few hours, and I will have them ready for you."

What was I supposed to do all that time? *The watch! Yes. I'll find a watchmaker to fix the watch for me.*

I couldn't help but wonder about what that old lady was doing with the sand in her tray. I had to know, so when I finished at the watchmaker, I returned to the narrow alley. The ground beneath my feet felt slightly uneven, the cobblestones worn smooth by years of footsteps. There, I found her in the same spot, her gnarled fingers caressing the grains of sand. The subtle crunch of the sand beneath her touch filled the air as I approached. I had no idea what came over me because as soon as I was close enough, I stuck my pinky into the sand and felt the cold grains brushing against my skin, sending shivers up my spine. I felt ice touching my bones, seeping into the core of my being. I immediately knew that it wasn't real, that it was just a vision, but it was clear as day, even more detailed than my own visions. I saw myself forcing something down my own throat—I was drinking blood, drowning in it. The metallic tang of iron flooded my senses. I could taste the sharp, distinct flavor that sent my mind reeling. With a jolt, I pulled my finger out of the sand, the grains slipping away like time through my fingers. I stumbled back, my heart racing.

"What was that?" I said. The reality of the vision still clinging to me, the taste of iron lingering on my tongue.

"A glimpse. You'll be back when you need me again. Off you go," she said and shooed me away.

٢٧

TWENTY-SEVEN

Adam

Earlier, in Egypt . . .

I couldn't seem to get used to sleeping in this house. Anywhere else in the world was fine, except under my father's roof. All I could think of was Maya. I refused to believe she died when they never recovered her body. There must have been a very good reason why she had faked her death and disappeared. Perhaps she was running from someone and was too scared to tell me. Maybe she was running from my father and knew how closely he was watching us. Perhaps she didn't think she could trust me.

The last time I checked on her brother, Dissie opened the door and asked me to leave before Maya's father saw me. He was still angry because of my outburst at the funeral and didn't want me near their house. Sometimes, I went to the diner where Dissie worked and asked her how Milad was doing. Talking to Dissie gave me hope; it felt like I still had something. In the beginning, Dissie was really weird about it, but the more I came over, the more she opened up. She got very comfortable with me. I remember thinking how much Maya would have resented that I became friends with her because of Dissie's relationship with Maya's father. And I could see how a simple man like Jack would fall for that. She was a flirt by nature, and I honestly didn't think she knew what she was doing to the men watching her. One time, she was serving me food when she bent over the table for an unnecessarily long time with her breasts all up in my face. Then it suddenly struck me. I couldn't believe that I didn't remember this 'til now. That day, her necklace slipped from her shirt and swung back and forth. It was a turquoise gemstone hanging on a thick silver chain, long enough to hide beneath her shirt.

It was still in the middle of the day back in Mist Creek, so I could still catch her at home or work. Immediately, I put on some clothes, adhāred to an alley behind the diner, and walked to the front door. I couldn't see Dissie anywhere, but her sister was behind the bar.

"Adam! How are you?" she said.

"I'm actually here to talk to your sister." She looked at me like I was crazy. Before coming to me, she served a beer to an older gentleman. "I don't have a sister," she said.

"Your sister, Dissie—I need to talk to Dissie."

"I'm an only child, Adam," she said, not understanding my confusion.

"My mistake. I thought she was your sister."

"There is no Dissie working here. Maybe you're thinking of a different place?"

I definitely wasn't, but I wasn't going to argue with her, so I just walked out of there. She was definitely one of them, and she was hiding something. I just didn't see a gemstone on her. Perhaps she was hiding hers the same way Dissie was. She wasn't wearing any jewelry or anything, but she could still carry a stone in her pocket. I wasn't sure if visiting Jack and asking about his girlfriend was a good idea, but I decided to go anyway. The memories came back when I got in front of their house. I knocked on their door and heard footsteps running down the stairs. I just wanted to see her again. It would be enough just to see if she was okay.

Milad opened the door and looked at me for a second. "Hi."

"Hi, Milad." I didn't know what to say or how to begin. It seemed a bit insensitive to ask about Dissie now. "How are you holding up?"

"I'm okay, I guess."

"Is your father home?"

"No."

"How about Dissie?"

"Who's Dissie?" he said. How could he not know about her if she lived there? Or maybe she didn't live with them and was just over the last time I came here. Another alternative could be that Dissie didn't exist, and I was losing my mind. The fact that I couldn't find her was driving me crazy. I just saw her a month ago, if not less than a month.

I went straight over to find Elias at home. Maybe he had seen her in the past few days; if not, Lena must have, but they weren't home, and I had to wait for them. I had never bothered to get Dissie's number. She was always working at the diner on Tuesdays and Fridays, so I didn't need her phone number. Then

I rummaged through my old room and found Maya's phone, but it was dead, so I had to charge it. Even if it turned back on after all this time, I wasn't sure if there was a password. I thought I would lie down and rest for a second, and before I knew it, I had slept just about three hours. Elias barged into my room and woke me.

"Hey, you called. I'm sorry. I didn't even check my phone."

"I'm looking for Dissie, Lena's friend. Have you seen her lately?" I said, rubbing my eyes, trying to shake off the nap.

"No, why would I see her?"

"I just need to talk to her. Maybe Lena knows?"

"Baby, can you come in here? Please," Elias called. I heard her footsteps echo heavily on the stairs. Despite her petite frame, she treaded on the hardwood floor like an elephant.

"Can you call Dissie? Adam wants to talk to her," he said.

"Who the hell is Dissie?" she said. As expected, her memory was wiped as well. I figured as much.

"What do you mean, who?" Elias was surprised, though. I hadn't given him any details. "Don't worry about it. I thought she was one of your friends. She was Maya's friend," I interrupted. I couldn't believe she had vanished. As if she was sucked into the ground and forgotten about. "Oh," Lena said. Elias was about to balk, but I glared at him.

Maya's phone was finally working again, but I couldn't guess her password for the life of me. After being suspended for the third time, I called Milad.

"Hey, Milad, do you happen to have the password for Maya's phone?"

"I do. I know everything," he said, but there was no cocky spirit in him. "Do you have her phone? My dad asked about it."

"Yes, I just found it. Can you please give me the password?"

"It's either seven two, seven two or . . ." he was quiet for a brief moment. "Or my name." He sighed.

"It worked. Thanks. I'll bring the phone over one of these days," I said. I was torn between going through her pictures or calling Dissie. I figured it would be better to call her now before it got too late. I had all night to go through her phone and be miserable. I also had to clean it out before giving it to Jack. I knew for sure she sent me a few pictures that were considered inappropriate, and I didn't want her father to stumble on them. I called Dissie, and she didn't pick up until the third time I called.

"Maya?" Dissie said as if that was a possibility.

"Um. It's Adam. I hope I didn't wake you."

"Oh! No, I just didn't hear it." She was almost whispering.

"I know it's random that I'm calling you. I kind of just thought about you. So, I was wondering if we could meet up . . . alone."

"Right now?" she sounded surprised.

"I know. It's weird. I'm sorry for bothering you," I said as if I wanted to hang up. She fell right in. "No. Wait. I can't right now, but I can meet you next week because I'm out of town at the moment."

"I can come to you if that's easier," I said.

"Um, no, that wouldn't work." *Of course it wouldn't. You fled town.*

"Then, Tuesday, maybe? At Olympia?"

"Okay, I'll meet you there," she said.

This was my chance to find out if she was one of them. I had a shot at getting on my father's good side and winning some trust. Maybe then he would relent and tell me what he knew. If I could just get my hands on her necklace to see if it was indeed the real deal. I had to play this right, or she might get suspicious. I had to get close enough to feel the energy of the stone. It could be an ordinary necklace, but since everyone had forgotten about her, she couldn't be anything but a witch. She must have done something to their memory.

٢٨

TWENTY-EIGHT

MAYA

Every night, I would have some sort of lucid dream that fucked with my perception of this family. That night was no different. I woke up in the middle of the night again after dreaming about how Seema kept going behind our backs and putting her relationship above everything else. She had never left this place to meet her boyfriend, but it still felt real. Whether the dreams showed me the future, past, or the present, I didn't know. I tried going back to sleep but couldn't because I had to pee. I lay there for such a long time, forcing myself to fall asleep instead of getting it over with. I hated getting up from the bed in the middle of the night. It was such a hassle, but I had finally made my way out of bed and into the hallway.

I noticed one of the bedroom's lights was on after I got out. Then a noise came from that same room. It sounded like a heavy dresser being pressed up against the wall. Of course, I had to check. I didn't even hesitate to open the door.

I was instantly frozen in time, my senses engulfed in the scene unfolding before me. The air crackled with tension, carrying the scent of her intoxicating perfume. The room seemed to hum with anticipation. My eyes couldn't escape the vivid image before me. She was a vision in lace, her lingerie delicate against her skin, which seemed to glow in the room's dim light. His hands, warm and possessive, traced a fiery path, exploring every contour of her body. I could almost feel the electric charge in the air as his fingers grazed her mouth, leaving a trail of heat in their wake before gliding down her neck and breasts. A touch that was once so familiar to me. Her back arched in response, her breaths becoming shallow, as she unbuttoned his shirt, the fabric yielding under her fingers, revealing the firm muscles underneath. I could practically feel the urgency in his touch, the way he grabbed her waist with one hand, fingers pressing into her skin, while the other hand entwined in her hair, tugging gently. She responded in kind, wrapping her legs around his body, their kiss deepening.

I could suddenly feel my lungs collapsing, my windpipe closing with no warning, as if invisible hands were tightening around my throat. I gasped for air, but there was none to be found. Panic surged through me, sending electric jolts down my spine. My hand instinctively shot to my neck when I realized it was another lucid dream. I forced my eyes open in shock, finding the dream dissolving into the darkness of my room. Yet the pressing need for air remained. It was a matter of seconds before I would throw up. The acidic taste of nausea rose in my throat. I clamped my hand over my mouth as I stumbled toward the bathroom and reached the toilet by a mere microsecond. My body convulsed involuntarily as I retched. It seemed to have no end. I almost didn't get a chance to take a breath between each heave.

I was such a fool. *Fool! Fool! Fool!* How could this happen to me? And why did it hurt so much? My body physically hurt from the images in my mind. The insides of my body were trying to crawl their way out while I was silently weeping in bed. I wished I could make this pain go away. *Stop feeling sorry for yourself. He never truly loved you and only used you to gain access to your soul. It's all he wanted. It's all he wanted. It's all he wanted.* I wanted this pain to go away, to feel nothing at all, to shut it all off. I had a goal, a prophecy, to fulfill. *Yes.*

At breakfast, there was an awkward silence for no apparent reason. I tried to make eye contact with Sepideh, but she was completely lost in her food. Leyla started talking to one of my aunts and freed my bleeding ears from listening to people's chewing.

"Can anyone tell me where Dissie has been the last few days?" Shirin asked without looking at any of us.

"She's out of town for a week," I said. The image of them resurfaced in my head.

"Who gave her the permission to do so?" Shirin asked, looking at no one in particular. Or maybe she did. I didn't pay attention.

"I did!" I said carelessly. The room got quiet again. Even the chewing stopped. I looked up and saw Leyla put a hand on Shirin's arm to calm her down; she was pissed.

"I'm sure Maya had a good reason, letting Dissie leave us," Leyla said, letting me know that she wanted an explanation.

"I can't treat these girls like prisoners as you would want me to. Trust is earned. They need to know that I trust them and that they can trust me," I said to Leyla as if the other girls weren't there. However, last night, I was proven wrong. I was glad I did. How else would I have seen what I saw? It seemed like Dissie would do just about anything to get laid, but she wasn't the one I was disappointed by. After what she did with my father, nothing surprised me about Dissie. It was more heartbreaking knowing Adam would sleep with her of all the girls on earth. He could sleep with anyone, and he still chose her! *Fool!* I guess I expected him to get over me, but I didn't think it would happen so fast. I couldn't suppress my feelings; they controlled me more than I liked to admit it. I never thought I would be motivated to fight them with all my heart, but I had nothing left to lose.

٢٩

TWENTY-NINE

We were halfway through October, and she finally decided to make the announcement. One of us was to go with her on the journey ahead. Ever since Maya woke up, everything changed. The stories we had grown up with, and everything we knew of the prophecy was replaced with something else. I couldn't wait to hear who would be burdened with the task of assisting the leader. The girls thought it stood between Lara and me, but I hoped they were wrong. I deliberately did nothing to impress her because I didn't want to be chosen. I was relieved when I heard we weren't all going and wouldn't need to sacrifice more Sāher blood for a stupid prophecy. Not that I didn't want to help my family—I did, but I was just not built for war. The sad reality was I could be forced to kill one of my own. So many people kill in the name of love; I just hoped I didn't have to be one of them. If my family ever found out Samuel and I were still together, we would both be screwed. We promised each other we would stand together to the end, no matter whose family was in our way.

I promised Samuel I would make time for him, but I didn't know how to get out of the damn house without getting my head chopped off. One option was to ask Maya if I could leave; she let Dissie go. At the same time, I didn't want her to think I was running away. Dissie was supposed to be back by then and wasn't. Lara says it was Maya's fault that Dissie went away. She had never disappeared for that long without an explanation, but I didn't think it was a lack of judgment on Maya's part. We had free will; Maya understood that. Lara was still hung up on the old ways.

Maya was sitting in the study, reading one of the books on protection spells and wards. I remember that book was so boring I always fell asleep trying to read it. She sat gracefully, her legs crossed, while a strand of hair twirled delicately around her finger, lost in the book. As I sat across from her, she closed the book and looked at me, smiling.

"What's on your mind?" she asked.

It's now or never. "My best friend is very sick, and I want to visit her in the hospital, so I was wondering if it's okay with you. I won't be gone for long. I promise," I said. She leaned back in her chair and raised her eyebrow at first but then her face relaxed.

"If you're home by tomorrow night—"

Lara barged in. She had been eavesdropping all this time. "You're going to let Seema leave as well!" Her voice sharp with accusation. "What kind of leader are you? You can't do this. You can't come here and split up our family."

Maya stood and took a step toward Lara. The room seemed to respond to the emotional storm, the chandelier above swaying. The books lining the shelves trembled, some falling to the floor, their pages rustling like leaves in a storm. Maya raised her right hand, her fingers curling with energy. Her face changed, her eyes showing the whites only. It was as if the very room held its breath, waiting for the eruption of power. Without warning, a force propelled Lara acrōss the room. She collided with the wall and slid up, pressed hard against the wall by an invisible force. The room seemed to blur, objects lifting off the ground like weightless feathers, suspended in midair. Lara, once defiant, now looked like a fly trapped on a bug strip tape.

Maya relaxed her right hand for a second and then grabbed the air again, which pushed Lara even harder against the wall.

"Tell me aziz, *dear*. What can I not do?" Her words dipped in mockery. "Do you think you can do better than me? Or maybe you think your powers can measure with mine." Her eyes were ablaze with anger.

Lara didn't answer. Maya had probably cut out Lara's voice herself because, when Lara opened her mouth, only empty air came out. Finally, Maya released her hold, and the room exhaled in relief. The trembling ceased, and the books fell to the ground with a resounding thud.

Then she took a deep breath, returning to her usual self. "I have the spirits of a thousand Sāhers within me, pulling and pushing me to do their biddings. I don't need you standing in my way. You can either choose to walk beside me or not be at all," Maya said with the softest voice, as if she hadn't tormented Lara five seconds before. She walked out of the wreck and left us to clean it up. I had no idea she was hiding all that power. The rest of us could only manipulate a Dūshev's strength, nothing more, nothing less. We all knew she would be more powerful than us, but we didn't realize how powerful she would become.

Considering it, I understood why Maya reacted the way she did. Lara hadn't been the nicest one of us since she came here. It was like everybody changed when it happened. They became so competitive and mischievous. We used to be best friends; now, it was all so calculated. Lara had doubts about Maya ever since we found out it was her. She would say some mean, stupid things to make Maya look weak. And after the demonstration, I was positive Maya wouldn't pick Lara for her quest. I was scared to be stuck with the task because Roya was too apathetic, and Sepideh was not mature enough.

Meeting Samuel wouldn't take more than a couple of hours, but the traveling time was what took the joy out of it. I wish I could have let him teleport here, but it wasn't safe for us. We always met at my family's mountain cabin in Cambasi, near the ski resort. It was where I met him the first time. I knew something was off but couldn't exactly tell if we were synching or canceling each other out. Usually, people took it as a joke when you said you came from a family of witches. No one actually believed witches existed. That's why I usually just told people; no one believed me. I told him, too. Within a week, he confided in me and told me he was a Dūshev.

Six hours later, I arrived at the cabin. When I entered, he turned from where he was seated. He was sitting on my favorite chair, staring into the crackling chimney. The fire cast a glow on his beautiful face. He looked at me and then down at my empty hands. "No bags!" he said. I didn't get the chance to defend myself before he continued. "How short will this date be? When do I get the chance to spend a whole day with my girlfriend?"

I loved him, loved him so much for wanting to be with me and spend time with me, but right now, we were both busy with our families, and he, of all men in the world, should have known how critical this time was.

"I'm sorry," I said and hugged him. Sometimes, it was just easier to hug instead of giving a frustrating answer. The scent of him was suddenly disturbed by the lovely smell of food.

"You got us food?" He smiled and slowly pulled away from me. He was so thoughtful, always one step ahead, trying to make me happy. Even though he didn't know how far I had traveled to get here, he knew I would be hungry when I arrived. The hours went by so fast when we were together. There were so many things we wanted to do as a couple. Maybe one day, we could realize our dreams. To get a country house with a vegetable garden and maybe have some kids and live a quiet life. It felt like mere minutes had passed before I had to get up and leave. With a sad expression, Samuel helped me put on my jacket and kissed me on the neck just before pulling the jacket over my shoulders.

We were standing outside in the snow, waiting for the taxi to come and pick me up, when he took my hand and kissed it.

"Is it true that this ring means everything to you and your family?" His thumb traced the contours of my Firuzeh ring.

"Who told you that?" I said. I wasn't aware they knew about the Firuzeh amulets.

"This tale is as old as time," he said.

"Well, it is very important to us because we harness our powers from them." He looked at my ring, twisting it around my finger.

"But don't worry about all that. I will never let them get to you. It's always going to be you before them." I reached for his cheek.

"As long as we can be together," he said and kissed me goodbye.

٣٠

THIRTY

MAYA

I was brushing my teeth, spitting out the excess toothpaste, when I saw all the swirls of blood. It never bled like this because I always made sure to floss. I opened my mouth and saw that I had been brushing my teeth so vigorously that my gums were bleeding. I shouldn't have put up with people screwing me over. I felt chewed up and spit out like a tasteless piece of gum. I hated Adam for not looking for me, hated my family for expecting leadership from me, and even hated myself because I kept second-guessing my powers. It wouldn't hurt to help my family and destroy the Dūshevs. They were a waste of space and didn't deserve to live, except for Adam. I had better plans for him. I was not letting him get away that easily. *He played me, and he is going to pay.*

It was just before 6 p.m. when Seema came home. "Don't start without me!" she shouted as she shut the front door. I knew she would come back in time. She was very adamant about preserving her good-girl image. We were sitting in the living room, drinking hot tea, with the cooler on medium, when she came in and sat with us. She had brought a cake with her. It was creamy, fluffy, and beyond delicious.

"I want to say this, not only to you, Maya, but to all of you," Lara said, gesturing to everyone, dragging my focus away from the chocolate cake melting in my mouth. "I was wrong about you, Maya, and I am sorry. I would be honored to serve this family beside you and give you my blood oath." *Too late, bitch.* I couldn't use such an opinionated person as my right hand. I needed someone moldable, someone I could trust with my life.

"I've already chosen someone, and it wasn't based on our disagreement yesterday. I made my decision long ago, and I haven't changed my mind since." I had brought a book with me that I was certain none of them had delved into before, except perhaps Shirin and Leyla, the ones who brought me back to life. It was a book with restricted information, and only the person I had selected would be able to read it. I had played around with a locking spell, ensuring that whenever anyone attempted to open it, they would only see blank pages. As I lifted the book from under my seat, the astonishment in some of the girls' eyes was palpable; they immediately recognized its distinctive cover.

"Necromancy!" Lara exclaimed.

"Yes," I replied.

"But we're not allowed to even touch this book." She looked at Leyla. "We can't! It burned me the last time I touched it."

Oh! I didn't know that. "Nifty trick," I said to Leyla. I didn't even have to put a spell on it. I stood to hand her the book and realized that they had all stood up with me. I didn't need to walk far; she was just one person away from me. "Let's see if your hands will burn, too," I said.

"Me?" Sepideh asked, not believing her own ears.

"Yes, Sepideh, you."

She hesitated momentarily, her fingertips gently brushing the surface of the book. Then, with newfound determination, she grasped it firmly and cracked it open in the middle. The other girls eagerly leaned over one another, their curiosity piquing, trying to catch a glimpse of its contents.

"But it's blank," Roya said.

"Not to her, it's not," I said.

"I won't disappoint you," Sepideh said, closing the book.

"The easy part is over, and the struggles are yet to come. When this month passes, we will have to be extra careful. They know we are coming for them, and they are prepared. So, while Sepideh and I are gone, the rest of you should perfect your protection spells like never before because I need you to be at your best when we go for the chalice. The fact that you have not been chosen does not excuse you to put your guard down. You will be attacked in this home, and you must be ready for it. I have seen this house burned down to the ground, so if you're not prepared to risk your life for the prophecy, you should pack your bags and go today before tomorrow."

With the help of Leyla and Shirin, Sepideh went into the forbidden realm of necromancy, a subject widely frowned upon. In the world of necromancy, there was always a sacrifice, the ominous requirement of a blood sacrifice; no matter how people tried to gloss over it, inevitably, it boiled down to a life for a life and a soul for a soul—no pun intended. Sepideh needed all the help she could muster, for the spell I needed her to master demanded a level of expertise only the most seasoned practitioners possessed. She was the only one I could trust to do this without ulterior motives. I had come to understand that intention was everything, but it couldn't take you all the way. The fewer flaws, the more substantial power produced. Some of the techniques I had used weren't described in the books. In my experience, preparation and timing were fundamental keys to achieving the purest form of magic.

Last night, I had a dream that might explain why Dissie never returned to Iran. I wasn't sure if it was merely wishful thinking fueled by my anger toward her or if it actually happened. Everything appeared incredibly vivid, yet I always sensed the disconnection from my own reality. The dreams grew more intense each time, with an unparalleled sense of presence. The dining room was adorned with intricately crafted sconces, their warm golden light casting a soft glow against the dark wood-paneled walls. Ornate chandeliers hung from the ceiling, their crystals shimmering on the smooth, polished marble floor. I felt the chilling draft of the house and sensed their powers stretching across the room. The focal point was a man seated at the far end of a long dinner table. Everyone present bore some resemblance to him; he was Adam's father. His features were etched with age—gray hair, bushy eyebrows, and wrinkles etched around his eyes.

Adam stood roughly thirty feet away from me. After detailing how he had killed Dissie, he turned, his gaze locking onto mine as if he had detected my presence. I found myself saying, *Well played.*

When I woke up, I told Leyla about my dream, but I may have forgotten to mention that Adam was the one who killed her. Despite my friendship with Dissie, seeing her dead in the dream didn't evoke anything in me—no sadness, remorse, and certainly no resentment toward Adam. Perhaps I was jealous that she got to see him, touch and kiss him. He was mine, and she took him from me like she did my father. She sold herself to them, sold us, trading away years of suffering and pain—for what? A quick fuck. *I should send him a thank-you note for getting rid of her.*

٣١

THIRTY-ONE

Adam

I carried her lifeless form in my arms, stepping into the dining room. The room buzzed with the clinking of silverware and hushed conversations. Carefully, I laid her cold body at the end of the long table, the wood smooth beneath my fingertips. My brothers stopped mid-bite, their eyes fixed on me, as I retrieved her necklace from my pocket, its metal cool against my skin. With a flick of my wrist, I sent it, gliding across the table toward my father. Samuel, seated nearby, followed its path, his eyes catching the glint of the necklace as it moved.

"You always get ahead of me," Samuel remarked, a sardonic grin playing on his lips.

"How did you—"

"I seduced her, tracing kisses along her neck while undoing the clasp of her necklace. She glanced back, warning me not to take it off, and that's when I broke her neck. Sometimes, brute force isn't necessary."

"You didn't exactly kiss her to death," Samuel said.

I tried to suppress my pride, not mentioning that I was the first to get one. I had brought her here to make a statement, but the elders remained unimpressed. Most of them rose from their seats to inspect her.

My father passed the necklace around. "Feel the weight of the stone. Sense its power beneath your fingertips," he instructed and turned to me. "Did she suspect anything about you? Was she wary?"

"Oh, she definitely knew about us and what I was capable of doing to her. I think that made her an easier target. She wanted the forbidden fruit."

"Is that so?" Edgar interjected.

"I'm guessing they all know about us," I added.

"Very well, but next time, leave the filth outside these quarters," my father commanded. The necklace returned to his hands, cradled like a sacred relic. As his palms closed around the turquoise stone, time seemed to stretch, sounds fading into a distant murmur. My senses blurred, and I felt a watchful presence enveloping me. Panic gripped my chest, and I turned abruptly, searching for the source. There she stood in the doorway, altered but undeniably real. It felt like a dream; I was paralyzed, unable to move or speak. Her voice broke the silence, familiar yet changed. "Well played," she said. Same demeanor. Even though it had only been a few months, there were signs of aging on her face. It looked like she was at least two years older. Her hair seemed to have darkened a shade—nothing people would notice, but I did. I knew her. Somehow, she looked more ethnic. Her hair was wilder and wavier. Her eyes were darker than the darkest brown, almost black.

It was a fleeting moment; I didn't have time to react. She vanished, dissipating like smoke in the wind. Sound rushed back, crashing like a tidal wave, and the world returned to normal. My father was explaining something about the stones, but my mind was elsewhere. *She is alive!*

Still processing what I had witnessed, I left the dining room, my thoughts consumed by her. I didn't know if the same had happened to the others or if I was the only one who saw her.

Samuel caught up with me, his eyes brimming with worry. "Can I ask you something? No questions asked?" he said, his tone hushed but intense.

"Anything," I assured him.

"Could you aďhār while she was around?"

"I'm sure I could if I wanted to."

"No, but did you try?" he persisted, his eyes searching mine for something deeper.

"No. Where are you going with this? I don't understand."

"Don't worry about it," he said cryptically, leaving me with more questions than answers. I would have pressed him further, but my mind was too occupied at the time. After all, I had just witnessed the impossible—my dead girlfriend standing before me as if she had never left.

٣٢

THIRTY-TWO

I had to do this all by myself because we couldn't compromise both of us. If I failed, Sepideh would have to step in my place and finish everything I had started. That was what the blood oath was for—to make sure she held up her end of the bargain. For me, it was different. I could try to derail, but inevitably, circumstances would conspire, aligning themselves whether I liked it or not. The prophecy, it seemed, was destined to unfold, with or without my cooperation.

Standing in line, I was trembling. A dead girl trying to erase her every step. I was screwed should I get caught, but I wouldn't get caught. They made sure of that. This wasn't their first or last fake passport. It was made by an American militant in Baghdad. They gave me a new name and assured me that Maya Ara Forest had ceased to exist. However, I could still be recognized by people I knew, which was why I came back in the first place. I wasn't even allowed to exist in people's memories anymore.

"Passport, please," he said as I approached his booth. He was an older guy with buckteeth, curly hair, and an angry frown stamped on his face. He checked my passport and scanned it into the computer; something on the screen made him look back at me, smiling.

"Welcome home, Miss Salehi." *I got through!*

It felt good to be back, even though I, soon, wouldn't exist to anyone. I walked through baggage claim with my duffel bag and headed to the exit. *What now?*

The question was what to do with Adam. To be completely honest, I didn't care what my family thought was best. I was going to decide what was best for me on my own. I had so much rage and so much hatred that they couldn't cloud my judgment about him. I just needed some time to figure it out. It would be easier to deal with if I made him forget but then there would be no way back. I would erase our history and be a stranger to him. He would kill me without hesitation if he found out what I was.

I couldn't just walk around town, so to avoid drawing any attention, I rented a car from the airport, did most of my grocery shopping in one go, wearing a cap and a scarf to cover most of my face, and drove to a motel in South Mist Creek. I had to stay in the next few days and prepare for this spell. Once perfected, the daunting task would be to pour it on my father's doorstep, a ritual that would wipe my existence from his memory and the memories of everyone I held dear. This spell would leave no trace of my existence behind, but it wouldn't extend to the spiritual community; practitioners would remain unaffected. The same applied to the Dūshev. I had to craft a separate potion specifically tailored for them so that, when I would pour the water on Adam's doorsteps, he and every Dūshev I had ever met would forget. The question remained: could I go through with it?

After four days of preparation, I stood in the dimly lit room, the black candle in my hand flickering like a phantom in the darkness. I chanted the ancient words over the moon water.

> *By moonlight's grace and shadow's duce,*
> *I cast a veil, the memories you lose.*
> *Forgotten footprints and whispers at night,*
> *Erased from thoughts and out of sight.*

Of course, it was so much more than a chant over a bowl of water. It was a strong infusion of valerian root in the charged moon water mixed with wolfsbane, and the essence of amnesia rose. Carefully, I put one drop of my blood into each bowl, repeating the spell three times at my altar beneath the open window, bathing in the soft glow of the moonlight. The potion shimmered like liquid moonlight as I poured it into a bottle. To seal the spell, I allowed the wax from the black candle to drip onto the bottle's lid, each drop representing the permanence of the spell. Once poured, this spell could not be reversed. The room was steeped in the aftermath of the ritual. My heart was heavy with both anticipation and uncertainty. Gathering my resolve, I stepped into the night, and I found myself standing in front of my dad's house, thinking only of my brother. What would happen to him? Who would take care of him? I certainly wasn't the best sister. Then, who would? *Who? Who? Who?* Cutting ties with him was destroying me, but I could do nothing about it. He had already mourned my death, and *dead*, I was. It wasn't written, but I knew I could never go back to my life before. I had no soul, no life to return to. *You have to do this. Be strong.*

I lit the candle and looked at the familiar silhouette of the place I used to call home.

Beneath the sky, a tree grows wide,
Branches stretch, and memories collide.
In every bough, my name departs,
And my whispers lost within their hearts.

I carefully poured the water on the steps of our entrance, the moonlight dancing on its surface. A flame flickered to life as the candle wax dripped onto the water. For a brief moment, panic gripped me. *What if I set the whole house ablaze?* The flame spread out in tendrils resembling tree branches, gracefully touching the doors of every house on the quiet street. My heart pounded in my ears until I realized the fire vanished as swiftly as it appeared. I sprinted to my car, following it. It went in every direction, but I had one specific route in mind. Would it hit Adam's house as well? The road stretched out before me, lit by the pale glow of streetlights. With each passing moment, I grew more fixed on the next step and parked the car two houses down from Adam's. I waited in the shadows until the blue flame passed by me. It didn't touch their door, and the realization was suffocating me, urging me to complete the task.

No matter how long I had stood there, I couldn't seem to find a good reason why he should forget. The bottle in my hand felt like an anchor, its cap seemingly impossible to open. I took a deep breath, setting the bottle down on the step beside me. My trembling fingers pulled out the candle and lighter from my back pocket. *Perhaps if I lit the candle first . . .*

"Can I help you?" A voice sliced through the night, jolting me from my thoughts. I turned, and dread washed over me at the sight of Elias, his eyes mirroring my own startled confusion.

"Holy shit," he whispered, and panic surged through me, urging me to flee. My skin prickled, breaths quickening. For a fleeting moment, I closed my eyes, hoping for a way out. *This is wrong!* When I opened my eyes, reality had shifted. Elias was gone, and the world outside vanished. Instead, I found myself sitting in the driver's seat, hands on the steering wheel.

"Did I just teleport?" I uttered in disbelief. Everything around me appeared normal, even my face reflecting back from the rearview mirror. *What the hell just happened?*

٣٣

THIRTY-THREE

Adam

I was having lunch with Samuel, enjoying myself for once, when my phone buzzed on the table. It was Elias calling. I dismissed the call initially, thinking I would catch up with him later. He had been calling me a lot lately, talking about all sorts of things. He was probably nervous about becoming a father—which was no small feat. Elias was persistent; he called again and then once more. It wasn't like him, so I excused myself from the table and stepped away to answer his call.

"Whe—are you doing anything important right now?" His words were rushed and jumbled.

"No, why?" My apprehension kept growing.

"Come home right this second," he said sharply before hanging up.

"Everything okay?" Samuel asked, his brows furrowed.

"I'm sure it's nothing. Just going to see what Elias wants."

"You have to go now?"

"Yeah, I think so. What if his girlfriend is in labor?" I said. Although I had a feeling it wasn't that. She wasn't even that far in her pregnancy. I changed into warmer clothes and adhared back to Mist Creek. It was around five in the morning when I got there. I found Elias sitting outside, huddled on the steps of our porch, knees pulled to his chest. The glow of the porch light illuminated Elias's figure.

"What's wrong?" I asked. Elias got up abruptly and started pacing back and forth. "Talk to me!" My mind raced with all the possibilities of what could have happened.

"I'm gonna say something that sounds fucking insane, but please let me finish before you dismiss it," he said and took another deep breath. I braced myself for whatever news he was about to say.

"I was—I just adhāred back from the gas station because Lena was craving chocolate ice cream, and I didn't want to drive all the way. You know how crazy she has gotten lately." He paused, his eyes wild. "You have to understand, I was not, no, I was tired! But I'm not delusional. Fuck—"

"Elias. Can you take a deep breath and tell me what the hell is going on? You are freaking me out."

"When I got back here, in the driveway, I noticed a girl on our porch. She had her back to me, and she was doing something weird. She put this bottle on the step." He pointed at the bottle, his hand trembling. "Do you see it?" he asked.

"Yes. I'm not blind," I said.

"Good! And then she pulled out something from her back pocket. That's when I took a few steps in her direction." He looked behind him and took a step back. "This was the distance between us. About six feet." He gestured with his hands.

"Get to the point, will you?"

"No, this is important. Look at me!" he said. "How clearly can you see me? Do you have any doubts if it's me or not? Because of the darkness or whatever!"

"I see you. Your face is lit up by the porch lamp—"

"Exactly!"

"Who was it?" I asked impatiently.

"You don't understand! She turned around, and I saw her, I saw her face. She was as shocked to see me as I was to see her. I saw Maya!"

"Repeat that." My voice was barely a whisper as I struggled to comprehend his words.

"I know it sounds crazy, but I swear to you, she was right here!"

"And where did she go?" I asked, trying to keep my calm.

"That's the thing. She adʰāred right before my eyes as soon as she realized I had seen her."

I let out a sigh, my mind whirling with confusion.

"Why are you not freaking out about this?"

"Because a while back, I saw her, too."

"What! Where?" He rubbed his face in disbelief.

"In Egypt, at the facility, where everyone was present. But it didn't seem like the others saw her, so I thought I was hallucinating. She just appeared in the dining hall and disappeared again."

A heavy silence settled between us. I approached the mysterious bottle, needing to see what she had left behind to find some sort of clue.

"Don't touch that!" he exclaimed.

"Relax, it's just a bottle." I unscrewed the cap and smelled it.

"Don't drink it. Are you out of your mind!" he protested, his hands moving in frantic gestures. Then he evaporated the whole thing.

"What did you do!" I yelled.

"Don't be pressed," he said. "It had the density of water."

I still had the bottle in my hand, waiting for an explanation that might never come. She had taken a risk by coming here. Everyone thought she was dead. She was running from someone and came here looking for me, but why did she come here if she didn't want to see Elias? I couldn't go anywhere; I had to find her.

I knew I would see her again. *I just knew it.*

٣٤

THIRTY-FOUR

Maya

I was on the brink of ruining everything the moment Elias almost caught me. Sure, I didn't have the chance to pour it on their house, but I didn't want to, either. Consequences be damned, I wanted him to remember—doubt himself. I wanted him haunted by uncertainty, questioning if I still existed in this world. And if, by any chance, Dissie told Adam what we were, Adam would try to hunt me down and do to me what he did to her. Not knowing what I had become.

Annually, Wright Park came alive with the spirit of Halloween, hosting a fair that drew in the crowds. For me, it presented an opportunity to step out of this motel room in a Halloween costume that concealed my face.

The turnout was beyond my expectations; a sea of people in costumes filled the park. "No play this year?" I asked a woman.

"No, not after Mrs. Roberts passed," she said.

"She died?" I asked.

"Yes, unfortunately, she died on August ninth. Do I know you?" she asked. I froze for a second because I wasn't sure if I did. She looked familiar, but I didn't know where I had seen her before.

"Of course you do. I'm the Grim Reaper," I said, hoping that would be sufficient.

"Good one," she chuckled, seemingly convinced. I walked away slowly, trying not to look suspicious.

I came to the park because I wanted to feel normal for a second. Be myself in my hometown for one last fleeting moment. The need to remove my mask, to simply exist without the weight of my predicament, consumed me. I didn't know if the spell had taken hold yet or if it had to be sealed before it worked. Regardless, I would finish the ritual during the *jadu* hour, but at that moment, I just wanted to be me.

I stood at the park's heart, acutely aware of time ticking away. The Firuzeh nestled against my skin seemed to throb in harmony with my heartbeat, a subtle connection to an ancient power. I traced my fingers over the pendant around my neck and then over the others I wore, each containing a sliver of magic.

Standing among all those people, enveloped by the chatter and laughter of unfamiliar faces, I felt transformed, unbreakable. A foreign source of power had surged within me, coursing through my veins.

I sensed someone's eyes on me, a lingering gaze that prickled the back of my neck. Despite the urge to look around, I resisted, knowing my eyes would inevitably meet theirs once I scanned the crowd. They had probably seen me, arms outstretched, head to the sky in a trance. They couldn't see what I felt inside. *Show them!* I just had to figure out what these newfound powers did so that I could look them in the eyes and provide them with the performance of a lifetime. *Show them true marvel!*

As much as I tried to resist it, I couldn't help it. I found myself compelled to glance to my right and look at the person who had been watching me. My heart plummeted. He was staring as if he knew who was hiding beneath the costume. I didn't have to do what I did next, yet his intense stare ignited a spark, a desire to engage in a game. Slowly but deliberately, I turned my body to align with my gaze, lifting my chin ever so slightly. I removed the hood, showing my face hidden behind the attached veil. Our eyes locked for a heartbeat, a charged silence passing between us. I broke it by winking, waking him from the trance. That simple gesture jolted him awake, prompting him to shove aside the people blocking his way. I couldn't help but smile as I pulled the hood back over my head and turned to leave. My pace quickened, but I didn't run. It was a subtle invitation for him to follow. *Why am I inviting this danger?* Maybe I wanted him to catch up with me, but what would I say? Would he try to kill me in front of all these people?

Fear gripped me when I realized he had disappeared in the crowd, and I couldn't see him. *I need to get the hell out of this park.* I turned the fast pace into a slow run, made my way out of the park, crossed the road, and slipped into the alley where The Nob was situated. My steps slowed back to a brisk walk. I convinced myself that I had shaken him off, at least for the time being. This alley was so much more creepy and depressing than I had remembered. The dumpsters were overfilled with trash, and the stench didn't disappoint. One block farther, I took a left turn; my car was parked on 7th Street. I kept the scythe firmly in my grip, maintaining the aesthetics of my costume.

"Please, don't run." His voice cut through the air, stopping me in my tracks before I could even turn around. How had he managed to teleport without being seen? How careless of him to do it in public. I really must have driven him mad.

He was so close I could smell him.

"Let go of my arm, or I'll make a scene," I threatened, even though, deep down, I knew I wouldn't. We stood in the shadow of a massive tree, right in front of a green triplex. Someone was walking on the other side of the street, oblivious to our existence.

"Just give me one minute—please," he pleaded, releasing his grip on my arm. He hesitated, then reached for my hood, pulling it back slowly to reveal my face. I could feel my hair was a little static.

He pulled me toward him, his arms enveloping me until my feet left the ground. I didn't resist—I couldn't. I realized I had missed him so much. The moment felt surreal, a bittersweet reunion that tugged at my heart until something unpleasant fired up in my chest like heartburn. Unwanted images of him and Dissie flickered before my eyes. I tried to pull away, to break free from his grasp. His forehead was pressed against my shoulder, and in that instant, I could have sworn I felt his body shudder.

"Let me go, Adam."

"I can't." His voice trembled.

I shook off his arms and fought my emotions. "I don't even know what's worse. That you took my soul or that you slept with Dissie."

"I didn't. I swear I didn't sleep with her. You don't understand—" he pleaded desperately.

"No, I understand plenty, Adam. I saw you kissing her, touching her—"

"Because I had to kill her. I swear it wasn't anything romantic. She was a part of a coven. They are dangerous witches, my fath—" I silenced his words with a sharp gesture. He choked on his own explanation, his face contorting in shock. Without laying a finger on him, I pushed him against the rough bark of a large tree. I didn't care if anyone saw. I would get out of this town and leave him to the mess.

"*We* are dangerous. You're right about that," I declared. With that, I released him and walked away. He remained rooted to the spot. He didn't chase me, but part of me wanted him to.

٣٥

THIRTY-FIVE

<h1 style="text-align:center">ADAM</h1>

I was outside of myself, suspended and disconnected from my own senses. My heart was pounding in my chest. Confusion and questions swirled in my mind, obscuring my thoughts. She walked off as if she didn't care, as if I was a forgotten chapter in her story, a tale she had outgrown. She had chosen a path that didn't include me, but it wasn't supposed to end like this. I didn't think she would leave me.

Had Maya been one of them all along? The realization clawed at the edges of my mind, the taste of betrayal bitter on my tongue. *No! It's not true.* Why didn't she tell me? Why wasn't she wearing a turquoise gemstone? I trusted her with my family's secrets. So, why didn't she trust me? How did we end up here, my family, against her coven? If I didn't partake in whatever my father had planned, my brothers could find her before me and kill her, and if I submitted to my father's schemes and went looking for her, she would see it as a dagger aimed at her heart. Would my family put two and two together if they saw her? I know I didn't because my grief shattered all rationality within me, leaving my mind in ruins. If she just hadn't based our entire relationship on a lie, then maybe this wouldn't have happened. I wanted to say I wasn't hurt, but I was. I didn't know where to go from here, what clues to follow, or how to protect her. Whether she liked it or not, I wasn't going to let her be slaughtered by my family. She had no idea who she was up against. If I could kill Dissie so easily, then so could everyone else. I was the one who kicked off the hunting season, and my brothers felt pressured to follow my lead. I had to get the witch hunt under control and keep them away from her.

٣٦

THIRTY-SIX

Maya

He clearly still loved me. I could tell he had missed me as much as I had missed him. It was all very conflicting. *Get a grip! You can't dismiss your duties as a Sāher because of a boy!* They were right. I had to stop the Dūshevs from taking any more souls. My ancestors were more bearable now that I was on the right path. They did everything to help me focus and grow stronger. Though, sometimes, they crossed some of my boundaries. Whenever I didn't veil, I could feel them meddling, whispering in my ears. They weren't harmful or destructive, but I still felt violated. Sometimes, I just wanted to be alone in my head.

Back in Iran, the task of finding the first four oldest sons was the only thing on my mind. Because of their abilities, they could be anywhere, making them seem impossible to locate. I tried to gain perspective by sketching the world map on my bedroom wall, hoping the visual representation would spark an idea. Removing my veil, I stared at the map as if the continents held some secret clue. Perhaps, if I stared long enough . . .

I stepped back from the wall and instinctively touched my necklace. The moment I touched it, a vivid flashback flooded my mind of the day I shattered the Firuzeh into pieces. Her face, hauntingly pensive, illuminated my thoughts, and suddenly, clarity washed over me. I knew what I had to do. I grabbed my shawl from the bed, my fingers trembling with a newfound determination. *I have to call Ashrafi and ask him to take me downtown, specifically to the gold market.*

Ashrafi stopped a few blocks from the market, the same spot he had waited for me last time. When I finally got there, the hollowed wall was empty. She wasn't there; there was absolutely no sign of her or the tray of sand. I asked around, but no one knew who I was talking about. The shopkeeper told me that the hole in the wall was once a mailbox. I trudged back to Ashrafi, defeated, uncertainty pressing down on my shoulders. *What now?*

As I neared his car, I noticed Ashrafi engaged in a heated exchange with a woman. His back was turned to me and covered her entire silhouette.

"*Khanum*, I'm waiting for someone else," he told her.

"We can take her first, then you can drive me home," I said.

However, when he moved out of the way, I saw it was the sand-tray lady. This couldn't be a coincidence. She was holding what looked like an urn.

"My mistake, Ashrafi. This lady is coming home with me. She is my guest."

He drove us back home, and neither one of us spoke on the way. I couldn't understand why, but she didn't utter a single question or show any hesitation to come along. As we entered the house, I sensed Shirin's watchful gaze from the living room, her eyes following our every move. Upon entering my bedroom, the sand-tray lady's attention was immediately drawn to the world map that covered an entire wall. Her eyes locked onto it, studying the details.

"I need you to help me find them," I said.

"We are not alone," she said. I knew that. Someone was holding their breath outside my bedroom. Sand-tray lady didn't care; she gently lifted the lid from the urn, allowing the sand to cascade like a waterfall onto the floor. Instead of forming a pile, it spread out, snaking its way across the room, enveloping every inch of the floor. I took a step toward the door and saw the sand around my feet fill out the footstep. I opened the door and found Lara eavesdropping.

"I thought maybe you needed help," she said.

"I do. Get me Sepideh, then go to the market and find me the biggest world map you can find." Lara forced a fake smile and started shouting for Sepideh.

Sepideh came in and looked around the room, then at the sand-tray lady, and finally at me.

"I want you to mark every exposed area with a circle," I said and handed her a marker from the desk.

"What exposed area?" she asked, confused.

"You'll get it in a minute." I locked the door to my room and shut the blinds. "Let's hope this works," I told them both. It would've been smarter if I had drawn the world map on the floor instead of the wall. I took a deep breath and removed my scarf, realizing that this task demanded far more effort than I was used to. With some help from the spirits, I got a hold of the energy and enclosed it in my left hand. I struggled like hell to keep it there. My knees were trembling, and my body heated up. The sand responded, gliding across the floor and ascending the walls. The sand-tray lady approached, her fingers tracing patterns that vanished in seconds, replaced by the relentless advance of the sand. With her retreat, the sand began to swirl, forming a flat tornado on the wall.

I continued to hold the energy, my vision dimming, the room growing hazier until only shadows remained. My senses slowly shut down, making way for the energy to flow unabated. It felt like an eternity had passed before I sensed a hand on my shoulder.

You can let go now, I heard as an echo. I let go, my knees buckled, and I collapsed. *You did good.*

A long time had passed since I had been resurrected, but time was different. The hours and days blurred together like they weren't real. *They are real enough for now.* In the beginning, I thought I would somehow go back to my old life, but winter deepened, bringing the unyielding wind with it, and I finally realized there was nothing for me to go back to. I had no friends or family left. Everything changed, and I only had the Sāhers. *It's all you need.* How did I even end up here—*agreeing to all of this. No, it's the right thing to do.*

The journey was to begin, and I was here to find the fourth son. I only had a day or two before jumping into something I couldn't take back. It didn't help that I was in a country where I didn't speak the language. I had never heard anything about Romania, except for the mention of Dracula, if that even counted. The streets of Timișoara were beautiful and very European-esque, with colorful old buildings and historical charm. Also, they felt frightfully familiar. This was the city I would find him in, and it would also be the place where he met his end. Of course, he didn't have to, but I had seen his death. I didn't know exactly where it would happen, but it wasn't far from my hotel.

I strolled through the narrow streets and alleys multiple times to grasp their essence. Each time I passed a particular bridal shop, his face haunted my mind. I had Sepideh accompanying me this time; this was her moment to prove herself. Placing all my trust in her capability, or lack thereof, to revive me, I was putting my fate entirely in her hands. If the Dūshev decided to kill me, all my powers would be transferred to her, including his ability to teleport, if I had done my preparations right. She should be able to teleport and take me back to a safe place where she could perform the ritual. I wasn't even sure if I would come back at all. I could die, and it would be the end of it. The worst part was I was okay with that. I didn't care anymore. If we succeeded, it would be solely because of the Dūshev himself. He would be the blood sacrifice needed to resurrect me. He was the master of his fate, and nothing would befall him if he chose not to retaliate.

The next day, we set up the altar, preparing for the possibility that Sepideh might be forced to go through with the ritual. Dabbling with necromancy wasn't the desired method, but we didn't have much of a choice. A sense of anticipation was around me; I had a feeling the day had come, and I would finally meet him. I chugged a tall glass of water, ate a few dates, and left the room, carrying myself as though I might not return. It was pitch black outside. Sepideh hurried behind me.

"You can't follow me. If he sees you, we're both dead," I said.

"I know. Did you remember to bring the fake necklace?"

"Yeah, I'm wearing it," I replied, pulling it out from under my shirt. It wasn't exactly fake. It was still a genuine turquoise, just not the one they were on the lookout for. Sepideh went back in, and I ended up wandering the city for two hours. The shops hadn't opened yet, so why were people out and about at this early hour? I found myself back in front of the bridal shop again, contemplating how often they sold dresses. It seemed like a very fancy shop.

"It translates to *love doesn't cost*—or more like *you can't buy love*. That explains it better," an old man suddenly said. I hadn't noticed him approaching, so his words caught me off guard. He was talking about the graffiti written in Romanian between the shop's two windows.

"So, what are you doing in Timişoara? Are you studying here?" he continued. I probably looked like a tourist, given that he spoke to me in English. I couldn't seem to categorize my visit here and ended up staring at him mutely.

"Good day," he said when he realized I wasn't going to respond. I didn't want to be rude, but there was so much going on in my head that I couldn't even form a sentence. Even though he was long gone, I walked in his footsteps and ended up at the big square every little street had led to. The street with the bridal shop was called Strada Alba Iulia, and the one after that Strada Gheorghe Lazăr. I was hoping that if I remembered my way back, I could manifest a slightly less grim outcome. I strolled across the square, compelled to pause and admire the stunning yellow church with towers that rose gracefully into the sky. From a distance, it appeared to be supported by six massive columns, but as I approached, I realized it was merely an architectural illusion. Maybe this was the last piece of art I would ever see, so I might as well enjoy it.

In an instant, a shock wave jolted the back of my head, and I sensed his presence. Swiveling around, I noticed a sudden influx of people bustling from one spot to another. I caught myself freaking out just as I needed to appear composed. Taking a deep breath, I closed my eyes and counted to seven, my impatience not letting me get to ten. When I opened my eyes, I found him. His back faced me as he disappeared into a narrow street.

I pulled out a map of the city, nonchalantly trailing him. His pace gradually slowed, suggesting he might have sensed me shadowing him. Fuck! We got to this gloomy street with no shops or people at all. The creepiest thing was the Christmas trees hanging bottom side up from wall to wall on a wire. Rows after rows of fir trees executed after Christmas. I sensed his eyes on me as I pretended to study my map, a wave of anxiety washing over me. Just as I was about to catch up, he came to a halt, glancing into the alley to his right and checking his watch. With only a few feet between us, I realized it was now or never.

"Excuse me. Can you help me? I think I'm lost," I said to him.

He turned to face me, his smile disarming. He was an older man, perhaps in his mid-forties, his features lacking the typical Middle-Eastern appearance. He had pale skin, a heavy set of brows, and his teeth were all over the place.

"For a moment there, I thought you were following me. Where are you headed?" he asked, his eyes flicking down to my map. As he rummaged in his pocket for his reading glasses, I noticed the subtle movement of his hands.

"Strada Alba Iulia," I replied, my voice steady despite the growing tension in my chest.

"You are walking in the opposite direction, my dear. You have to go back to—"

"You have something on your neck." I interrupted him and extended my hand. My fingers reached out, and in one swift motion, I cut through his skin just enough to draw a single drop of blood. The instant my fingertips brushed against his skin, a surge of energy coursed through me. It was as if I had tapped into his very essence. In that fleeting moment, I felt his strength enveloping me as if I had become him, if only for a second. His sudden jump caused me to retract my hand instinctively.

"Oh, I'm so sorry," I said. My words were laced with feigned innocence. Then I looked at my nails for blood, and at that moment, I lost control. My thumb rubbed against my forefinger in a compulsive, circular motion until the blood vanished, absorbed between my fingers. I didn't want him to see it, but his eyes bore into mine, catching the brief lapse. I didn't even have a moment to blink before he yanked me into the narrow alley to our right. I attempted to scream, but his hand clamped over my mouth, silencing me ruthlessly.

"Don't play games with me, little girl," he whispered. I fought to breathe, to focus, to find a way out. I knew I could fight him if I harnessed his powers, if I tapped into his strength. His abilities were mine to command. I relaxed my body entirely and closed my eyes. As he loosened his grip, thinking he had me under control, I seized the opportunity. Bracing myself, I thrust him backward into the wall, breaking free from his clutches but not from the dark energy coursing through my veins. I gasped for air, feeling as if I couldn't breathe, but I pushed through it. He advanced toward me, and I didn't hesitate. Summoning all the power I had absorbed from him, I collided with him, slamming him against the cold brick wall. Surprised by my unexpected strength, he chuckled.

"You're feisty," he said.

I tried to throw a punch, but he moved so fast, causing my fist to connect with the wall. Pain seared through my knuckles from the failed punch, leaving me momentarily stunned, and there was no respite. Before I could recover, he seized me by the throat, his fingers digging into my skin. Gasping for air, I was forced to the ground, the rough surface biting into my back. His thumbs pressed mercilessly into my windpipe, cutting off my ability to breathe. I struggled beneath his grip, desperate for even a gasp of air, but his hold tightened, and the world around me started to blur.

"Your kind will never stand a chance," he said as he hammered his fist down on my chest, and everything went black.

I was freezing to the bone, my body seized by an icy grip that numbed my senses and fogged my thoughts. My eyes strained to perceive anything, but it was darkness that surrounded me. Had I gone blind? Each breath I took felt like inhaling shards of glass, suffocating me in the frigid air. I gasped for air, sounding like a wheezy old man had smoked his whole life. "Fuck!" I groaned, and suddenly, everything became bright. Sepideh sat upright on her bed and looked at me.

"I'm cold," I managed to say. It's like I couldn't move. *Fuck! Am I paralyzed?* I strained every muscle, attempting to move, fearing the worst but then a small victory: a wiggle of my toes brought an overwhelming sense of relief. I wasn't paralyzed; I was simply battered, my body aching as if it had been trampled by a truck. Sepideh, roused from her slumber, took a moment to register the situation. With a sudden awareness of my state, she hurriedly rose and fetched another blanket, her eyes reflecting concern and pity. I could see in her eyes the recognition of my dire condition. I was a wreck, a mere semblance of a person. I didn't know how long I had been gone. I didn't remember anything, as if I had been asleep without any dreams to anchor my consciousness. I had become so used to dreaming that it was odd being without.

In a desperate attempt to rise, I found myself screaming at the top of my lungs, the agony ripping through me. I didn't know where the pain came from or why it hurt so goddamn much. With another futile effort, I tried to push myself up, only to let out a guttural cry and collapse back onto the bed, each movement sending shockwaves of anguish through my broken body. Tears streamed down my face, and I couldn't make them stop. My chest was tearing up from the inside. The shards of broken ribs pierced my lungs with every breath and every move I made. Summoning what little strength remained, I dragged myself to the bathroom and met my reflection in the mirror. Dark circles clung to my sunken eyes, my forehead a grotesque landscape of swelling, my cheeks gaunt, and my hair looked like it had been blow-dried for six hours straight. My gaze fell to my neck, and there, in the hollow of my throat, a mysterious tattoo marked my skin—a Rune, perhaps, or a sigil. Sepideh came up behind me.

"What is this?" I asked.

"The tattoo manifested the moment you drew your first breath. A symbol—or a checkmark, if you will—of the first task completed," she said.

I put a hand on my chest and realized the bait necklace was gone. *I did it!* I wasn't sure if it was the fact that I successfully completed a task or if it was something else driving me, but I felt like I was finally good for something. *You are useful. You are needed. You are powerful.*

I finally healed and could walk again without the agonizing pain. The healing happened by itself after Sepideh had performed the ritual. My skin and bones, my cells, everything worked independently to mend me, to ready me for my next task. We were standing on Piata Uniri, enjoying a brief moment of peace on what was probably my last birthday. *The prophecy is in motion.* I closed my eyes and took a deep breath. *It's all that matters. Now, pay attention!*

I felt pressure against my back, butt, and the back of my head. The sensation of lying down on a hard surface slowly registered, pulling me out of the void of unconsciousness. With a jolt, I opened my eyes, greeted by a surreal scene that unfolded before me. Rough, polished wooden floors contrasted sharply with the cool, metallic touch of chrome under my fingertips. I had grabbed onto a chair for support. The air was tainted with the pungent smell of spilled beer. I was sprawled out on the floor of what appeared to be a café-type bar. Every detail seemed etched into my mind: the faint hum of conversation, the flickering neon lights casting eerie shadows, and the occasional clinking of glasses in the background. I understood—this was no ordinary blackout. My eyes fixated on someone at the bar, a fierce determination burning within them. At that moment, I knew I wanted the bartender. I wanted his blood on my hands, his soul in my grasp, a craving that clawed at the very core of my being, threatening to consume me whole.

٣٧

THIRTY-SEVEN

Adam

Housekeepers hurried around, their footsteps echoing in the empty halls, packing everything from the art on the walls to the books in our library; all of it was put into boxes. I had returned after being away from the facilities for a few days, left in the dark about the upheaval. Per usual, the Elders treated me with indifference, like I didn't matter. Blind to the countless hours I spent with their children, guiding them, teaching them the ways of our kind to hone their skills and transform them into adept Dūshevs. In all my frustration, I walked upstairs and rapped on my father's office door.

"Can I have a word with you?" I asked.

He motioned me in. "Just the one I was looking for," my father said. "Have you decided on a place to stay?"

"I don't understand. Why is the house being emptied out?"

"Were you not informed this morning? This is not a matter we take lightly. Surely, Edgar told you." His brows knitted with concern. I bit back a retort. Of course, Edgar didn't tell me anything. I would bet my soul he forgot to mention this small fact on purpose. If I told my father this, he would think me a brat not able to get along with yet another brother.

"Our facilities have been compromised, and in order to protect the institution's secrets, we must evacuate immediately."

"Compromised how—who are we running from?"

"Adam, for God's sake," my father sighed. "Their high priestess has initiated the first step of this war. She has humiliated us, and I will not stand by and let my whole legacy fall because of a mere girl. She and her coven must be eradicated." This was serious. Was he talking about her? Had she been here, or was it someone from her coven? My father never mentioned other covens or their high priestesses. We knew of them and the regions they occupied, but they were of no threat to us because we were vastly different from them. We had real powers and did not cast imaginary spells or boil herbs and powders to make potions. It was hard to believe my father felt threatened by one of these mere witches. Did he really believe anyone could stand a chance against us? Even Maya, I could take if I wanted to. She had power, but not enough to take me down.

"Adam . . . Adam!" My father said twice before I reacted.

"Yes?"

"Have you decided on a specific place you will stay during all of this?" *During all of this . . .* He wanted me to stay out of it. He didn't even deem me worthy of fighting for us.

"I have a small place in Scotland. I think I will go there," I lied. I would be a part of this whether he liked it or not. Of course, I wasn't entirely sure what Maya's part was in this, but I was going to stop her from getting herself killed. I had to weigh my options and pull in some favors amongst my brothers because this could very well end horribly. Maya had no idea what she was getting herself into.

"There is one more thing," I said. "I heard Zaki and Erik talking about volunteering for the vaults—"

"Don't be concerned with everyone else. Keep a steady head and an eye on your own path," my father answered vaguely. I had no more patience left in me for his games and riddles, and I wasn't going to accept being left out of absolutely everything.

"Father, I will make it my concern either way."

"Don't be ridiculous." He waved a dismissive hand. "We can't take any risks. I need my strongest to stay behind. You will stay in your place until I say so! Now, gather your belongings and stay away from here until further notice."

I left my father with the promise of keeping myself alive and away from the enemy, but I wasn't sure if I was going to keep my promise. It all depended on Maya. I knew my fate was entwined with hers, and I couldn't stay away. Perhaps it was time to find my own way instead of being an extension of my father.

In the middle of February, I relented and decided to visit Kristian. He had begged me to come because no one else would disobey my father's orders. He wasn't exactly on the list of brothers I was going to ask for help from, but he was a good time. I always had a laugh with him. The only annoying thing about Kristian was that he was so goddamn competitive. Even when he knew he was losing, he would never give up a fight or an argument. Everything was a game to him, no matter the cost.

Kristian owned a hybrid café that turned into a pub in the evening. Sometimes, he went there to actually manage the place, but most of the time, he was there to have fun. Kristian was a lady's man and very charming, but he was also a cheat. He never wasted an opportunity with a woman.

Kristian stood behind the bar because his employee had called in sick. He had started slicing lime wedges and was so focused you would think he enjoyed doing mundane tasks. Meanwhile, I was having another beer by myself, trying to enjoy the moment. Still, whenever the door opened, I felt the bitter air hitting the back of my neck, ruining my experience.

"Here's a shot to warm you up," Kristian said like he had read my mind. Then he went back to waiting on another customer. The door opened again, and this time, I actually turned to scowl at whoever entered. I almost fell from my stool when I realized who was at the door. She was dressed up; her hair was tied back, her lips tinted, and she wore all black. She saw me and didn't even flinch. *Is she joking?* She came straight to the bar and approached Kristian. I couldn't believe my eyes and stared at her like a maniac. *Why is she pretending not to see me?* Maybe I had one too many drinks, or maybe this was someone who looked like her. *I am losing it.*

"Heyya, what can I do for you?" Kristian said to her.

"Can I have a cup of black tea, please?" It was her voice! I was not making it up.

"The other end, love," he said, pointing to the opposite side of the bar where the kitchen was serving. "You can order tea and food there."

"What a shame," she said, her eyes flicking between him and the busy kitchen staff. Was she really flirting with him, knowing full well I was listening?

"I only serve liquor, love." He smiled, his eyes meeting hers with a mischievous glint.

"Then, I'll have a gin and tonic." Her body subtly shifted, leaning slightly toward him, her lips curling in a playful smile. I continued to watch her, captivated by her every move. She effortlessly slid out of her leather jacket, revealing a hint of a tattoo in the hollow of her neck. *This isn't her. It can't be.* Our eyes met briefly before she reached for the drink that Kristian had prepared for her. With a practiced grace, her fingers brushed against his in a way that made my heart skip a beat. She was doing this to me deliberately, and she had no idea it was my brother she was messing with.

She made her way toward the back end of the café, disappearing from my view. I was still not processing what had just happened, trying to make sense of the situation, but my mind was clouded with confusion. Maybe if I had another shot, things would go back to normal.

"Who are you looking at?" Lost in my thoughts, I didn't notice Kristian watching me closely.

"Um, nothing."

He chuckled softly, shaking his head. "I mean, you can shoot your shot, but I think she was into me."

The bar buzzed with activity around us. A group of guys approached the bar, their laughter and banter filling the air, creating the opportunity for me. This was my chance to talk to her without her making a scene. I walked over, pulling out a chair in front of her, my heart pounding in my chest.

"What are you doing here, and how did you find me?" I whispered to her and glanced back at Kristian.

"What makes you think I came here for you, baby?" Her eyes, dark and enigmatic, met mine without a hint of fear. I was completely stunned for a moment. *This is really happening.* "Maya, there is a war between our kinds. If my brother finds out what you are—"

"It's not a war . . . That would imply we both have an equal chance of victory. To me, it looks like your people will lose." Her words cut through the air like a sharp blade. She sipped her drink, and I couldn't help but notice the huge turquoise ring on her finger. So many thoughts raced through my mind, and I struggled to focus on one thing at a time.

"You need to hide that ring," I blurted out, my eyes darting back to Kristian. Did she understand the gravity of the situation? Could she see the storm of emotions raging inside me? This was no joke. My brother would kill her on the spot if he noticed.

"You need to get out of my way. I'm not here for you," she said with a dominance I hadn't heard before. She pulled away from me, her expression unreadable.

I reached for her hand, my fingers trembling. "I'm begging you, please don't reveal yourself to my brother. He will try to kill you." She pulled her hand back, her movements swift and deliberate, her eyes narrowing in response to my plea. She got up, scraping the chair against the floor. I rose, too, my movements mirroring hers as I refused to let her slip away from me again, so I followed her outside.

"If you would just mind your own business, you wouldn't be in the middle of this," she snapped and glanced from left to right, her eyes scanning the surroundings, before walking into a narrow alley that led to a parallel avenue.

"Can you stop walking for a minute, Maya?" I tried to stop her as delicately as I could. I couldn't afford to provoke her anger, not now.

She whipped around, her eyes ablaze with defiance. "What do you want?"

"I'm bending over backward trying to keep you away from my family, and you come here flirting with my brother!" I gestured toward the bar. "Last month, my other brother killed one of the witches and returned with her necklace. It could have been you! Don't you see that?"

Her lips curved into a smile. "How is your brother doing right now?" she asked.

"This is not a joke. What is wrong with you? Have you lost your mind?" I caught myself raising my voice, and she followed suit.

"No! I lost my soul!"

I shattered. I suddenly couldn't breathe. "Take it," I said, walking toward her, my movements unsteady. "Take everything I have. Just don't leave me again." My voice broke, and I fell to my knees. She let me fall into her, my head bowed, leaning on her. One hand found its place behind her leg, and another rested on her heart, seeking to return what I had taken. It felt like we had both stopped breathing, and suddenly, our hearts were in sync.

"Take it," I whispered, my voice barely audible, and I prepared to release the only soul I had left, but she pulled away.

"Whether you meant to do it or not, this was going to happen. I was meant to lose my soul. You just ended up being the one who took it," she said, her voice calm and resolute.

"You know I would never do this to you."

She was looking at me, her gaze unyielding, and then her demeanor changed. There was a shift in the air, a subtle movement of energy. "Tomorrow night, I'll leave you breadcrumbs. The trail starts at the Fremont Hotel. Catch me if you can," she said, taking a step back, and in an instant, she adʰāred, leaving behind a void and my astonishment. *How?* I had so many unresolved issues with this girl, and she was toying with me like never before, but what choice did I have?

٣٨

THIRTY-EIGHT

Maya

Meeting Adam was the last thing I had expected, and I had to think on my feet. Part of me longed for his touch, aching for the connection we once shared, while the other part suppressed those feelings. It was triggering, and for a moment, when his hand touched my chest, I was about to give in, ready to fall back into his arms and lose myself in the warmth of his embrace, forget what I was made of, who I was, and the mission ahead of me. Time stopped between us, and I felt a life force trying to enter my body, but I was jolted away from the moment. The pull felt involuntary and forced, like someone else was controlling me. When I stepped back and looked at him, I couldn't help but pity his ignorance. He had no inkling of the supernatural forces at play, no understanding of why he unwittingly took my soul, and what had to be done in order to restore the balance in the world. Despite my lingering affection for him, I knew what had to be done. The world was at stake, and the Dūshevs had to be stopped. In my heart, I hoped to spare Adam, now knowing he was innocent in his father's dark schemes. However, I couldn't afford the risk of jeopardizing my mission. I couldn't let my guard down, not even for a moment. If there was even the slightest chance that Adam might appear at the bar, all our efforts would be in vain.

I decided to take a different approach this time, determined to avoid the pain I had endured. I had no intention of getting hurt in his attempt to murder me. I would seduce him instead, making him believe I was an easy target, a quick hook-up. Who would say no to that? Certainly not a flirt like him. Knowing Adam could decide to drop in made the plan risky, but I was willing to play if it meant accomplishing my mission. I didn't come here to be nice.

The early evening cast a subdued atmosphere over the bar. As I entered, I noticed him immediately, his eyes lingering on me with unmistakable interest. There was only a handful of people scattered around, minding their own business. I met his gaze with a confidence I didn't truly feel. I walked toward him with purposeful strides, maintaining the intensity of our eye contact, silently displaying my intentions without uttering a word.

"Gin and tonic?" he asked.

I played my part convincingly, accepting the drink with a sly smile. "That's not exactly what I came for, but I'll take what I can get."

"No, I insist. How can I help you?" he asked and took the bait.

"I can think of a thing or two," I teased, luring him deeper into the game, watching as he eagerly fetched a bottle of tequila. With it, he brought lime wedges and salt. I dipped my finger into the tequila shot he poured, pressed it into the salt, and licked it slowly, making sure he saw.

I took the shot, letting the tequila burn down my throat to ease what I was about to do next.

"Can I borrow the staff restroom? I promise I won't tell a *soul*," I asked, flashing him a coy smile. He met my gaze, his expression turning playful. "Maybe you can even help me with my zipper—it always gets stuck," I added. His eyes sparkled with mischief as he gestured for me to follow him. Behind the bar, he led me into their back room. Once inside, I turned to face him, our eyes locking.

"You are a cheeky devil, aren't you?" he said.

I leaned in, my lips brushing against his ear as I whispered, "You have no idea." My fingers gently tracing the lines of his arm.

One thing led to another, and before I knew it, we were going at it in the staff restroom. His hands were rough, pulling my hair, his lips tracing a searing path along my neck. I bit my tongue, stifling any involuntary response of repulsion. His fingers, eager and searching, tore off my shirt in a frenzy of urgency. As he exposed my skin, I seized the opportunity, slipping one hand beneath his sweater. Gently, I trailed my fingernails across his back. He seemed to enjoy the sensation, his breathing growing heavier with each caress. I steeled myself for the real moment, knowing the wound had to be precise. It had to be deep enough to draw blood, yet not so deep that it would trigger him. I continued my charade, keeping him distracted, with my other hand sliding into his pants. The room pulsed with erratic heartbeats, muffled moans, and the occasional gasp of my *pleasure*. My nails finally scratched his back hard enough to draw blood, but he seemed to enjoy it. His hand slipped under my bra, his grip firm as he pulled my hair back, exposing my neck.

I thought I had it under control, but a sudden surge of instinct pulled me back and forced me to push him away. My focus shifted to my fingers, now stained with his blood, moving in circles, a ritual meant to harness the power I needed to fulfill my mission and protect the world from the Dūshevs.

His eyes widened in horror as he spotted the blood on my hand and the turquoise ring. *Fuck!* I ruined it. Panic flickered across his face. "How could I be so stupid?" In an instant, he lunged toward me, his fingers closing around my throat like a snake, cutting off my air supply. The world blurred, and a suffocating darkness crept at the edges of my vision. I didn't fight him. It was almost impossible to resist the urge to fight back. Every instinct screamed for survival, but a strange calm settled over me. It was easier to let him kill me. My last thoughts were of the prophecy and the world I sought to protect.

٣٩

THIRTY-NINE

Sepideh

Gosh, how I love this feeling of power. I thought she had failed, but she came through. A surge of immense energy and strength entered my body, and I knew it was done. I felt transformed, my senses heightened and my abilities magnified. Maya told me this Dūshev was even more powerful than the last, and facing him had probably been a great challenge. She had located him yesterday at a bar, accompanied by another Dūshev, so we both had to be extra careful. I don't know how she managed to separate them, but she did, and now I was standing in her power. This was only my second time channeling Maya's powers, and I still felt a lack of control. So, I surrendered, allowing my ancestors to guide my actions. I closed my eyes and offered to become a vessel for their ancient wisdom and strength. In an instant, I found myself teleported to a dimly lit bathroom with two stalls. Maya's lifeless body lay sprawled in the stall, her eyes open and empty. I checked for a pulse and found none. Her state was a grim testament to what the Dūshev had done. She was still wearing her pants, but her shirt and jacket were tossed on the floor. I couldn't tell if he had raped her, then dressed her or if he didn't get that far before killing her. Swiftly, I collected her belongings and held her hand, preparing to transport both of us back to our hotel room.

It was nearly impossible to carry her to the bed because the powers were wearing off. Still, I managed. Then I cast a protective circle around her bed, calling upon the protectors of the towers and assistance from our ancestors. With practiced precision, I scraped off the remaining dried blood from Maya's fingers with the obsidian athame, blending it with potent ingredients from the earth: mandrake root, graveyard soil, baneful marsh water, and belladonna. The mixture ground into a paste, which I used to carefully inscribe a sigil on her chest. I let the ancestors guide my hand and mark her. Soon enough, she would wake up, gasping for air, as if she was drowning, and all the signs of her death would slowly disappear, except for the second tattoo that would mark her skin. Just like the scar of my blood oath to her, the tattoos would prove her loyalty to the Sāhers.

٤٠

FORTY

After looking for her for nearly twenty-five minutes at that damn hotel, I knew something was off. I thought she was avoiding me and never thought she would return to the bar after seeing me there. I only realized what a moron I had been when Kristian called me.

"That girl from yesterday. Did she try to scratch you with her nails?" he asked.

"No?" My heart was racing, my mind trying to process his words. I had no idea where he was going with this.

"Can you come to the bar real quick?" The urgency in his voice spurred me into action. I retraced my steps, and I hurried back to Kristian's bar. I couldn't afford to waste another moment but couldn't exactly aďhār in broad daylight, either. I swung open the door to the bar and scanned the room. My eyes darted around, searching for any signs of her, but she wasn't there. Kristian motioned for me to follow him to his staff room.

"What's going on?"

"I had my head so far up my arse I didn't realize she was one of them until it was too late," he whispered. His confession sent a shiver down my spine. "Did you know?"

"What do you mean?" I tried to stay composed, the movement of my hands steady, hoping he couldn't hear the tremor in my voice, though my fingers trembled slightly.

"She came in, flirting with me, saying all these things, and you know I'm an idiot—didn't even see her ring until it was too late." He pulled out her ring from his pocket. I almost had a heart attack. I took the ring from him to examine it.

"This doesn't feel real," I said. *Please tell me she got away.*

"The ring is the least of my problems. I don't know if she performed a ritual on me or whatever the fuck she did—my head was somewhere else. I swear she got me good. She was tearing at my clothes, scratching me with her nails. My dick was pulsing, and I couldn't get in fast enough, then suddenly—"

"You had sex with her!" I blurted out involuntarily. I almost couldn't breathe. She had sex with my brother to get back at me. *She had sex with Kristian . . .*

"No, the bitch didn't even let me fuck her before she dug her nails into my skin. When I realized what she was doing—because I would have fucked her, but you know, Idris told me about Timișoara, so I killed her and—"

"YOU DID WHAT?"

"Shhh. Stop yelling. That's why I called you. What are we going to do with her body? I can't leave it here."

"Where is she, Kristian?" I asked, my voice sharp with dread. *This is not happening again!* I couldn't deal with it. I couldn't survive another round of this mayhem.

"Calm down. You're fuming. She is still in the stall where I left her."

I took a deep breath, attempting to steady my senses, and slowly walked to the bathrooms, with Kristian trailing behind me. I didn't rush, hoping against the odds that something would change in the time it took us to get there. I reached for the door handle and turned, but the door resisted.

"Obviously, I didn't leave it open," Kristian said, unlocking the door and walking in before me.

"Where is she?" I asked as he pushed both stall doors open.

"I swear this is where I left her." He was suddenly frantic. This was some sort of trick. Clearly, she had a way of escaping death. Either Maya had become immortal, or she was really good at playing dead. A drop of sweat slid down my temple, and a sigh escaped from me. Something I hoped he didn't take note of. I don't know what I would have done to him if her body was in that stall. Kristian was too flustered to notice the change in my breathing.

"You don't understand. I strangled her. There was no pulse when I left her."

Then, he described everything that had happened in great detail. I tried to block the images of his hands all over her body. She would have gone all the way with him hadn't he noticed the ring on her finger. Was she punishing me? Seeking revenge by going after my family?

"We have to meet with Father. He will know what to do," Kristian said.

"He will have a fit when he finds out we were hanging out." In truth, I didn't want my father to know of my involvement with anything concerning Maya. Not that Kristian had any inkling about who she really was.

"I know, but we both need to tell him everything we know about her. You talked to her for quite some time. She must have said something," Kristian urged.

I nodded. I had no choice but to go along with this charade, the flow of events spiraling beyond my control.

Edgar only gave us the location of my father's whereabouts because Kristian called for an emergency meeting. Despite being one of the youngest elders, Edgar had significant influence. His whispers in my father's ears carried weight, guiding his decisions. My father had chosen to self-exile in Tuscany, residing in a modest home he used to live in when he was young and childless. The house had remained empty ever since. We had a lot of property like that around the world. Some of the houses were falling apart because they had been abandoned. This particular house, however, stood well-maintained, as if time had forgotten to touch it. He had brought two maids with him to help out around the house. I couldn't figure out what had changed about my father, but something was different; he looked a little frail.

Kristian began recounting the events that had unfolded, and when he finished, my father looked at me.

"Why did you initially approach her?" His gaze probing, as if he sought the truth hidden within my words. He had asked me that before. That exact sentence. It felt like he knew, trying to make me confess to the crime.

"Because she was good-looking, and I was bored," I said.

"Can you describe her to me?" His eyes shifted between us.

"She had long black hair and black eyes, too," Kristian said.

"You mean dark brown," my father said.

"No, they were really black. Like a demon."

My father turned his attention to me, his gaze penetrating. "Was there anything familiar about her?" Drops of sweat slid down the back of my neck. *He knows.* I wanted to be honest with him. I really did.

"She looked like any other Middle-Eastern girl, I would say. But, yes, she did remind me of the girl I killed." I had to give him something.

He crossed his legs and looked at Kristian. "There was a ring?"

Kristian immediately got up, retrieving the ring from his jacket. "But isn't it odd that I experienced the same thing as Idris?" he said and handed my father the ring.

"Idris is dead," my father announced nonchalantly while inspecting the ring.

"What!" we both exclaimed.

How is your brother doing right now . . . Did she do that? I should've told my father from the beginning. I was way too deep into the lie, and if I were to have said something, he would never forgive me.

"What happened to him?" Kristian demanded, fear flickering in his eyes.

"This is another replica. These women are cunning. We do not know what happened to Idris. It seems like he slept in," my father said, placing the ring on the side table.

"Adam, I need you to meet me in Egypt in two days. Kristian, I will need you to stay here for the next couple of weeks."

"Weeks, what for?"

"You need to be examined. There might still be traces of her on you."

"And what do you need me for?" I asked.

"To begin your duties, of course." His words hung in the air, laden with implications. Uncertainty clung to me like a ghost. Maybe he wanted to separate the two of us, or perhaps he was apprehensive about Kristian and thought he would die.

Two days later, I was in Egypt, as per my father's request. I had no idea what to expect, my mind a whirlwind of thoughts and concerns. My father hadn't explicitly stated his intentions, but his insinuations were enough. All of a sudden, he wanted my participation, and he wanted it before time. This meeting could very well have been an ambush, a carefully laid trap waiting for me to step on.

For the first time, this place looked haunted to me. There were already cobwebs and dust collecting in the corners. Every step I took made an echo on the walls. I walked up the stairs and had a look around. All rooms were empty, shrouded in shadows. In the unsettling stillness, Nashir emerged, slithering through the air like a snake on the prowl. She moved with a predatory grace, her eyes gleaming.

"They are waiting for you in the grand hall," she said.

I could hear the faint murmur of voices seeping through the cracks around the closed doors. As I raised my hand to push the doors open, the voices ceased abruptly. I pushed the doors open and stepped inside. The room was bathed in a dim light, casting long shadows across their faces. They were seated in their customary positions, their eyes closed, lost in a deep meditative state. Their traditional attire consisted of modern-day black suits that stood stark against the opulent golden great hall. Edgar's eyes met mine as he rose from his seat.

"We're glad you could make it," he said, as if I had a choice. He closed the door behind me, the sound of the lock clicking into place resonating in the room. Locking the door seemed silly, but I understood the need for secrecy, especially with the maids around.

"Father, shall we begin?" Edgar asked.

My father was the only one not meditating, fully occupied with a book.

"Very well," he said sand closed the book he was reading. As he did that, the other elders woke from their trance. They all got up from their seats, my father with them. He approached me, his hands reaching out to grasp mine, the elders standing behind him, their presence commanding.

"What's going on?" I asked.

"Adam, do you vow to stand by and protect this family?" my father asked, his words carrying the weight of his expectation.

"Of course. When have I not?" I replied, even though I sensed something deeper at play.

"We never doubted your loyalty. This is just a ritual necessary in times of chaos," my father reassured me, though his words only deepened my concern.

"What ritual?"

"The line of succession," Herman said, stepping forward, presenting my father with a gleaming dagger. I felt a chill creeping up my spine as the significance of the moment settled in. Closing my eyes briefly, I attempted to adhār, but something was hindering me. A feeling of powerlessness washed over me. Did my father notice that I tried to escape? I looked like a fool, a coward.

"What about it?" I pressed, my heart pounding in my chest.

"Collectively, we decided it was best for everyone if you became my direct successor," my father said.

"Not because of your great love for me, I'm assuming."

"Don't be foolish. This is not the time to mess around. This is about who can and cannot take my place when I'm gone. Idris made me question the safety of our future. Prophecies against us are aligning, and it seems only you can take my place," my father explained. Until now, the position of the head of our family had always been my eldest brother's birthright, determined by age. My father, driven by a desperate need to alter our fate, wanted to change the rules, putting the weight of our family's future squarely on my shoulders. My father was the first Dūshev. He had learned valuable lessons as he ventured through the world, shaping his understanding of our unique powers. He loved the idea of a massive family so much that it went overboard. He didn't know it would be his last when he had his twenty-seventh son. And since a witch had killed Idris, my father was angsty. His reign had never been threatened before.

"What if I deny it?" I asked.

"It's your birthright to be the thirteenth in line, and we will not force you to step ahead of your brothers."

"Adam—"

"No." My father's firm voice cut through the room, silencing Herman. "It is his decision entirely."

"It's no big deal. I'll do it. Just know you wanted this." I turned my attention to the elders. "And I have no experience nor desire to rule over this family."

"Hopefully, it won't come to that," my father said and reached for my right hand, seeking my consent. "May I?"

I nodded, allowing him to proceed. The elders encircled us. My father took the dagger and carefully etched a symbol into my palm, the sting of the blade oddly distant in my mind. He then closed my hand into a fist and wrapped his own around it, completing the ritual that sealed my fate. That moment was the last coherent memory I had. Everything after blurred into a haze, my mind consumed by the weight of my new responsibility.

٤١

FORTY-ONE

Maya

Choosing not to fight back turned out to be the best decision, as waking up was significantly more manageable. The witch marks that had manifested this time were tiny dots at the tips of my fingers except my thumbs. Both hands were symmetrical, and the pattern of the dots didn't look like anything to me, unlike the first mark that I had mistaken for a rune.

Following each encounter with a Dūshev, I had to go back to Iran for a cleansing ritual. Casting a circle powerful enough to do that, I needed Leyla's help. There was also the matter of my Firuzeh. I felt more aligned with my higher self but utterly dependent on them. The thought haunted me—without the pieces of Firuzeh, did I even matter, or was I just a pawn? I still felt like a stranger in my own body, and I needed to fix that. I needed to know if I could achieve anything without the Firuzeh anchoring me.

I woke up this morning to find the world map on my wall wiped clean. There was no trace of it, and I was sure it was there when I went to sleep. Someone in this house didn't want me to continue hunting them. Perhaps Seema was scared her boyfriend was next and tried to sabotage us. I was only meant to get the first four sons and, honestly, didn't know what would happen to the remaining Dūshevs, Adam included, and frankly, I didn't care.

I asked Leyla to gather all the Sāhers because I wasn't playing games. I was concerned about our safety and wasn't about to risk my life again for these bitches to ruin everything *we had worked for*.

"I think we have a mole in our family," I stated bluntly. I knew who I thought it was but didn't say that exactly. If she continued seeing him, she would put everyone's lives at risk, and they needed to be told that. "That's why I need all of you to swear a blood oath to me." It wasn't enough with Sepideh. I needed this as a binding guarantee.

"I feel like you're changing the rules as you go. What are we supposed to do? Change our ways and blindly follow you? Every time you come back, there is something new, and now, you think someone in this family will sell us out! You were the last to join us, might I add," Lara retorted.

"Lara!" Leyla warned.

I, on the other hand, was amused. How I had refrained from dealing with Lara's insolence was beyond me.

"I mean, I agree with Lara. I think what you're saying is offensive," Seema said. So, she was basically asking for it.

"I need a blood oath so I can be sure you don't run back to Samuel whenever you see something."

Seema fell silent, realization dawning upon her, her eyes darting between Lara and her mother.

"If anyone didn't catch that. I was referring to the Dūshev she has been meeting behind our backs," I said.

"You're still with that loser!" Lara said, launching herself toward Seema and grabbing her by the neck. Before I could intervene, the darkness overpowered my vision, and everything in front of me disappeared. I wasn't astral projecting this time. Instead, disjointed scenes played out before me, looking like poorly edited clips from an old movie. The images told a story without any sound. I saw Adam being crowned as if he were a king, seated arrogantly on his throne, wearing my decoy turquoise ring, exuding a sense of invincibility. Then the setting shifted. A slideshow of trails, roads, and hills unfolded, all pulling me backward. The images came to an abrupt end, plunging everything into darkness again. I didn't know how long I had stayed in the nothingness before finding myself back on solid ground, surrounded by towering trees that seemed to stretch into eternity. The biting cold wind crawled up my shirt, giving me chills. The wooden cabin wasn't completely wrecked, but it was missing a window, replaced by crisscrossing planks. Rusty bells hung in front of the main entrance, ringing in the wind. I entered a maze of a house I had never set foot in, yet my steps were confident. My focus was solely on the creaking wooden floors beneath me and the blood dripping from my hand.

I knew where to go and understood what needed to be done. The real question haunting my thoughts was whether I had the strength to see it through.

"Maya," Sepideh said, cupping my face. "What did you see?"

I exhaled slowly, my gaze locking on Seema. "The location of my victim." I wanted to strike fear through her bones, even though it had nothing to do with her boyfriend. I hated her. She had managed to preserve her fairy-tale life while I was forced to sacrifice mine. I had nothing left to wager except my influence over their fate. I lost control over my own worthless life when I made the choice to erase myself from the memories of my friends and family. *You did the right thing.* There was no way to undo the spell. *And there is no reason to.* I had regrets, but there was no way back, and I didn't want to let this family down, too. *Yes.* They had fought for so many years for peace and justice. The Dūshevs built their whole legacy on lies about helping humanity, and we had to stop them—I had to stop them. *Yes.*

"When are we leaving?" Sepideh asked.

"In a couple of days, when he settles in his new home."

Landing in Glasgow Airport, I did not know what to expect from what was to come. I was beyond afraid of getting caught with the fake passport, but we made it through airport security without even a blink.

"They sure advertise Loch Ness a lot," Sepideh said, looking at the brochure stand at the car rental.

"And Fort William," I said, nodding to the huge poster.

"The Highlands are braw, absolutely stunnin'. An' ye should definitely visit Fort William, nae doot aboot it," the guy behind the desk said, smiling. "Ye wanted the warranty wi' the breakdown assistance package an' unlimited mileage, correct?"

"Yes, please."

"Aye, I'll tak' a scan o' yer documents an' will be richt back," he said and left. His accent was so heavy I was questioning if I understood English to begin with.

Only when the car was in front of us did I realize I would be driving on the wrong side of the road.

"Do you want to drive?" I asked Sepideh.

"Only if you want to get us both killed." *Fuck.*

Thankfully, I reached the hotel without any mishaps. The drive hadn't been as challenging as I'd anticipated. I did bang my right hand against the door a couple of times while trying to shift gears, only to remember I needed to use my left hand instead. Sepideh and I would split up from the hotel, but first, I needed a nap. I was exhausted from the trip and hadn't gotten any sleep during the flight. I had nothing but the images from my head to guide me before driving one and a half hours north to find him. I had no specific address or landmark to follow, just the mental snapshot of the Balquhidder highway sign etched in my memory. Previously, it had been relatively straightforward to track the Dūshevs down because the visuals in my head were of busy cities, landmarks, and street signs. This time around, I just knew the general direction and a bunch of trees that all looked alike. If I was lucky enough to spot the abandoned cabin, I would recognize it for sure, but it was a long shot.

I followed the GPS directions for Stirling and then merged onto M80, relieved that driving on the highway was far easier than navigating city streets. All I had to do was keep within the dotted line on my left, and I was good. It seemed like everything was going great until I was finally in Balquhidder an hour later and had no idea where to go. The cabin was in an area next to a river, and that's all I could go by. The road grew narrower, eventually turning into a gravel path along a cliff. It was disconcerting how dark it was getting already. I couldn't see where I was driving, and people were getting frustrated behind me. After two hours of winding through various trails, I stumbled upon an oddly familiar path. Its uneven surface and potholes triggered a déjà vu feeling. The deeper I ventured into the forest, the more certain I became that I was closing in on him. I parked the car somewhere on the least steep hill I could find, where it wouldn't bother people driving by. I closed my eyes for a second, and when I opened them again, I let my intuition guide me down a pathway through the trees.

There, I found the remains of what was once a nice cabin now reduced to a dilapidated state. The rusty bells weren't ringing this time. He was in there; I felt his powers crawling in. For a second, I couldn't decide whether I wanted to run back to my car or knock on the door—I let my nails bite into the skin of my palm and chose the latter.

"Hey, baby," I said when he opened the door.

٤٢

FORTY-TWO

Adam

The ceremony with the elders turned out to be an unexpected plot twist, catching even me off guard. I thought I knew what my father was up to, but this revelation was a surprise. It seemed like he wanted to change the trajectory of my life every once in a while. First, he wanted a grandchild, then he didn't, and since then, I was going to take his place whether I liked it or not. He sort of tricked me into the ceremony, and the only option was to do it. I mean, I would have complied anyway had he approached and asked me with sincerity. Of course I cared about the future of my brothers and nephews. It was the manipulative way he had lured me in and posed those questions that left a bitter taste.

Midway through the ceremony, I blacked out, and when I woke up, it was just the two of us. The elders had retreated into hiding while my father was waiting for me to wake up and tell me to find a quiet place for the next month. I was instructed to avoid big cities, so I ventured to my cabin in the Highlands of Scotland. The place that had been untouched for years. Thick layers of dust shrouded every surface, and the entire place desperately needed cleaning. Sheets and comforters were stashed away in closets, thankfully spared from the musty odor of mold. The windows were boarded up, but I planned to change that, so it didn't feel too depressing living here all by myself. I was cleaning the kitchen when I heard the subtle whisper of a knock at my door. I thought it was inside my head, but then there were three firm knocks.

I opened the door, and I stood there, stunned into silence.

"Hey, baby," she said, gently pushing the door open and walking in as if she owned the place.

"Missed me?" she said, gliding through the hallway and into the kitchen and living room area. I closed the door and followed her like an idiot. She shrugged off her jacket, tossing it casually onto the couch.

"Why are you doing this to me?" I finally said.

"What do you mean?" Her expression remained innocent, a facade of normalcy that denied the chaos she was causing me.

"Why are you playing games with me?" I pressed.

She approached me, her hands reaching out for my face. "Can't a girl visit her boyfriend?" She cooed, her lips tantalizingly close to mine, when I seized her wrists with both hands and pushed her away. She didn't trip, but it got her off balance for a second. She feigned shock, placing a hand dramatically on her chest.

"Stop messing with my head."

"Here, I thought we were in love," she said and came close to me again. "And you push me like that?" she said softly, her hand gently finding its way to the back of my neck, caressing me as if to soothe the storm raging within me. I felt like a monster, questioning the sincerity of the person I had once claimed to love.

"Adam, baby," she purred, her demeanor shifting entirely. Before I could react, her iron grip clamped around my neck, forcing me to the floor. For a moment, shock immobilized me. I could easily overpower her. Maybe she forgot what I was capable of because she certainly didn't see it coming when I drew the air from her lungs, watching the panic flood her eyes as she gasped for breath. Her grip weakened, desperation etched on her face. Tears welled up, and her complexion turned red. I released my hold, allowing her to breathe.

"I spent years learning to use my powers, and you think you can come here and use it against me!" I spat out.

She got herself back up, steadying herself with one hand on the kitchen counter. The room seemed to tremble as her breathing slowed. Suddenly, appliances began hurtling toward me, crashing against the walls with tremendous force.

"I don't need to harness your powers to kill you," she sneered.

"YOU CAME HERE TO KILL ME!?" I couldn't believe what I had just heard.

"This time, I came here for you, baby," she said. A chair hurtled in my direction, sending me crashing into the wall. It was evident that she had learned a few things during our months apart. Summoning my strength, I sent a shock wave through her mind, hoping to halt her. For a moment, she faltered, but it didn't last long. She picked up where she left off, and the microwave came right at me. I had no choice but to strike back once more. This time, she clutched her temples, letting out a shriek. Seizing the opportunity, I forced out air from her lungs again. Tears streamed down her face, and when her nose began to bleed, I released my hold. I wasn't going to kill her, and she knew that.

"I'm done," I said and put my hands up. I couldn't recognize myself. I felt like a stranger in my own skin, a shadow of the person I used to be.

"We're not done." Her eyes were devoid of any emotion. She made a hand gesture in the air, and without a touch, I backed into the door, my spine hitting a doorknob.

"If you want to kill me, then, do it," I said, meeting her empty gaze with defiance. I searched desperately for a glimmer of the person she used to be, but there was nothing left in those eyes, only a void. "I'll even make it easy for you. I'll walk away so you don't have to look me in the eye when you do it."

I was ready to face the consequences of whatever fate had in store for me and my family. What I wasn't going to do was kill her and live with it for the rest of my pathetic life. I took a deep breath and, without another word, walked past her. To my surprise, nothing happened. The air remained still, and the silence in the room was deafening.

I heard the faint sound of something small hitting the ground behind me, followed by more delicate clatters that echoed through the silence of the hallway. Curiosity got the best of me, and I couldn't resist turning around to see what she was doing and why she had fallen silent. When I peered back, I found her deep in concentration, gazing intently at her hand. She didn't even look at me when I walked back into the room. Instead, in a moment of inexplicable calm, she slowly unfurled her fingers, revealing a thin chain with a golden teardrop pendant. The chain was wrapped around her fingers until she loosened them and let the chain slide through. The pendant dangled in midair for a fleeting moment before gravity took hold, causing it to drop and bounce on the hardwood floor. Her eyes, once empty, now held a glimmer of warmth. She turned her head and caught me watching her.

"I'm sorry," she said before collapsing on the floor.

She lay there, lost in unconsciousness, her face contorted in a restless semblance of sleep. Hours passed, and her distress only seemed to deepen. Each moment, her body twitched and writhed, her eyelids fluttering rapidly, showing the whites of her eyes. I had carried her to the bed and tried to heal her, but I didn't know what was broken. I was drained of energy from fighting her and couldn't think clearly, but I had to try one last thing. I knew I would survive fine without it. I didn't care; I just wanted time with her. In the end, it was never mine to keep.

Seated beside her, I placed my hand on her chest and released it, my body leaning steadily over hers. I was rigid, afraid my joints would buckle and that I would collapse on top of her because of the impact of losing my soul, yet I felt oddly detached from the situation.

Her body stopped twitching and squirming. For a moment, she lay motionless, her form eerily serene. Then her eyes snapped open as if gasping for air after a near-drowning experience. She took a deep, desperate breath, her eyes darting frantically around. She half-rose with a surge of energy, yet her eyes remained elusive, refusing to meet mine.

"It's so quiet," she whispered, her voice breaking the silence as she rubbed her eyes, trying to make sense of her surroundings.

"Are you okay?" I asked, placing my hand gently on hers.

"Adam," she breathed, her face slowly turning toward mine, her eyes finally meeting mine. She drew another breath. Her eyes burned red when she reached for me. I longed to lose myself in her, to breathe in her scent and feel the warmth of her skin against mine. Tentatively, I let her embrace me, afraid that if I wrapped my arms around her, she would disappear.

"I know I put you through hell the past few months. I'm so sorry." She pulled away, cupping my face in her hands and pressing her lips against mine. "I've missed you so much. You don't understand. I wanted to tell you, but they wouldn't let me. They're in my head." Her words tumbled out between sobs. Her cheeks were wet with tears. She kissed me again and again.

"It felt like my own thoughts and actions. It felt like I was in control when I truly wasn't."

Gently, I wrapped my arms around her waist, lifting her up and settling her onto my lap. Her head rested on my shoulder when she told me her side of the story, from the moment of her death to her gradual descent into the intricate world of the Sāhers. With each word, the weight of her burden became more palpable. She described how she gradually lost her train of thought and her grasp on reality. It could have been someone else's fate to fulfill the prophecy. She could have been free from the forces that bound her hadn't I taken her soul. In her newfound state as a Sāher, she had gained powers that didn't truly belong to her. She was capable of siphoning all the energy around her and was made for one purpose only—to kill my family.

She confessed to going after Idris and Kristian and the ritual she was forced to perform on them. Worst of all, she wasn't supposed to come looking for me. The prophecy had initially singled out my four eldest brothers, but something had changed, redirecting her path to me. What hurt the most was the betrayal by my own father. He had concealed the truth, manipulating events to serve his desperate desire to stop her. He had known everything and willingly chose to place me as the sole heir to his throne, sacrificing me in the process; a bitter reminder of the lengths he would go to protect his legacy, even at the expense of his own blood.

Maya rose from my lap and settled at the edge of the bed. "In my next life, I'll make our story a novel," she said.

"In your next life? What makes you think there is a next life?"

"I saw it," she said, with a hint of fear in her eyes. "When I got rid of the Firuzeh and went unconscious, I saw a life that was familiar."

"What happens in your next life?" I asked, wanting to know if she saw me in it, secretly hoping to find a place for myself in her future existence, even though I understood the impossibility of it.

"I'll be an immigrant child," she began. "Moving to a Western country, somewhere mundane. Every winter, I'll question my parents' decision to settle there. At twenty-five, I'll marry someone, and life will be pretty uneventful until I meet you in my late twenties." Her expression turned sad, regret etching across her features.

"Me?"

"Yeah. Well, not you, Adam. The next version of you."

"Oh! Will we date?"

"I don't know—you tell me. I'm a married woman, Adam," she responded, a playful grin curving her lips.

"Maybe you should leave your husband for me," I said, attempting to break the tension.

"Oh, I will leave him but not for you. Because you will be too scared to come forward. You'll be resisting the undeniable connection that you cannot make sense of. So, you'll settle with a nice girl. She will make you happy and give you a beautiful daughter. Years will pass until you realize we have always been two halves of the same soul. And by then, I will have moved out of that country because there will be no reason for me to stay," she said.

"You know, my father mentioned the twin flame connection."

She paused, studying my expression. "Twin flames don't always work out because not everyone is ready for a connection this deep. People across the world will read the book and wonder if it was real. Wonder if we ever met again to join our souls."

"If you were forced to dance in hell—" I started to recite the last part of the poem, but she leaned over and kissed me, and while sharing my breath, she finished the poem. "I would carve out the inferno through my shell."

It didn't matter to me; her beliefs about future lives held no significance for me. I would go through hell with her. She was back in my arms, her presence a reassurance that the nightmare was over. All I wanted was to hold her close, feel the warmth of her skin against mine, and trace the contours of her body with my fingertips. I kissed her repeatedly because it would never be enough. It was all I wanted and all she wanted. I was already halfway on top of her when she pulled the T-shirt over my head. Her hands were all over my body, feeling me out. She bit down on my shoulder, marking me.

"I have had so many sleepless nights thinking of you. Thinking of how you used to touch me, thinking if I would ever get to feel it again," she said while I undressed her, peeling away layers of clothing and revealing matching black underwear.

"You little siren," I said and pushed her back down on the bed. She hoisted back up on her elbows. "Stay down."

"Make me," she said, challenging me. She truly was my undoing. I withdrew slightly, sinking to my knees between her legs. I kissed the sides of her knees, then her thighs, until I was at her middle and tore at the fabric of her underwear. She gripped the sheets with one hand and the back of my head with the other, squirming. The sound of her drove me crazy, but she didn't let me finish and wrenched my mouth off of her.

"Fuck me, Adam."

I had never heard her scream so loudly when I thrust inside her. Again and again and again until I was sure she was sent to oblivion.

"More," she moaned as her nails dug into my back and scratched me the moment I erupted. I pulled out, my body half on top of her, my face buried in her hair.

"Give me a minute, and I'll make you come again." I panted.

She let out a chuckle that sounded foreign. "I told you, baby. This time, I came for you."

I forced myself up and saw a startling transformation in her expression. She wasn't looking at me. She was looking at her hand. Instinctively, my eyes followed hers, and there, I saw the blood between her fingers.

I let myself fall back to a sitting position across from her and felt an overwhelming numbness wash over me. I wanted to say something, but the words had knotted in my throat.

"I would lie if I said I didn't enjoy myself," she said with deliberate calmness, and rose from the bed, gathering her clothes. I was still frozen in my place. My jaw clenched in an attempt to suppress the tears. I wouldn't allow it. I wouldn't let her destroy me, not like this.

"Everything I told you is the truth, but I am no longer the master of my own will. The soul was never mine to keep. You can't change the prophecy."

The weight of her revelation settled, and I realized she was right. The soul was back in my core, even though I had released it.

"If you want to stay alive, stay out of my way." She pressed a kiss on my motionless lips and was gone.

www.ingramcontent.com/pod-product-compliance
Lightning Source LLC
Chambersburg PA
CBHW031835310726
48972CB00005B/1287